The
LABRYS Reunion

Terry Wolverton

Spinsters Ink
2009

Spinsters Ink
P.O. Box 242
Midway, Florida 32343

Printed in the United States of America on acid-free paper
First Edition

A portion of Chapter 15 was published as a short story, "Seduction," in *modern words*, San Francisco, CA, Summer 1995.

Editor: Katherine V. Forrest
Cover designer: Linda Callaghan

ISBN: 1-935226-02-9
ISBN: 978-1-935226-02-4

Acknowledgments

We may accept that "it takes a village to raise a child," but we don't always acknowledge that it takes a community to write a novel. From idea to publication, this novel took twenty-one years to complete. Over that span of time so many individuals were helpful in so many ways, it may be impossible to name them all. Mary-Linn Hughes, my "art buddy," gave me the courage to write a novel. Susan Silton, my partner during the first decade of the book's development, provided me ongoing practical as well as emotional support. Nine women invested in this project at the very beginning: Liz Bremner, Linda Griego, Debra Hirschberg, Deborah Irmas, Willette Klausner, Ginger Lapid-Bodga, Linda Preuss, Leslie Stone and Jeri Waxenberg. It is not overstating the matter to say that their early faith and support made possible my writing career, and their patience is deeply appreciated.

Robert Drake represented this book between 1991 and 1998 (at which time he closed his literary agency); his unwavering belief in the project helped to keep me going as well. Charlotte Sheedy read an early draft and told me to "put a murder into it." She was right. Nancy Aranda advised me on Cuban expressions of endearment.

Members of my Monday night writing group, as well as my students in Making It Better, Women At Work and One Page At a Time all provided crucial feedback on various drafts of the book. For this final draft, I would especially acknowledge Elaine Katzenberger and Gwin Wheatley for their assistance, and Donna Frazier for outstanding and unflinching editorial input. Thanks as well to Judith Stelboum, Ph.D., editor-in-chief of Alice Street Editions, and above all to Katherine V. Forrest and Spinsters Ink for finally giving this book a home.

About the Author

Terry Wolverton is the author of seven books: three novels, *The Labrys Reunion, Bailey's Beads,* and the novel in poems, *Embers;* a memoir, *Insurgent Muse: life and art at the Woman's Building;* and three collections of poetry, *Shadow and Praise, Mystery Bruise* and *Black Slip.*

She has also edited fourteen successful compilations, most recently, with Sondra Hale, the anthology, *From Site to Vision: the Woman's Building in contemporary culture,* published on the Internet at <u>www.womansbuilding.org/fromsitetovision/</u>.

Terry has taught creative writing since the late 1970s; in 1997, she founded Writers at Work, a center for creative writing in Los Angeles, where she offers several weekly workshops in fiction, creative nonfiction and poetry. She is currently an Associate Faculty Mentor for the MFA Writing Program at Antioch University Los Angeles. She spent thirteen years at the Woman's Building, a public center for women's culture, eventually serving as its executive director.

She is also a certified instructor of Kundalini Yoga.

She welcomes your response to this book. E-mail her at <u>wtrsatwork@aol.com</u>.

Prologue

Friday, May 10, 1996

If she'd thought about it, Gwen might have said that Emma Firestein seemed destined for trouble. It wasn't the blonde young woman's tight, black mini or her leather vest with nothing under it but bare skin. It wasn't the requisite studs in her nose and eyebrow. Or her backpack with a sticker for the Riot Grrrl band Bikini Kill.

If Gwen had thought about it, she might have noticed a certain uncontrollable spark in Emma, a reckless flame that was essential, in Gwen's view, to any artist but which she also knew from experience led to chaos in one's life.

But Gwen was not thinking about it. She'd just come offstage after performing a piece she'd intended to challenge and provoke the audience out of its mid-1990s complacency and in this, at least, the piece had succeeded. Her adrenaline high was just beginning to wane, and was slowly being replaced by the inevitable crash that followed her performances. Once she came back into her senses, all her muscles would throb; her rigorous athletics onstage had begun to take their toll now that she was in her forties.

She dragged a sweaty, leopard-print T-shirt over her naked torso, shimmied into purple overalls, and was jamming her feet into ankle-high boots when the two young women accosted her.

Convinced they were poised to pounce and harangue, Gwen was trying to decide whether rudeness or cunning would best serve her when the skinny blonde with a tattoo on her neck piped up.

"Gwen, Gwen, your performance was totally *stoopid!*"

Gwen knew from her girlfriend JJ that this was not an insult; the current vernacular used "stoopid" the way she would have said "cool."

"It really pisses me off the way the seventies get so dissed," the blonde continued. As she launched into a monologue idealizing seventies feminism, Gwen took a moment to study her. The young woman looked streetwise but well cared for. A poser, she wondered, like so many of the art students she met these days? Gwen took a certain pride in having made an art career while never having sought an MFA.

"Hey, I'm Emma, and this is Ayisha," the blonde added.

For the first time Gwen looked at Emma's companion, who hadn't spoken a word. She seemed a different type, more wholesome, jeans and turtleneck topped with a neat blazer. Curly brown hair framed ivory skin. Eyes obscured by sunglasses long past dusk.

"Great, thanks for coming," Gwen said, wanting to wrap this up so she could leave in search of a double shot of espresso, anything to give her the juice to make her way back downtown. Although the young women seemed friendly enough, she'd been on the defensive about her art ever since her last performance, Unsafe Sex in the Urban Jungle, had been reviewed for the *Voice* by a Gen X'er who called it "...warmed over seventies feminism...witless essentialism that neither titillates nor inspires...theoretically and artistically retrograde."

"So, we were on our way to have coffee." Emma's brashness turned a little shy. "There's not too much right around here, but we know a place that's pretty major. Would you...uh, wanna come with us?"

Gwen didn't, but the lure of coffee was irresistible.

In minutes she found herself sitting across from the two of them in a Cuban café, shoveling forkfuls of black beans and rice into her mouth, suddenly ravenous. As she ate, Gwen learned that Emma was twenty-three, an art student concentrating in video art; she'd seen all of Gwen's video pieces and believed Gwen deserved to be more famous than she was. "*You* could have been one of those artists that got dissed by the NEA!" she exclaimed.

No doubt that would have been glamorous to Gwen too at age twenty-three. Now it was with weariness that she answered, "Actually, I just found out that my grant was pulled by Jesse Helms and they're circulating it around the Senate as an example of 'degenerate art' that the NEA shouldn't fund. It was just in the paper."

"That is *soooo cool!*" Emma's eyes gleamed with admiration.

Gwen didn't bother to explain that it could end her already stalled career.

Ayisha had remained silent, so Gwen turned to ask her, "What about you? What do you do with your life?"

Ayisha was set on ultra-low volume; Gwen had to strain to catch every word as she explained, "I was in law school for a while, but I didn't like it. Now I work in a law office and..." She shrugged, as if to demonstrate her lack of direction.

Clearly accustomed to interpreting for her friend, Emma broke in, "We're roommates. Isha's mom died last year, breast cancer. I moved into their place with her."

Over a shared plate of fried *platanos*, Gwen learned that Emma was bisexual, which disappointed her mother. "She really wants me to be a lesbian," Emma said regretfully.

Gwen smiled. "There's a switch." She thought of her own Catholic mother, who still got on her knees every morning to pray that her daughter might miraculously come back to Chicago with a husband.

"My mother's pretty rad," Emma acknowledged. "You might even know her, she's a big feminist. Dana Firestein?"

Gwen felt a peculiar rushing together of past and present. "Your mother is Dana Firestein? I knew her a long time ago, from this thing called Labrys."

"You were at Labrys?" the young woman practically squealed. To Ayisha she explained, "Labrys was this really radical feminist...thing...my mom started—what would you call it?" She turned to Gwen. "A camp? A school?"

"A phenomenon," Gwen supplied. "Actually it was conceived of as an institute, a kind of think tank, but because it was held in the summer, it ended up feeling sort of like camp, only one where the campers tie up the counselors and set the cabins on fire."

"What do you mean?" These were the first words Ayisha had volunteered.

"We fought like crazy. We spent eight weeks bitching at the organizing collective for how everything was set up, we laid trips on each other about being working class, or lesbian, or whatever. One group of women even split off and tried to form an *alternative* alternative institute on the other side of town! It was 'Psychology of Oppression 101!'"

Emma nodded. "That's what my mom says, too. So how come you two didn't stay in touch?"

"By the time it was over, the collective made it pretty clear they'd just as soon not see any of us ever again."

"You really oughta call her up," Emma suggested. "I bet she'd love to hear from you."

Gwen was noncommittal; she dug in her backpack for money to pay the check.

"Hey, can I ask you something else?" Emma zeroed in with her intense blue eyes and didn't wait for a response. "I'm in school here at NYU, and I'm trying to do this performance and video thing but I feel like the professors don't get me. My critiques are really lame."

Her expression grew more serious. "The people at school act like feminism is over, you know? But it isn't! I mean, really messed up stuff still happens to women, violence and sexual abuse. So I was wondering..."

She trailed off as if she expected Gwen to take it from there. Gwen was already busy shaping her refusal. *Too busy, overcommitted, need to put my energy into my own work, don't do that sort of thing.*

She watched as Ayisha inclined her head in Emma's direction, the slightest nudge of encouragement.

"I'd like to show you some of my work," Emma finally got

out. Her cheeks flushed. "I think you would really understand what I'm trying to do. And your work is so rad, I think your feedback would really help me."

No. Uh-uh. Sorry. Can't do it. Wish I could help. Too bad. This was the music floating through Gwen's head, along with JJ's soft, insistent, "Just say no, *nena*."

She was just about to do that when Ayisha added, barely audible. "It would be a chance to further your legacy."

Emma stared at Gwen with naked expectation, hope. She was exactly the age Gwen had been when she'd gone to Labrys. And when Gwen looked at her this time, she saw that spark, the one that flashed *She could be an interesting artist. Fuck!*

Damned if it wasn't Gwen's mother's voice that joined the chorus in her head. "For once in your life, think about someone besides yourself"—the mantra with which she'd admonished Gwen since she was five or six.

To her chagrin, Gwen heard herself say, "I guess I could look at a piece or two, if you want to send me your tapes." She knew she would regret those words, but it was too late to take them back. So she fished out her card, a lime green rectangle with her address stamped, off-center, in purple ink.

As they said goodbye outside the restaurant, Emma squealed her appreciation for Gwen's black denim jacket, decorated on the front with strips of zebra print fabric, on the back with a velvet painting of Jesus. Then she hugged Gwen, promised to call soon. Ayisha merely mumbled a few words and turned her back.

Watching them walk away, Gwen felt a strange list in time, recalling herself at their age, her first year in New York just after Labrys. She ached for how young she'd been then, how grown-up she'd believed herself to be, ready to fight the revolution with spotlights and handmade props and her naked body. That spark of Emma's, she recognized it. She was surprised to realize she was curious to see the young woman's art, to see how feminism might be rearticulated in her vision.

If she'd thought about it, watching Emma disappear down the crowded block, Gwen might have felt a stir of foreboding, a premonition of what can happen to that kind of light.

Chapter 1

Monday, June 10, 1996

"So where are you going, again?"

Ayisha didn't think Emma was being very smart. Ayisha perched on the closed seat of the toilet, watching her roommate smear dark vermilion lipstick over her mouth.

"Ayisha, if I wanted to live with my mother, I wouldn't have moved in here." Emma accentuated the bow of her lip. She studied her reflection further, then added a pair of earrings, thick silver crosses that dangled nearly to her shoulders.

"Emma, believe me, I don't wanna be anybody's mom. But you met this guy at a club, for God's sake. You don't know anything about him." Ayisha hated the worry and accusation that turned her words to a shrewish whine.

Emma put a hand on her hip and turned away from the mirror to face her friend. "Isha, I'm gonna be fine. I'm twenty-three. I've been, like, how you say, 'sexually active' since I was fourteen. I'm down, okay?"

"All right, girlfriend. 'Scuse me I forgot I was dealing with a woman of experience." Ayisha began rummaging around in the basket that sat on top of the toilet tank. She fished out a foil-wrapped condom and tossed it in Emma's direction. "Just don't forget this."

Emma grinned in appreciation, tucking it into her backpack

along with the dark lipstick. "That's great. Listen, I'm gonna meet this guy…" Seeing the question forming on Ayisha's face, she added, "Jersey, all right? His name is Jersey! Anyway, I'm gonna meet him over at the Mercury Lounge…"

"That place on East Houston, right?" Ayisha interjected.

"That's the one," Emma sighed with exaggerated patience. "And then, if I'm lucky, I'm gonna get laid!" Turning to catch Ayisha's frown, she appealed, "Isha, I *need* to cut loose after the stress-o-rama day I've had."

"You met with that artist, right? What's her name–Gwen?"

Emma wilted against the doorframe to illustrate the trauma of the experience. "The esteemed Ms. Kubacky told me I had to watch my tendency to *romanticize* violence against women in my work. She could have been a little more encouraging, don'cha think? What ever happened to sisterhood?"

Ayisha crossed her arms over her thin torso. "So, I guess you won't be meeting with her again?"

Emma bugged eyes at her. "Are you kidding? Even if she's a psychobitch from hell, it's a fabulous opportunity! I'm meeting with her again next week. She's gonna give me an assignment. I'm just trying to tell you why I *deserve* a little positive attention on a Monday night." Emma turned the deadbolts and opened the door.

Ayisha pushed at the door to close it again, blocking her roommate's exit. "Hey, just don't bring him here, okay?"

"I know, I know." Emma held up her hands as if to fend off another lecture.

"It would be one thing," Ayisha continued, "if he were someone you were seeing, you know—going out for dinner, talking on the phone, getting to know each other? This dude is no more than a trick, and I don't need him knowing my address."

"O-kaaay, don't wait up for me, okay?" Emma swept an arm around her friend's neck, gave her a clumsy hug, then grabbed her leather jacket and was out the door.

"Be careful, please," Ayisha whispered to the wood. She could hear Emma's heavy heels stomping down three flights of stairs as she secured the deadbolts.

After those footfalls disappeared, Ayisha sat in the living room of the quiet apartment with the lights out as she did most nights. The apartment was an old brownstone on West Tenth, the same five rooms where she and her mother had lived since Ayisha was nine. Ayisha had wanted to move after Marilyn's death, but rent control made it impossible.

Ayisha caught a glimpse of her face in the mirror on the opposite wall. She scowled at the ivory skin, the green eyes. If she caught just the right angle, she could see the trace of African in her features, the slight spread of her nose, the fullness of her lips, but these were subdued by the colonizing genes of Europe.

Her own father's vision had failed him. When his daughter was born with her mother's pale complexion and eyes like new olives, all he could see in her face was the enemy. Lincoln Cain had departed before Ayisha was a year old; she'd never seen him again. Now that Marilyn was gone, Ayisha believed it was only her light skin and Caucasoid features that kept her father from coming back to claim her.

Turning her gaze from the mirror, she rocked, and as she did, she imagined her mother. The Marilyn she remembered from her own childhood—energetic, passionate, raising her fist high, shaking her short dark hair—threatened to blur into Marilyn in the last few years of her life, wreathed in pot smoke, defeated, bitter, dying.

Ayisha dozed then until the sky began to lighten, until the streetlights winked out, until the night sounds rising from the street dimmed to the rhythms of morning.

She was still asleep in the rocker, wrapped in an old chenille robe of her mother's, when the downstairs buzzer blasted through her dreams. Ayisha regularly ignored the buzzer—too often, it was neighborhood kids playing a joke, or suspicious types trying every buzzer to get into the building—but this blare of sound was deliberate and relentless. At the fifth blat, she stumbled over to the wall panel, and with her most truculent attitude, snarled, "Yeah?"

"Do you know a Miss Emma Firestein?" It was a male voice,

and sounded older, not like any of Emma's friends or tricks.

"Who *is* this?" Ayisha demanded.

"Detective Howard O'Hara, NYPD. I need to ask you a couple of questions." His voice retained a hint of an Irish brogue.

Ayisha pressed the button to release the door lock. Her fingers had turned suddenly cold. She could hear the long trudge of footsteps up the stairs, and was already fumbling to undo the deadbolts when she heard the knock on the door.

"Where's Emma?" were the first words she hurled at the gray-haired, red-faced man who stood before her in a rumpled jacket. He was large, a little overweight, and walked with a pronounced limp. The detective showed her his badge, took out a notebook and said he needed her name.

"Ayisha Cain. Emma's my roommate."

"Could you speak up, please? And would you spell that for me?" The portly detective recorded her words with a ballpoint pen. "Do you know how to get hold of her family?"

Ayisha thought of how Emma would handle this situation, how she would be insistent and powerful, how she wouldn't rest until she got her way. "Look, Detective, you've got to tell me what's happened. Emma would want me to know. We've been friends for a long time."

The detective sighed. He ran a hand through his thinning hair, and his face flushed a deeper shade of red. "Miss Cain, I'm sorry to inform you that your friend Emma Firestein was found assaulted and strangled under an on-ramp of the FDR..."

"Strangled?" Ayisha asked as if the word were not one she understood.

"She's dead," the detective explained in monotone. "I'm sorry for your loss. Can you tell me anything about where she was going last night?"

Ayisha dropped heavily into Marilyn's rocker. Her entire body felt swaddled in cotton, making it hard to hear the detective's words, hard to hear her own responses. Still, she told what she could about Emma's plans for the night before.

"This man—Jersey—what night did she meet him?"

"Maybe it was last week. Wednesday or Thursday, I think it was."

"And did she meet him at the same club, the Mercury Lounge?" The detective consulted his notes.

"I don't think so. She's been going out a lot lately. Maybe it was the Fez, I'm just not sure."

"And this guy, Jersey, do you know what he does?"

"I think maybe he was a musician? I don't really remember."

"And when she met him last weekend at the Fez, do you know if she had sex with him that night?"

"No, I don't think so."

"Did Emma tell you, or how do you know?"

"Well, she was eager to see him again, and usually that's not the case once she's slept with a man."

"Did your roommate often pick up men she barely knew?"

"Often? I don't know. She'd done it before."

The detective continued. "And do you have any idea where I might find this Jersey?"

"I don't have any idea." Ayisha found that she was shaking. "Do you think he killed her?"

The buzzer screamed again. She turned involuntarily toward the noise, half-expecting it to be Emma, who sometimes forgot her keys.

The detective pressed the button on the wall panel and said, "That will be my partner. He's going to need to search Emma's room, Miss Cain."

They waited for the second detective to reach the fourth floor. The apartment felt stifling. Ayisha pushed open a window, relieved to feel the air on her face. The man who came through the door was African-American, tall and slender. He showed his badge, which read Johnson. She searched his eyes for some acknowledgment of her, but his face was a closed mask.

Mechanically, she showed the detective to Emma's room. When Ayisha was growing up, this space had been hers; now she slept in the room that had been her mother's. She thought how vigorously Marilyn would have protested this invasion; her mother had hated cops, a hostility honed by her years of activism.

"Miss Cain?" The Irish burr cut through her musings. "Can we continue? I've got a few more questions."

Ayisha nodded as if anesthetized. She had not yet begun to feel beyond the shock, her sleepless state conspiring to make it seem as if these events were taking place in a parallel universe, unconnected to her waking life.

"Did Emma have a regular boyfriend?" the detective was asking her now.

"No. She identified as a bisexual. She's had some steady girlfriends over the years, steady for a few months anyway, but she says...said...that she just liked men to have sex with, not to really hang out with." Ayisha spoke in a monotone, betraying none of her own judgments about her friend's stance.

The detective asked, "Any of these girlfriends she was still in touch with?"

"Not that I know."

He turned a page in his notebook. "Let me ask you something else—was Emma into drugs that you knew of?"

Ayisha shook her head. "I'm pretty sure she wasn't. Maybe a little weed now and then, but that's it. Why?"

The detective was about to answer when the officer emerged from the bedroom. In his possession was a collection of dildos, a pair of handcuffs, a whip. He kept his face expressionless as he showed them to Detective O'Hara, who turned to her.

"Do you know anything about these?" he asked her.

She shrugged. "What's to know?"

"These belonged to Emma?"

"I suppose so, if they were in her room. It's not like she ever talked to me about them."

The detective frowned. "Would you say she was into kinky sex?"

Ayisha sucked her teeth. "I'd say you'd have a hard time finding a young white girl living on her own in this city who doesn't have some kind of collection like this. It's a fad, I think. Like piercings."

"So you don't think she might have sought out rough trade?"

Ayisha knew this line of questioning would have made Emma furious. A woman is assaulted and what the cops wanna know is about her sex life. "Detective, I never slept with her. I never watched while she slept with someone else. I can't really comment about what she did in bed."

Detective Johnson returned to the living room and spoke in a low voice to the detective. O'Hara turned to Ayisha and said, "There's a message from the guy Emma went to meet on the answering machine. We're going to take the tape so we can have a record of his voice."

Ayisha didn't bother to nod; it had not been a request.

Detective O'Hara closed his notebook. "You said you knew how to contact Emma's family?"

"Her mother's name is Dana, Dana Firestein. She lives uptown; here's her address." She scrawled the information on a scrap of paper and handed it to him.

"Thanks for your cooperation," he said, as he and Johnson prepared to go. "I'll be in touch with you again after I talk to her mother. I'm going to ask you to give me the names of her friends, anybody she went out with."

His features seemed to crumple inward. "It's a terrible thing that happened to your friend. I really wanna catch this scumbag."

The two men plodded out of the apartment. She heard them making their way down the stairs, and then they were gone and the apartment seemed unnaturally quiet. It was only then that the emptiness of the rooms seemed to swell, a chasm big enough to swallow her.

Ayisha moved quickly to the telephone, her fingers making quick jabs against the keypad. She heard the ring, imagined its echo in a room uptown, and then the voice in her ear, and her own voice saying, "Dana, it's Ayisha. I don't know how to tell you this..."

Later that morning, Ayisha waited with Emma's mother in the chilled basement of the city morgue. She felt profoundly grateful not to be there alone, although she realized that she would never have been the one they asked to identify the body, even though she felt as close to Emma as a sister. Both only children of mothers engaged in radical politics, they had known each other since they were kids.

Leaning back into the hard folding chair, Ayisha studied the woman across from her, dressed in a black T-shirt imprinted with the faded face of Che Guevara. This she wore with aging combat pants, their military green bleached to gray. Her attire was understated and uncalculated except for a pair of black work boots, polished to a military shine.

Dana Firestein had a beautiful face, though acne scars had left it pitted. This, coupled with her propensity to scowl, made her seem older than her fifty-one years, and forbidding. Blue eyes penetrated from behind thick, black-rimmed spectacles. Her dark frizzy hair was worn longer these days and was shot through with silver, but it was as unruly as ever, appearing, as it always had, as if she never combed it.

Although she'd shared a common politics with Dana, Marilyn Horton Cain had been a different kind of woman: rounder, softer, more concerned with how other people felt, more easily wounded. Perhaps, Ayisha had sometimes pondered, this was why her mother had been defeated by the political setbacks—she'd taken them personally—while Emma's mother was a warrior still, fierce and uncompromising.

Dana had been fighting with Detective O'Hara ever since he and his partner had shown up at her door, as if they held responsibility for her daughter's death. She'd raged at them when asked about her daughter's sexual history. She'd chastised Ayisha for allowing them to search her daughter's room; they'd had no warrant, and no judge would have granted one, she insisted. Now they had the evidence they needed to turn this crime against its victim.

Emma had always said that the only emotion with which her mother was truly comfortable was anger. Dana had demanded that Ayisha be allowed to come along to the morgue, arguing it as a point of fairness, that "the fascist state refuses to recognize extended, chosen family," but Ayisha could not help but wonder whether Dana also dreaded facing this task alone.

An odor permeated the basement that frigid air and

antiseptics did little to dispel, a scent of sweet and rot and chemical. It reminded Ayisha just a bit of the smell of her mother's room, the smell of sickened flesh, of death.

"How dare they think they can make us wait all this time?" Dana's gruff voice broke into Ayisha's musings. The older woman rose and strode down the hall, toward the door through which the detective had led them, half an hour ago.

She returned a few minutes later with Detective O'Hara, whose face was redder than ever and whose patience was beginning to fray. "Lady," he was explaining, his temper barely contained, "I can't let you view the body until the medical examiner has finished with it…"

"First of all," Dana cut him off, "do not call me 'lady.' Second, I have the right to see my daughter at any time, and if I need to get a lawyer in here to make that case, believe me, I'll do it."

Ayisha closed her eyes against the harsh voices. She wanted nothing more than for time to rewind, to be rocking in her chair in the dark apartment, watching a breeze stir the shadow of leaves. She wanted Emma to be out having a sexual escapade from which she would return with the morning light, sore and satisfied and recommitted to looking for a girlfriend.

"Ayisha, come on," Dana snapped, and then they were following the detective down the hallway, through a set of double doors like in a hospital. They were led into a cubicle; on one wall was a window, with a shade drawn.

"I'm not going to look at my daughter from behind glass," Dana protested. "You have to let me see her."

"Look, this is the department policy…"

"Fuck department policy! And if you can't get me in there, let me talk to the person who can!" She was fearless about approaching him, yelling right into his face. While Dana was a full six inches shorter than the detective, and half his girth, her intensity made her seem more massive than O'Hara.

The detective left the room, returning a few minutes later with a tired-looking woman in her late thirties, whose pallid skin was made even paler by her white coat. Her hair was a nondescript brown, and the stench Ayisha had sensed earlier emanated from her pores. Ayisha did not quite catch her name, but understood that this woman was the medical examiner.

In a soft, faintly Eastern European accent the woman began to recite the department policy, but Dana wasn't having it. "You need me to identify the body," she reminded them. "What I'm telling you is that I won't do it unless you let me in there with her. Let *us* in there." She gestured toward Ayisha.

Ayisha wanted to interrupt, to say, "No, really, I can just stay here." She had been alone with her mother when Marilyn died, and she'd sat with that body for a long time, listening for the next breath, watching the features turn waxy and hollow, too afraid to move. She had no wish to resume a vigil with Emma's corpse, yet she did not dare cross Dana.

There was no other option than to give Dana her way; she'd made that clear, and eventually the medical examiner gave in with a tired shrug. "Follow me," she said, and led the short procession through the door and into the room beyond the window.

If the entire basement was cold, this room was frigid, and Ayisha began to shiver. Despite her thin T-shirt, Dana paid no notice of the temperature. Nor of the odor, which had grown overwhelming. She walked over to the gurney on which her daughter's body lay, covered by a white sheet. "Show me," she demanded, her voice steady.

Ayisha forced herself to cross the space between the door and the gurney; her feet dragged across the white linoleum. The medical examiner slowly drew the cloth down to reveal Emma's body. To Ayisha, her friend looked childlike, naked and motionless on the sheet. Her dark lipstick was smeared across her cheek. Dreadlocks hung like pigtails from her head. The studs in her nose and right eyebrow had been removed and her face looked undefended.

Her left eye was swollen and bruised; more bruises purpled her slender arms and delicate hips. At Dana's insistence, the medical examiner showed her the ligature marks on Emma's neck, just above the tattoo—a hexagram from the *I Ching* that was translated as "flaming beauty"—she'd had since she was eighteen. "They're consistent with those made by rope. See, there are slight burns to the skin as well."

"We didn't find the weapon at the site," the detective added, "although it's possible she wasn't murdered there, but killed somewhere else and dumped beneath the expressway ramp."

"And you said she'd been sexually assaulted," Dana continued; she was perfectly calm, dry-eyed. Marilyn would have been in need of sedation by now; Ayisha could not help but make the comparison.

Without pointing these out, the medical examiner explained that there were bruises on the pelvic area, as well as tearing and some bleeding in the vaginal walls, and the presence of semen.

"We're assuming," O'Hara interjected, "that this was assault, against your daughter's will. Although, given her history of sexual experimentation, it is possible that the sex was consensual."

Dana's expression gnarled with hatred. "I assure you, Detective, that this *murder* was committed without my daughter's consent."

The medical examiner hastened to intervene. "Two of her fingernails are broken, see?" She lifted one of Emma's hands. "Under the others, we've got samples of skin. It's clear she fought her assailant. We'll run DNA tests on the samples."

"She never had sex without a condom." Ayisha heard her voice before she knew she was going to speak. "I saw her put one in her purse that night. She had some friends who were sick with AIDS, and she was always careful."

The detective noted that in his book. "We've got her belongings. I'll check and see if the condom is still in her purse."

The medical examiner made a move as if to cover the body once more, but Dana put out a hand to block her. She bent nearer her daughter's face and stared for a long moment, as if trying to memorize each detail. Then she lifted her right hand and grabbed a fistful of Emma's hair, clutching it tight. It was as close to tenderness as this vehement woman could come. Finally the detective cleared his throat, and Dana released her grip and turned away. Then she raised her fist and slammed it against the wall, hard enough to rattle the glass window, before she strode abruptly from the room.

Ayisha lingered just a minute more. She too wanted to reach

to touch her friend, but she was no longer sure she could make her limbs move at will. Even her breath felt too heavy to force in and out of her lungs. Finally she pressed her lips to Emma's forehead, the skin cold, unyielding. "Girlfriend," she whispered, half-scolding, half-lamenting, "Oh, girlfriend…"

Chapter 2

Gwen had three New York State Council grants to write for a Friday deadline. One of the ways she supplemented her rather meager income as a performance artist was to write grants for arts organizations and for other artists, though she drew the line at writing grants that might be directly competing with her own. She'd tried having a job, but she wasn't good at being an employee; she always thought her way of doing things was better than the boss's way, and this inevitably resulted in conflict. So she taught a few classes around town, hired herself out as a director for other artists' performances, wrote grants to advance the careers of those other artists and, once in a while, got paid to perform. In these ways did Gwen eke out what passed for a living in the Big Apple.

She didn't like to think about her mother's views on her career choices. Gwen's family had groomed her to grow up to be a traditional housewife, scrimping every penny, making herself small enough so as not to antagonize the man of the house, and cleaning as if her life depended on it. The Kubacky women had been trained to scrub the corners of the linoleum with a toothbrush and wash down the walls every spring. Gwen's sisters had all bought into it, even Pauline, the only one who graduated college.

Every one of them would have had apoplexy if they'd seen Gwen's studio. It was an unfinished industrial space on Rivington Street, a block that had somehow managed to elude the wave of gentrification that swept the East Village and Alphabet City in the eighties. Gwen occupied two thousand square feet, one gigantic room with a bed, a makeshift desk and homemade bookshelves, a sagging couch and a couple of chairs in front of an aging TV, a hot plate and small refrigerator, and, in a far corner, a sink, toilet and old-fashioned bathtub behind a makeshift wall of old brocade drapery. But all this was dwarfed by the jumble of props, costumes and set pieces from performances past. Huge wings of lavender gauze, an enormous grinning clock face. A colossal neon cross was propped in a corner. Piles of boxes spilled a chaos of stage lights and extension cords, cassette cases and slide boxes, rope and reels of duct tape. These vied for space with racks of clothing scavenged from thrift stores, one of Gwen's few remaining vices. Every spare surface was littered with *tchochkes*—her choice collections of cocktail napkins, wind-up toys, snowshakes—and all of it covered by a fine layer of dust.

She often quoted Quentin Crisp, who'd said of housekeeping that, "After the first four years, it doesn't get any dirtier." That, in essence, was Gwen's philosophy of domestic science. Her mother never had, and if Gwen could help it, never *would* see where she lived.

Gwen's mother had told her that if she couldn't be a nice girl and keep a tidy home and give her grandchildren, at least Gwen should be socking away money for her old age. "Nobody's gonna take care of you," Wanda Kubacky complained in their infrequent phone calls. "Your father and I can't do it anymore." The niceness she'd drilled into her daughter kept Gwen from asking—*When did you ever?*

She'd had girlfriends who'd gotten on her case about the same thing—*Why don't you do something with your life, you have to think about the future, why live such a marginal existence*, blahblahblah. That was one reason she liked JJ. JJ never bugged her about that stuff. Of course, that might have had something to do with the fact that JJ hadn't hit thirty yet. But Gwen believed it was also because JJ too was an artist, a musician. She seemed to share Gwen's understanding that life wasn't about owning a snazzy car and having a retirement account and being able to shop at DKNY. JJ got it when Gwen said, "When I get to the point where I can't make art and I can't take care of myself any longer, I'll just jump in front of the F train."

Several times a week she had to stop and ask herself just exactly what a forty-two-year-old lesbian feminist was doing with a twenty-eight-year-old Cuban butch who played guitar in a post-punk band. It wasn't a relationship, she told herself, even though they'd been seeing each other for two years. It had no future, Gwen repeated like a mantra, although JJ would sometimes talk about their growing old together. Whenever JJ brought that up, Gwen would remind her that she'd be seventy-five before JJ even qualified for Social Security, and JJ always said, "*Cosa linda*, you know there's not gonna be any Social Security by that time."

This morning Gwen was yelling at her girlfriend to get off her computer so she could get started on her grants. Ever since JJ had talked Gwen into going on the Internet, she'd had to fight for access to her own keyboard. "JJ, don't you have to get to work?" she queried pointedly.

"Nah." JJ was only half listening as she surfed the Web. "No one's booked in the studio till noon." In between gigs, JJ worked as an engineer for a small record company that produced alternative bands.

Noon was still two hours away. For about twenty minutes Gwen fidgeted conspicuously, standing right behind JJ's chair, leaning over her to fuss with file folders inches from where her hand gripped the mouse, pushing aside her legs to get into one of the desk drawers. All the while sighing audibly. JJ just stared at the screen, oblivious.

Finally, in desperation, Gwen peeled off her antique lace shirt and lime green bra, and plopped herself onto JJ's lap. Lust was the one thing that could still disrupt JJ's link to cyberspace.

The dark-haired woman chuckled as she disconnected the modem. "You don't fight fair, Miss Kubacky." Her mouth began moving up Gwen's bare shoulder toward her neck, JJ's breath hot and sweet on her skin. JJ's hands found Gwen's breasts; the nipples swelled beneath her fingertips. Gwen's challenge now would be to keep from sinking under her own strategy.

Gwen pulled away from JJ's kiss, but JJ's lips pursued. Her right hand inched under Gwen's skirt, and Gwen was beginning to fear she'd never get started on those grants this morning when the phone blasted through the sound of heavy breathing.

"Forget it." JJ tried to pin Gwen so she couldn't reach the phone, but Gwen squirmed off her lap and captured the receiver before JJ could stop her.

"Hello." Gwen tried to assume a businesslike tone but a giggle rose up like carbonation, threatening to spill over. JJ now wanted to turn the tables; she began slowly sucking Gwen's left nipple, wanting to test how long she could carry on the conversation before she lost it.

This was a game they played, but Gwen withdrew abruptly when the voice in the earpiece said, "Gwen? This is Ayisha Cain. I met you a few weeks ago."

"Ayisha!" Gwen was astounded to hear from her. Gwen had already received Emma's videotapes in the mail, six of them altogether, and they'd had one fairly contentious meeting, but Gwen never expected to hear from her roommate. "What's up?"

"Bad news," the voice spit out, and only then did Gwen recognize the strain in Ayisha's tone. Gwen reached for a shirt of JJ's that was strewn over the back of the chair, and wrapped it around her body to signal that the game was over. In the cloth of JJ's shirt Gwen could smell the oil of musk her lover wore as cologne; it always gave her a weird flashback to the early seventies.

"Are you okay?" she asked Ayisha.

"It's Emma," the young woman began, and when Ayisha said the words, "She's dead," all Gwen could do was nod, as if something had been confirmed.

Seeing Gwen's face, JJ knelt down beside her, pressing her face against Gwen's knee. Her eyes stared up into Gwen's, dark and full of concern, and she reached for Gwen's hand.

In a few stark sentences, Ayisha recounted what she knew of

Emma's death. She didn't dwell on lurid details. As the young woman spoke, Gwen covered the mouthpiece, saying softly to JJ, "That girl I met, the one who sent me her videotapes? Some bastard raped and strangled her."

The deep wells of JJ's eyes filled; although she was easygoing, she was also deeply emotional.

"Shit," Gwen muttered inanely into the mouthpiece. She couldn't bring herself to think about Emma, who'd been straddling a broken chair right next to the desk just the day before yesterday; Gwen didn't want to picture her dead, bruised, violated, so she tried to focus on other things.

"How's Dana?" she asked as though she'd last seen the woman yesterday, instead of twenty years ago.

"Furious," Ayisha answered, and a picture of Dana burbled up through Gwen's memory: Dana was always enraged about something, her face contorted in a permanent grimace. "But I think," Ayisha continued, "it's the only way she can deal."

Something in her voice reminded Gwen of what Emma had said about Ayisha that day in the cafe: *Isha's mom died last year, breast cancer.* Gwen felt a surge of protectiveness for the stoic young woman on the other end of the phone.

"So what about you? Are you holding up okay?" Gwen asked, in a voice she hoped sounded maternal and caring. It was not a role that came naturally to her.

Nor, apparently, to Ayisha. She brushed off Gwen's inqury with a brusque, "I guess," and then proceeded with the purpose of her call. "Dana wanted me to call you. Emma had told her about running into you again. There's gonna be a memorial day after tomorrow. Friday morning at Judson Church. A lot of people are coming into town. I guess someone from that place...Lab—whatever," Ayisha faltered on the unfamiliar name.

"Lab—like the dog—then, -riss," Gwen enunciated it for her, "Labrys."

"Right, that place you both went to. Dana's got her family staying at the apartment, and Emma told her you live in a big studio space. This woman, Peg Morrison, is coming in with her partner. Anyway, Dana's hoping you could kinda put people up, those women, I mean. Since you know them." It wasn't easy for Ayisha to ask for things, Gwen could tell, even on behalf of someone else; the effort seemed to exhaust Ayisha, because her voice trailed off, leaving nothing to fill the void except Gwen's answer.

"Ayisha, I'm sorry, I can't possibly." Her memory of Peg Morrison was of her voice, a kind of braying, bombastic, ceaseless instrument that set her teeth on edge; Peg had never met an opinion she didn't feel the need to harangue about.

Ayisha's silence pressured Gwen to continue.

"Where I live is my work space. It's a seedy neighborhood. It's not set up for visitors. And I've got grant deadlines on Friday." Her voice lifted an octave.

"Dana really needs help," Ayisha insisted, as if Gwen's refusal made it easier, not harder to press her case. "She charges around like she's got it all together, but she's really whacked. It would just be for a night or two."

"I'm sorry," Gwen said again, although she didn't sound sorry. "What's happened to Emma is a hideous thing. It breaks my heart, and I can't even imagine what you're going through, Ayisha, you and Dana both. But I can't take on the responsibility of housing anybody. It's just not something I can do."

"Well, okay, then," Ayisha said, her voice betraying nothing but fatigue. "If you want to come to the memorial, it's Friday at ten, okay?"

She offered her phone number and signed off quickly, leaving Gwen to wrestle with relief and guilt.

She fell against JJ's slender frame, gave herself over to the strength of her lover's embrace. If JJ had an opinion about Gwen's decision, she kept it to herself.

Well after midnight, Gwen's entire body was streaked with dust and sweat. Her shoulders ached from a day of lifting cartons and pushing racks and scrubbing the painted wood floor, which likely hadn't seen water or soap since the loft had been built sixty years ago. She'd filled the large trash bin eleven times, hauled plastic garbage bags four flights down to the street, finally letting go of all those stacks of newspapers containing articles on which she might some day want to base a performance. She'd doused the windows with ammonia, giving herself a new, clear view of the decrepit neighborhood. She'd scrubbed the worst of the water stains out of the sink and tub, and dumped whatever was rotting out of the small refrigerator.

All day she'd kept telling herself that she was doing it for Emma, not that she'd ever know or care. Now Gwen was exhausted, none of her clients' grants was written, and the place still looked, in her view, like hell. She was halfway to working herself into a good fit when she started to think that what she really needed was a drink. Twelve years clean and sober, and still she could conjure the blue-black interior of a bar, its smoky light and sour smells, the way scotch would burn into the back of her throat and make it all feel better. For an hour or two.

At times like these she was supposed to call Howard, her AA sponsor for the past ten years. In the beginning she'd had to talk to him every day, but now that she was an old-timer they just checked in occasionally. She loved Howard; he'd been a lifesaver, the first straight white man she'd ever learned to trust. Tonight, though, she felt too beat to drag herself to the phone and listen to those AA slogans pour from his lips, so she curled up on the couch with a pillow pressed into her belly and whispered the serenity prayer, over and over again.

She was still in a fetal position when JJ came in, still high from playing a gig. She burst into the loft looking full and satisfied. The way some women are after sex, that's how JJ looked whenever she'd been making music. "¡*Cosita!*" she greeted, "I wasn't sure you'd still be up."

She stopped, looked around the room, then gave a long, low whistle as her eyes took in the studio. "Damn!" she murmured, sounding amazed, "you worked your butt off, didn't you?"

"Oh JJ, it's hopeless," Gwen whimpered, and JJ walked over to her then, perched on the edge of the couch.

"It's not hopeless, *nena*," she crooned, rubbing the tight muscles of Gwen's back with a strong hand.

"I didn't get one grant done today!" Gwen wouldn't have done this with just anyone, but she knew JJ had the patience to indulge her despair, at least for a little while. She wouldn't try to fix it, and she wouldn't get mad that she couldn't fix it, two qualities Gwen had come to really appreciate in a woman.

"Sshh, sshh," JJ whispered, kneading her fingers along the sides of Gwen's neck. "You don't have to solve it all tonight," she reminded. Gwen closed her eyes and let her muscles surrender to JJ's touch.

She almost drifted into sleep when JJ stood and Gwen moaned like a child, "Don't go." JJ assured her she'd be right back. A minute later Gwen heard the sound of water rushing through the pipes, spilling into the old bathtub.

After a time JJ returned, and gently lifted Gwen off the couch. They walked across the chipped floor, making their way toward the brocade curtain. Candles illuminated the small, makeshift bathroom. In their light Gwen could see that the tub foamed with bubble bath. The scent of lavender enveloped filled the room.

JJ helped her off with her dirt-caked clothes and held Gwen's hand as she stepped over the steep side of the tub. Gwen eased into the hot water gratefully, letting it soak the strands of hair trailing down the back of her neck.

JJ removed her own tight jeans and T-shirt; she too stepped into the tub, settling behind Gwen so she could rest her head on JJ's chest. With a washcloth she slowly scrubbed Gwen's face and neck, her arms, her shoulders. Then the washcloth sank beneath the surface of the water as her hands came to rest on Gwen's breasts. Gwen could feel her nipples rise to meet JJ's fingers. JJ leaned to kiss her and Gwen's lips found hers, but then Gwen stopped her.

"I'm sorry, baby," Gwen murmured to the water, "I can't tonight. I keep thinking about Emma…"

"Sshh," JJ put a finger to her lips, "It's okay." She wrapped her legs around Gwen's thighs and held her close until the water grew tepid. Then they crawled out of the tub and dried off, leaving the damp towels in a heap on top of their discarded clothes. JJ had heated water in the old kettle; she offered a cup of herbal tea. Gwen made a face; she hated herb tea. She wanted coffee, but JJ protested, "Despite what you say, your body does not really want caffeine at two o'clock in the morning."

So Gwen meekly took the cup from her and said, "Yes, dear."

That was another game they played: "Obedience." JJ insisted Gwen was the most stubborn woman she'd ever met, so on the rare occasions when Gwen did what JJ wanted, she liked to make a big show of her acquiescence.

JJ believed they were headed for bed, but instead Gwen pulled a robe from the wardrobe rack, draped her body in faded pink chenille and headed back to the couch. "I wanna watch something for a minute," she explained. JJ reluctantly slid into a denim shirt and followed her to the battered sofa.

Gwen pulled a tape from the stack of six videos on top of the TV, slid it into the VCR, and waited for the image to crackle to life. By this time, JJ had caught on to what Gwen was up to. "Are you sure you wanna do this now?" she asked, but they'd been together long enough that she knew not to try to talk Gwen out of it.

Then Emma's voice rose over the title credits, which read "The Essence of Desire." Petals floated from above as the artist's disembodied voice chanted. *"He loves me, he loves me not. She loves me, she loves me not. Me loves me, me loves me not. He loves she, he loves she not. She loves she, she loves she not. Me loves she..."*

Like so much art seemed to these days, the piece dealt with gender. And, like most video Gwen saw by young artists, the piece was self-conscious, with lots of arty effects thrown in to cover a lack of technical confidence. But the formal aspects of the work soon fell away as Gwen watched the vibrant presence of Emma. She appeared first dressed as a "woman," her hair styled, face made-up, wearing deliberately sexy clothes, high heels. She spent several minutes in this guise kissing a skinny, red-haired man, passionate, responding to his lead.

Then a quick cut. Now she was dressed as a "man," her hair disappeared beneath a baseball cap, no makeup save a mustache glued to her upper lip. Baggy pants. Shirt and jacket that robbed her body of all shape. In this scene she kissed an Asian woman with equal fervor; this time she was in charge, and the woman responded to her.

Other combinations ensued. Emma the "man" made out

with the red-haired man; Emma the "woman" tongue-wrestled the Asian femme. Then there were threesomes with Emma first as "woman," then as "man."

In the final scene, Emma was naked but for her tattoo and the rings in her nose and eyebrow. Her hair was loose, unstyled, her face devoid of makeup. She knelt before a large mirror and began pressing her lips deep into its silvery pool, kissing her reflection. At various times the reflection changed into her image as "woman" and as "man." The tape ended with a shot from behind the mirror, the live woman embracing the flattened, two-dimensional plane, the blackened surface of the looking glass all but obscuring her image.

The tape ended and the screen was full of snow, hissing in the darkened loft.

"Who would do this to her?" Gwen raged. "Men are just fucking evil, you know?"

"*People* are evil," JJ corrected, as she drew Gwen close. "*Some* people, *nena*." JJ was culturally and generationally inclined to reject a separatist view of the world.

Gwen ducked from her embrace to hunt for the telephone.

"Who do you think you're calling at two thirty in the morning?" JJ protested, but Gwen was rooting around to find a particular scrap of paper.

When she found it, she punched the numbers into the phone. Ayisha answered on the first ring; as Gwen had suspected, she wasn't sleeping.

"Ayisha, it's Gwen. Listen, I've been thinking, and... Peg can stay here, okay?"

Listening, she grimaced. "Yeah, fine, her lover too."

Then she warned, "It's an industrial loft, not *Better Homes and Gardens*. And I hope they're bringing sleeping bags, because I don't have a bed for them."

Once she'd hung up, JJ beamed her approval. But Gwen felt shame for even being concerned about her own comfort, or territorialism, or vanity. Emma was dead, brutalized and discarded, and Gwen was worried that someone she hadn't seen in twenty years might find out she was a bad housekeeper.

"Come to bed, *nena*," JJ urged in a voice of warm silk.

Gwen shook her head. "Can't," she said ruefully. "I've got three grants due Friday. Now I just have tonight and tomorrow."

JJ swallowed her argument; they'd been through this so many times before. She merely kissed the top of Gwen's head. "I'll be waiting for you."

I count on that, Gwen realized, as she hauled her body toward the salvaged door-on-two-sawhorses that functioned as her desk, turned on her computer, and picked up a file folder.

Chapter 3

**Wednesday & Thursday,
June 12 & 13, 1996**

A staccato of gunfire punctured the quiet of a late Wednesday afternoon. "Ted!" Luanne had to holler to make herself heard, "Te-ed! You know you don't watch TV until you've done your homework!"

The gunshots died abruptly and Ted appeared in the kitchen doorway, his hand gripping one sneakered foot while he balanced precariously on the other. "What if I don't have any homework?" The question brimmed with innocence, but the sheepish grin curling at the corners of his mouth acknowledged that he knew this ploy was feeble.

"Aw, Mom, how come I can't watch first and then do my homework?"

Still wiping up remnants of peanut butter from Ted's after-school snack, Luanne Ingersoll was in no mood to argue. "Because those are the rules, Ted, and if you don't like them you can speak to your father about it tonight." She did not raise her voice, but slapped the sponge against the tabletop for emphasis.

Without another word Ted spun on one leg and zoomed out of the room, arms spread, roaring like a jet airplane as if to prove she could not hold him back forever; he could fly away. As Luanne wiped a milk ring from the kitchen table she cursed herself for invoking Mike's authority. *What a throwback*, she chided. The problem was, it worked.

Her entire history of raising Ted seemed to consist of cleaning up after him and trying to rein him in. Her son possessed a willful yet unfocused energy she did not understand, and against which she struggled constantly to exert herself. This was not how she'd imagined motherhood when she first decided to get pregnant nine years ago.

She'd imagined a tiny girl, with eyes full of stars, who'd grow up to be someone utterly unlike her: stronger, smarter, more sure of herself. And Luanne would watch, amazed that such a being had come from her.

When Ted was born Mike had been so goofy with pride that Luanne never had the heart to tell him she was disappointed. But the image of the tiny girl with eyes like novas had never stopping haunting her, this ghost of the child she had conjured but not borne.

The heavy footfalls of the mailman against the wooden planks of the front porch broke her reverie. A splash of sweet air stirred against her skin as she cracked the screen door to pull the bundle from the mailbox. Spring had come to Michigan so late this year, the extended winter dragging on her bones these last months, and now it seemed they were moving directly into summer. She was unprepared. In another week Ted would be out of school, and what was she going to do with him while she worked, now that her mother had grown so forgetful?

Luanne hung in the doorway, reluctant to return to the chores that called her inside. Her part-time job as a dental technician did not leave her much time to attend to the care of the house, which still fell entirely on her shoulders. The screen door slammed at her back as she began listlessly sorting the mail. A catalogue snared her attention: Hudson's was having its Home Sale. She browsed, pausing for a moment to covet glossy pictures of carpeting.

A sigh of discouragement blew from her lips. The economy was down, car sales had been sluggish, and Mike would insist they couldn't afford new carpeting, even though they'd lived in this townhouse for six years, and the carpeting hadn't been new when they'd moved in. *Maybe I can talk him into patio furniture*, she mused, licking a finger to turn a page.

The phone rang and she searched for the cordless receiver, finally turning it up underneath a sofa cushion—*damn this stupid new technology!*— and said hello after the sixth ring.

It was someone she'd not spoken to since Ted was a baby. "Luanne. It's Dana." The voice still spoke in short staccato sentences. Luanne did not have to think to know it was Dana Firestein.

Without waiting for Luanne's response, the voice continued, spitting out those same gruff bursts of sound. Her daughter. Raped. Murdered. A memorial. In Manhattan. Would she come?

"What? Emma…?" As usual, Luanne lagged a few steps behind Dana's rapid-fire speech.

Dana repeated the information without any deviation of word or inflection, as if she were reciting from a prepared sheet.

"But who?" Luanne was still grappling with the fact of Dana's news. "Someone she knew?"

"Of course, the fucking cops don't have a clue." The derision in Dana's tone was familiar to Luanne.

In the aftermath of the call, Luanne would question her memory of the brevity of the conversation; had she really said so little, had she even expressed her sympathy? Then she would wonder if perhaps the conversation had been designed to deflect just those expressions, so that Dana would not have to deal with anyone else's grief.

Luanne clicked off the cordless. In her lap sat the catalogue onto which she'd scribbled a date and a time, an address. Dana's daughter. Impossible to imagine that Emma could be twenty-three. Impossible to believe she could be dead.

The dam separating past from present broke and Luanne was awash in a current of sorrow and memory. There was no one like Dana in her life now. Luanne had been another person when she'd known her.

Summer of '75. Luanne Conley had driven all the way from Detroit to Massachusetts in her '67 Tempest, metal-flake blue, black vinyl-roofed muscle car, Aretha wailing on the eight-track. Needle pushing ninety, escaping Detroit, the squeeze of the oil embargo, two winters of unemployment and nothing the union could do about it, the cramped yellow room in her parents' home that still sported the detritus of high school.

Without work, she'd enrolled in community college. When the class in Labor History had proved full, she'd signed up for History of Women. The instructor was a skinny, intense woman, long red hair pulled back in a clip, and more fire behind the eyes than any woman Luanne had ever known. Her words were darts, pointed and carefully aimed, hurled through the air, so different from the hushed plaintive timbres of Luanne's mother, the musical burble of her girlfriends.

Her words had ruptured the membrane that stretched over Luanne's life. Luanne had lived in that skin, sealed off, protected, confined and, once it had broken, she'd begun to bleed rage that sluiced over the men in her life—the stranger in front of her in the unemployment line; the man in the gas station who tried to flirt with her; her father, laid off from the plant, watching game shows all day—and she'd seemed unable to staunch the flow. It was her instructor who'd told her about Labrys.

The sound of Mike's car crunching on the driveway yanked her back to the present. The back door swung wide. "Hi, honey!" Mike kissed her quickly, at the same time surveying the kitchen. "You haven't started dinner?" There was a whine to his voice. "I'm starving! I spent my lunch hour taking some Bloomfield Hills debutante for a test drive. Her first car, and daddy wants it to be a Cadillac!"

"I'm sorry, Mike, I…" She started to tell him, then stopped herself. "I don't know where the afternoon went." Solicitude dripped from her voice, a warm, slippery oil. "How 'bout if I make some tacos? That'll be quick."

"I know! Why don't we just pile in the car and go out for pizza?" Mike spoke half to her, half to Ted, who'd just come whizzing into the room.

"Yay pizza! Yay pizza!" Ted took up a little chant, hopping around the kitchen. Mike looked to her for a response.

What she wanted was to send the two off by themselves; she

wanted time to digest the death of Emma, whom she'd known as a little girl. She needed to figure out how she was going to get herself to New York by the day after tomorrow, where she would find the money, how she would explain it to Mike, what she would do about Ted. But all that would have to wait.

"Yay, pizza," she parroted and made her mouth relax into a grin. "Just give me a minute to comb my hair."

"Don't take all night, Mom," Ted called after her in such a flawless parody of Mike that it stopped her heart.

Luanne hurried upstairs and into the bathroom, where she pulled a comb through her short graying hair. Both Mike and her mother were always telling her to dye it, but she wanted to look just like she looked. Lines sprouted around her eyes and mouth like tributaries on a map; soft padding cushioned her chin. Forty-six years old.

She hadn't even liked Labrys; she'd spent the entire eight weeks of that long-ago summer in a state of fury. Fury at the theorists who spouted abstractions so removed from women's daily lives. Fury at the politicos, puffed with self-importance, their rules of correctness. And especially fury at the lesbians, who were there in abundance, their boots and crew cuts, their accusations that straight women like Luanne were traitors, consorting with the enemy.

Dana was a politico and a lesbian, but in Dana she found a woman whose rage matched her own. Dana respected Luanne's union work, her class background. Also, as one of the organizers of Labrys, Dana had been besieged with criticism, and this too had drawn Luanne's sympathies.

Mike knew nothing about that summer of her life. Why should he? She had fled Labrys, disgusted with the women's movement. Her old life opened to welcome her back, then folded securely around her as if she'd never left, the membrane once more intact. She never again saw the skinny red-haired instructor of the History of Women. For several years she'd corresponded with Dana, writing about her union organizing activities, asking for advice. But in the Eighties she'd quit her union work, gone back to school for dental tech training. She no longer wanted to live inside the kind of anger that had fueled her twenties. She'd met Mike while cleaning his teeth.

She stared into the bathroom mirror, trying to find the evidence of the person she'd once been. The mouth had gone soft, the cheeks drooped in surrender, but in the eyes she found it, a kind of steel, determination reborn.

"Mom, come on! We're hungry!" Ted yelled up the stairs.

"Be right there." Luanne swiped a lipstick across her mouth, her one concession to vanity. As she turned to go, she caught one more look at herself. The eyes gleamed back at her.

She would use the money she'd been saving for a family vacation. And she'd have to impose on her mother, forgetful or not, one last time. The face in the mirror reminded her of her younger self, stubborn and resolute, sneaking out of the house at night to meet boys at the bowling alley. She'd never gotten caught.

The road hummed beneath the wheels of the camper as the blacktop stretched before them. The back roads of Pennsylvania were lush and lined with trees; fields spun past the windows in a green-gold haze.

Ruthie liked to imagine the camper as a rolling world transiting through the larger one, contained and safe. A world suffused with the smells of everyday comfort—the must of bedding, the sweetness of apples entwined with the pungency of coffee, the creamy herbal waft of hand lotion—and with the melodic tones of Peg's conversation, as pleasant and as mildly distracting as a chorus of musical birds. Easily navigating the two-lane road, nearly deserted on a Wednesday afternoon, Ruthie drew a sigh of contentment from deep in her senses.

Ruthie was driving and Peg was talking, an arrangement so natural that it might have always been just so. Although they'd been "on the road" for nearly seven years, inhabiting this moving world like twins floating in their amniotic sea, Peg had yet to fully master the Westfalia. The gearshift still made her nervous, after a lifetime of automatic transmissions. Besides, Peg loved to talk while she drove. Talking, for Peg Morrison, was an art form, one that involved her entire body and captivated her full attention, frequently to the detriment of her driving.

"You have no idea what it was like, Ruthie!" Peg's round face puckered, ringed by a puff of gray curls that bobbed with every shake of her head. "I was a good Catholic girl. My whole life was like *Ladies' Home Journal.* I was The Wife: my job was to stay home, polish the furniture, raise the kids, soothe George. He wasn't a brutal man, not like my father; he just saw me as his nanny. It seems so *primitive* now, but back then there were no other options. At least," she added with a sidelong glance at Ruthie, who'd been a lesbian since she stepped from the cradle, "none that I knew about. For God's sake, I was even a virgin when I got married!"

Half-listening, Ruthie was lulled by the rhythm of the road, by the rise and fall of Peg's voice. Like all of Peg's stories, she had heard this one a hundred times in the sixteen years they'd been together, but she never tired of the Irish lilt, the round full notes of Peg's speech. Ruthie reached across the gearshift to rest a hand on Peg's ample thigh, the tan skin seamed below navy blue shorts. "I would have loved to meet you when you were still a virgin." She grinned. "I could have shown you a few options."

Peg blushed with pleasure, her pink cheeks deepening to rubies, her grin disclosing large white teeth. It had taken her till age fifty, half a lifetime, to find someone who made her feel so courted, so lusted after. Were it not for Labrys, she reflected, she might never have opened to the possibility of loving a woman. Were it not for Labrys, she might still, in fact, be serving out the sentence of her marriage, *till death do you part.*

"Twenty-five years," she picked up the thread of her narrative as an expert knitter retrieves a dropped stitch, "I don't know how I survived! I grew to hate George—it got so the sight of his dirty clothes made me nauseous! I started burning them in the backyard, big bonfires fueled by jockey shorts and recent issues of women's magazines."

Ruthie Cowan nurtured her own private image of Peg as she would have appeared then—barefoot, hair loose and wild, face streaked with soot–reeling around a blaze in the neat backyard of her suburban home like one of Macbeth's witches, the neighbors stunned silent, pretending not to stare. But all Ruthie said was,

"What time do you have?" The hum of the wheels receded as she slowed the camper, approaching an entrance to the turnpike. She was sorry to leave behind the meandering roads they'd been following all day for the hurtling pace of the highway.

Pulling one plump, freckled arm closer to her eyes—for she was vain about wearing glasses—Peg squinted at her watch before reporting, "About twenty after three." From the glove box brimming with maps and cassette tapes, gum and Life Savers she extracted a red plastic coin purse emblazoned with the words, Put Your Money Where Your Movement Is. A souvenir of the Decade for Women, Houston 1980, the first year they had been lovers. Recalling that time, a smile played across her lips as she counted out the proper coins and dropped them into Ruthie's outstretched palm.

"We should make it to Ann's by about six thirty," Ruthie surmised, accelerating onto the road. This time the song the tires sang was urgent, its rhythms insistent, pulling them forward, faster, faster. "Do we need to stop and call her?"

Peg snorted. She'd branded Ann "my *yuppie* daughter," in a voice thick with distaste. Curls bobbing, she said, "Annie's not waiting on *us*. She told me she'd be working late tonight, but *Hank*"—this name uttered in a tone that suggested she had come upon a very bad smell—"should be home by eight. I guess that's 'early.' *Consuela* is there with the twins. Whoever thought *my* kid would turn out like *that*?"

Try as she might, Peg could not let go of a vague sense of disappointment, like a stone in her shoe that both irritated and caused her pain. It wasn't merely her own progeny; a whole generation of women had dismissed and discarded feminism at the same time their lives were irrevocably altered by it, and they provoked Peg to fury and despair.

It seemed her life had traversed an impossible distance, the way travel to the moon must once have seemed a quixotic yearning. Its span encompassed two entirely different beings, the housewife and the radical dyke, and all the space between. She could never understand how the daughters of moon travelers could be content to explore no further than their own scraps of ground.

Her sigh then was so loud and so melancholy, seeming to exude from the cave of years, that Ruthie picked up her hand and gently kissed it. Peg ran the same hand over the yeasty flesh of Ruthie's arm, bared by a white sleeveless shirt.

"At least she's alive," Peg said, giving voice to Ruthie's unspoken thoughts. It reminded them of why they were making this particular trip, in such great haste. "I can't imagine what it must be like for Dana. Not just to lose a child, but in that way..." She shuddered and closed her eyes against the thought.

She recovered fiercely. "We can't just go there to mourn this like some inevitable tragedy. We have to do something to make sure the predator gets caught and never does this to another woman. We owe Emma that at least."

They drove on for several miles in silence, then Peg spoke again. "I really wonder who's going to be there from Labrys. When I was there I felt so alone, like a refugee from the nuclear family. It seemed like everyone else paired up, women with women, this strange country where I didn't know the customs. Everybody was younger than me, I felt like a den mother at a slumber party. I never would have imagined that twenty years later I'd be traveling back to see them in my home on wheels with the love of my life."

A journey to the house of the past is likely to invoke unwelcome traveling companions, Elena Martínez reflected. Ghosts of one's former selves appear and disappear from rooms cramped with nostalgia, bitterness, regret. Unfulfilled longings reawaken, roam the halls like restless beasts at night. Still, the invitation arrives, unbidden, and one cannot help but go.

Elena believed herself to be, above all, a pragmatist, with scant patience for mysticism or sentiment. Yet the report on her lap, one of several that bulged from her leather briefcase, blurred in her vision, its seraphs dancing as memory wound around her like a noose.

High overhead, lights twinkled from the domed ceiling into a gray atmosphere that bleached blood and nerve from everything it touched. The airport enfolded her in its damp embrace, breathed its chill, chemical air against her cheek. This would be her fifth flight in three days, she whose fear of flying was surpassed only by her refusal to indulge it. Her throat ached and her skin was dry as parchment. In the bathroom at the Denver airport this morning she'd noticed a dark blue vein throbbing below her left eye, like a river pulsing toward the delta of her hollowed temple. It was her exhaustion, she reasoned, this flattening of the senses, dulling of the nerve sparks, that caused the veil between past and present, between the dead and the living to be worn so thin. Her Tia Rosa used to say, "There are spirits with us tonight," but Elena did not believe in ghosts; they belonged to a world she had left behind, such a long time ago.

Something was being announced over the indecipherable loudspeaker. Straining to hear through the static, she surreptitiously slipped off one black suede high-heeled pump and allowed herself the momentary pleasure of stretching her toes.

Thus pampered, Elena sternly redirected her lapsed attention to the report spread open before her, which would next week be distributed to select members of Congress. Her pen scratched desultory notations, but the hand that gripped it was slow and leaden. *Coffee*, a voice stirred inside her, and her mouth began to water. Coffee, she knew, would restore her edge, her keenness, but that dark brew, blood of her life since childhood, was now forbidden. Four years ago a heart attack, last year the ulcer. *Slow down, you're almost sixty*, commanded the white-coated doctors standing over her with their creased foreheads, but although Elena had surrendered her coffee and her cigarettes, she would not let them take from her her work.

Her work, which she sometimes dreamt of as weaving, the way her father's mother and aunts had loomed their blankets, colors of earth and sky, and she, Elena, like a shuttle negotiating the warp, zigzagging the country, spinning an unbroken web of fund-raising, congressional testimony and community organizing, keeping all the threads taut. Elena had founded the Committee on Reproductive Rights in 1972, stringing together a network that now spanned the fifty states.

The early days had been so heady, a whole movement taking

shape, pulled from the bright skeins of her vision. In the last decade, though, the enemy had descended with blades to slit the filaments, threatening to unravel the entire tapestry.

It was not so much the political losses that weighted her spirit, for Elena Martínez was a warrior; she loved nothing better than contesting a formidable opponent; that made the eventual victory all the sweeter. It was the human cost that ate at her insides.

She thought mournfully of Emma, whom she scarcely knew, who existed for her more as an idea than a person, a young woman snuffed out in her prime. Then her thoughts turned, inevitably, to Kay. Once again she felt herself sucked back through the veil, the airport dimming into shadow as Kay's sassy, exuberant laughter filled her ears. The last time she'd seen Kay was at an airport; it was raining in Tallahassee and she'd stepped down onto the tarmac to see her holding a bouquet of white flowers. Kay, radiant at age sixty-five, like a flower herself.

It was at Labrys that Elena had met Kay Vlasick; in that rocky soil were sown the seeds of an association that had lasted eighteen years. Until her death, Kay had served as Statewide Coordinator for CORR in Florida. What sprouted from those seeds was not a friendship; Elena was perhaps incapable of friendship. The two women never socialized, never shared a meal that wasn't a meeting, never exchanged the bits of gossip and personal history that baste one life to another. Yet there was a rare blooming of trust. It was with Kay, and no one else, that Elena would divulge her doubts about a given strategy; from Kay, and no one else, she would seek counsel.

Kay was gone, two years now, dead from a bullet in her brain. Her husband put it there, before he closed his lips around the barrel and took the next one himself. In eighteen years of political work, Elena had never met Kay's husband, something she'd only realized once it was too late.

Through a haze of static, Elena heard the boarding announcement for her flight to New York. Wearily she gathered her things—pen slipped into handbag, file stuffed into briefcase—and rose slowly, stretching her cramped muscles, straightening the creases in her dark silk skirt.

Rain was streaking the Chicago twilight as she settled next to the window in coach, strapping the seatbelt tight across her lap. Her staff was forever trying to book her into business class, but Elena always refused. "That's not what our donors are paying for," she insisted.

Reflexively she bent to retrieve the neglected report, rummaging sightlessly through the stack of manila folders. Kay was gone, now Dana's daughter too, dead of the violence that no amount of political action had been able to stem.

The plane began to roll away from the gate, picking up momentum as it hurtled down the runway. Elena clutched the arms of her seat and pressed her eyes shut; she would have offered a prayer had she believed there was anyone to pray to. Instead she drew in long, shuddering breaths, trying to modulate her anxious heartbeat. Once airborne, she relaxed her posture, wiping her damp palms on a crumpled tissue, ignoring the curious, sympathetic gaze of the man in the aisle seat.

Chapter 4

Friday, June 14, 1996

Gwen was sure it was immoral to be having a fashion crisis when she was on her way to a memorial. She confronted six portable racks sagging with clothing, and not one item among them was truly appropriate for the occasion. When she had decided she would never again work in an office, she'd made a big ritual out of giving her office clothes to a homeless woman on Astor Place (and even had her friend Tiger videotape her doing so, an act she now deeply regretted), but today she mourned that cast-off navy blue suit, that demure black wool dress.

Now it appeared that the most sedate thing in her wardrobe was an old black cocktail waitress uniform from the 1950s. It was a tasteful length, falling just below the knee. True, it was a little form fitting, but this was offset by the garment's fabric, heavy cotton that suggested nothing of skin. In theory it should have worked—it was black, it was a dress—but as she studied herself in the mirror she concluded that she looked ridiculous, as if she were in costume, which of course she was.

So she tried the layered look, sliding into a man's suit jacket, but the ensemble only grew more ludicrous. Not to mention that the temperature on this June morning had soared to a few degrees shy of sweltering. She had been to any number of funerals and memorials over the last ten years, but they'd been for gay men dead of AIDS, artists mostly, and the concept of appropriate attire was entirely open to interpretation. It was hard sometimes to remember that other people died, and of other causes, and that in such cases sequined evening gowns and feather boas were not necessarily suitable mourning attire.

She was stuck with the dress, she realized, and next came the quandary of footgear. When she'd worn this uniform in that long-ago performance she'd had waitress shoes, of course, dyed black, but even if she could have found them, it wasn't the look she was going for. Normally her shoe wardrobe was scattered over the floor of her studio, making it easy to spot at least one of whatever she was looking for, but in her fit of cleaning she'd dumped everything into a box. Now she was forced to dredge through its contents, strewing cowboy boots and fuck-me pumps, plastic jellies and chewed-up flip-flops in her wake. She foraged until she broke into a serious sweat, panicked about what in hell she was going to do, when she pulled out a pair she'd had so long she'd forgotten them. Black suede wedgies, with a delicate T-strap and an open toe, that had belonged to her grandmother.

Her grandmother's feet had been a full size smaller than Gwen's. She'd kept them more as coveted objects, a memento of her grandmother, than as something to actually wear. Which was why they were still in good shape—as her mother had told her a thousand times, Gwen tended to be hard on shoes. Still, she could just squeeze her feet into them and close the buckle at its very last hole. The pain was nothing compared to her relief at finding something to go with the dress.

She glanced at her watch; JJ would be here any minute. She hadn't wanted to go to the memorial, but after some serious persuasion had reluctantly agreed. Gwen was still trying to convince her to stick around after, not make her deal with Peg and her partner alone, but she hadn't yet broken through JJ's resistance. "I think I should just stay at my folks' this weekend," she'd told her this morning, but Gwen still hoped to sway her. She stared once more into the mirror. The dress was crackpot, no getting around it, but at least the shoes looked like they were part of the outfit. Her red hair was in need of a touch-up—she spotted a corona of gray-brown sprouting from the roots—and piled in a heap on top of her head, held by an assortment of barrettes and clips, pinks and yellows and greens; her lipstick was a flattering shade of purple. She was sure to get shit from somebody about wearing lipstick, but that was just the way it went.

As she heard the horn from JJ's van in the street below—three long blasts followed by three short, their signal—Gwen grabbed several inches worth of bangle bracelets and slid them onto her wrists.

She took a panicked look around the studio; already the disarray had started to return like a fur of mold no cleaning solvent can destroy. She could only pray she'd have an hour or two between the memorial and the arrival of the women who were supposed to crash here. Then the horn blasted again; was it Gwen's imagination or did it actually sound more impatient this time? She remembered to snatch up the clutch purse into which she'd stuffed keys, ID, some money, a few tissues and her lipstick, and then, limping only slightly, she rushed down four flights of splintered stairs to the street.

JJ had dropped her off while she looked for a parking space, so Gwen made her way down a side aisle of the church and stood there to wait for her.

Judson Church on Washington Square looked nothing like the churches of her childhood, stone monuments to Jesus and the Pope. Nondenominational, it was refreshingly free of the cloying self-righteousness that too often pervaded houses of worship. Still, Dana's parents had worked up a good head of steam over the fact that this ceremony was not being performed in a temple or a Jewish mortuary, and were freely venting their distress from the front row of pews. The word from Ayisha was that Dana had chosen this site at least partially for the purpose of making her parents crazy. Dana hadn't seen them in over thirty years, though she had allowed Emma to have a relationship with them, which Emma apparently chose to do at least partially for the purpose of making Dana crazy.

There were several distinct groups present, clustered in

separate regions of the church. Up at the front by the dais was Dana's family, dressed expensively and looking around the room with disgruntled expressions. Near the side door was a collection of young women and men whose severe haircuts and wistful angst identified them as art students and Emma's friends. In the back were clustered a ragtag bunch of club hounds, rough trade, and apparent substance abusers—evidently a different set of Emma's friends—sporting herds of leather. Then there were the indifferently dressed middle-aged women with bad haircuts who had for the last three decades been Dana's comrades. As Gwen studied each group it was not at all clear where she fit in.

Eventually, Ayisha spotted her; she was wearing a simple black cotton shirt and pressed pants. Gwen could already feel a sheen of sweat sprouting at her hairline, but Ayisha appeared unaffected by the heat.

"A couple of changes," Ayisha announced by way of greeting. She avoided looking Gwen right in the eye. "There are a couple of other women in from Labrys who need a place to stay, and I've set them up at your place."

"What?" Gwen started to protest, but Ayisha had more in store for her.

"*And* Dana's inviting everyone to come over to your place after the service."

"What exactly do you mean by 'everyone'?" Her voice climbed a register in panic.

"Well, not everyone," Ayisha explained, so calmly that Gwen suspected she was on autopilot. "Just the Labrys women, and some of Emma's friends. *Women* friends," she emphasized, in case that was a concern.

"Wait a minute," Gwen blurted too loud, before the sudden turn of heads in their direction reminded her to lower the volume. "I told you I'd put *two* women up for a night. That's all. Not a few more women, and not host a reception."

"Look, Dana just sprang this on me when women started to get here." She lowered her voice to a conspiratorial whisper, "She's completely freaked out. She won't cry, but she's acting totally wigged, firing off orders, then changing her mind every five minutes. If you've got a problem, you better deal with her about it."

Dana's always like that, Gwen was tempted to argue, but she reminded herself to practice compassion. Ayisha looked about ten years older than the first day they'd met, as if she were carrying about eight people's burdens for them. Gwen wanted to put her arms around the younger woman, but nothing in her bearing invited it. This reception thing was really not her headache, and Gwen decided not to make it any harder on her.

"Do you know where Dana is?"

"Around, I guess." Ayisha shrugged and moved off to greet a young woman with a totally shaved head. The minute they embraced, they both dissolved into tears.

JJ was taking forever to park; Gwen feared her lover must be cursing her for dragging her out on this sweltering day to mourn someone she'd never met.

Gwen recognized a few faces among the Labrys group, but she blanked out on most of their names. One Latina who was a big leader in abortion rights. A nondescript woman who always used to complain about being oppressed by lesbians. The ones who'd shown up were those who would have been voted "most likely to remain politically active," the ones with whom Dana must have kept in touch.

It was almost noon, and still no sign of Dana. Gwen had to stop and mutter a quick Serenity Prayer, because she could feel her anger rising like the wing of a huge dark bird. She tried to make herself hear each phrase of the prayer, to absorb the message, not just rattle off the syllables like some meaningless jingle for processed food.

Then, as if the simple prayer had conjured them, Gwen suddenly saw Dana standing in the vestibule with the one person she never expected to run into here: Howard, her AA sponsor. He was wearing a suit, which was how she knew he was on duty. Though she was curious about his presence here, she was more confounded by how in hell she was gonna give Dana Firestein a good chewing out at her own daughter's funeral in front of the person to whom Gwen most owed her sobriety and emotional health. Moving closer, though, she realized that

Dana was giving Howard a browbeating, yelling actually. She noticed another suited man, African-American, standing to one side, alert, but willing to let Howard handle this.

"You have no fucking business being here, O'Hara, no goddamn right to invade–" Dana blustered.

Gwen recognized the flush on Howard's face that meant he was trying his best to keep a civil tongue. "Ms. Firestein, we're not here to intrude. I'm just trying to do a job here, and we need to talk to some of your daughter's friends. One of them may have some information about what happened to Emma."

"You don't really think one of her *friends* would do this to her?"

"We have to look at every possibility. We canvassed the club where your daughter was supposed to be that night. A few people remember her coming in—the bouncer, the bartender—but nobody remembers seeing her leave. Ms. Firestein, guys who commit this kind of crime don't tend to do it just once. Whoever he is, we want to find him before he does it to someone else's daughter."

It was into this fray that Gwen walked, trying for nonchalance. "Dana," she said, "it's Gwen Kubacky. I'm so sorry about Emma."

She looked like she was about to yell at Gwen for interrupting, but then her face rearranged itself as if she remembered that she planned to impose on Gwen—big time—in the very near future, and she managed a hollow, "Gwen, thanks for coming."

"Hey, Howard." Gwen hugged the burly detective, who acknowledged her with a simple, "Gwen." They were both looking at her bug-eyed like neither could believe she knew the other.

Dana whirled around and muttered, "I've got to get this thing started," but before she moved away Gwen said, "Dana, I need to talk to you."

"We will," she agreed, but then her attention was caught by the arrival of Chi Curtis, a dark-skinned Black woman who'd taught martial arts at Labrys. There'd been rumors that they were lovers at the time, though it was hard to imagine Dana letting down her guard enough to be lovers with anyone. Chi wrapped her in a long, muscular hug, and led her down the center aisle before Gwen could make her stand.

"You know her?" Howard's exaggerated Bronx vowels insinuated themselves into her ear.

"From a long time ago," she told him. "I only recently met Emma. I was kind of her mentor. So you caught this case, huh?"

"Yeah, I been workin' some late shifts to try to help out my ex-wife with her car payments, sort of making amends, y'know? Jesus, I hate when shit like this happens to little girls like this one."

"Not so little," Gwen reminded him, "and what, you think it's better if it happens to old ladies?"

JJ arrived just as Dana began to call everyone together, and they scrambled into a back pew with Howard and Detective Johnson as a boom box was brought to life with the voice of Me'Shell NdegéOcello. JJ began to snuffle softly; Gwen handed her a tissue. People took the music as their cue to settle down, falling into an expectant silence, but as the song played for a while and nothing happened, a current of restlessness rippled through the crowd.

As much as Gwen couldn't abide services conducted by priests or rabbis or ministers—especially if the deceased was a nonbeliever, and especially if the sermonizer never even met the deceased—still, the religious figure served as a kind of Master of Ceremonies for the event. These secular memorials, devoid of an authority figure, always seemed to have a centerless, anti-theatrical quality that frustrated the hell out of the seasoned performance artist.

Finally Dana rose to stand before the group. She hadn't bothered to dress up; she wore faded, ink-streaked Levi's—Emma had mentioned that Dana worked in a print shop—and a "Stop Violence Against Women" T-shirt. Gwen couldn't tell if she'd chosen this message in tribute to Emma or just pulled the first thing out of the laundry basket. Dana had an awkward time, fighting to speak over the music, until a too-thin young man with violet hair mercifully lowered the volume on the boom box.

"A few people told me they had some things they wanted to say," she announced without fanfare. As pugnacious as Dana could be, she'd never been a great public speaker, always seeming embarrassed to have the spotlight. It occurred to Gwen that her perpetual anger could be a front for some kind of pathological shyness. "It's not really organized," she added without apology, "You can just stand up whenever you want."

Dana sat down again but still nobody was sure what was expected. The now barely audible music couldn't fill the uncomfortable silence that dragged on for several minutes. The director in Gwen wanted to leap from her seat and start orchestrating the ritual. She felt lucky to be sitting next to Howard, whose very presence reminded Gwen that the occasion was not about her. She could almost hear him say, as he'd done so many times, "Humility means you shut yer trap and try to learn somethin'."

Detective Howard O'Hara was somebody she'd never have known in her life if it weren't for AA. She hadn't even been aware what Howard did for a living the first time she heard him speak at a meeting. Now he'd been her sponsor for a decade. There was a time in her life when Gwen would have sworn she could never love or trust a man. Any man. Let alone a straight white cop. For his part, Howard called her his "lezzie friend" with the deepest affection. It was a first for both of them.

It was Dana's mother who stood to break the silence. She was a tiny woman, barely five feet tall in her pumps. Her features had the unnatural sharpness that came from serial face-lifts, and her hair was salon-styled. There was no shortage of gold jewelry adorning her black wool dress. With the exception of the two friends who'd accompanied her, she was the only woman in the room with porcelain nails.

Looking at her Gwen couldn't help wondering if Dana had been adopted, so unalike did they seem, mother and daughter, yet when the mother began to speak Gwen recognized a defiant spirit that was surely passed on to her daughter. Her voice was nails-on-chalkboard abrasive, utterly without melody, despite the tears that etched their way through the layers of makeup.

"In our family's tradition, which is Judaism," she began,

aiming this in her daughter's direction, "it is customary to say a prayer for the dead. That prayer is called Kaddish. I'd now like to say Kaddish for my granddaughter." The whine in her voice also managed to convey "against the wishes of my daughter and despite her best efforts to prevent me from doing so."

"*Yit-ga-dal ve-yit-ka-dash she-mei ra-ba be-al-ma di-ve-ra chi-re-u-tei...*" she intoned. The small chorus of voices that joined hers came from her husband and the two other couples who'd accompanied them. Gwen mouthed the words silently, surprised she could still recall them.

It was because of Lee Bergman that Gwen knew the Kaddish. She'd met Lee at Labrys, when Lee was thirty-seven and she herself was twenty-two. Gwen hadn't been a lesbian when she'd gone to Labrys, but she sure as hell had become one eight weeks later when she left. Lee had been the reason she'd moved to New York; they lived together for six years. Lee had taught her to say the Kaddish when their cat, Meshugenah (Shuggie), died.

By the time the prayer ended Dana's mother was weeping in earnest; her pale husband stood and led her back to the pew. Her sobbing provoked others from every cluster; even Howard pulled out a handkerchief and blew his nose. For a few minutes everyone just sat and listened to these open expressions of grief.

Then a young woman whose jet-black hair did not match her skin tone wheeled a large video monitor to the front of the room. She was wearing a midriff-baring top (Gwen thought: *And I was worried about dressing appropriately?*), allowing the assembly to catch the glint of a gold ring in her pierced navel.

She too was tearful as she introduced herself as Kendra DeValle. The name was oddly familiar to Gwen; maybe Emma had mentioned her. Kendra was possessed of the convoluted manner of someone who knew she was really pretty but wanted to pretend that she wasn't aware of it, trying to both expose and erase herself in the same moment.

"Emma and I were really tight." She paused to wipe one eye, sending a streak of eyeliner across her cheek. "We were s'posed to collaborate on a tape together; we were gonna apply for a grant and everything. Her art was really dope, so I thought we should show something of hers." She managed to flick on the VCR and plop down on a pew in one smooth gesture.

The tape was cued, so the screen was immediately flooded with the image of Emma's slim naked body, white against a black backdrop, her face painted like a skeleton. Gwen couldn't follow it very well; she guessed that the tape was made earlier than the one she'd viewed the other evening. It had an immature verbosity, as if the artist had not yet discovered that a picture really can be worth a thousand words.

On the tape, Emma was talking about death, and evidently someone thought the tape would be appropriate for that reason. It was a young person's view of death, romanticized and unreal. From where Gwen was sitting in the back, she could only catch about three words in five, so she could easily be projecting her own meaning onto it. It was brief, though, maybe no more than three minutes long, which was good, because no other image was visible than the talking skeleton-head.

Gwen worried it was bad to be so critical of something shown at a memorial. It wasn't even that the artist had chosen to show it; maybe wherever her spirit was now she cringing and longing to utter a disclaimer.

The young man with the violet hair, who announced his name was Devon, got up to sing, unaccompanied. The song he'd chosen was Billie Holiday's "Don't Explain," but he seemed unaware it was a Billie Holiday song; he introduced it as a song off an album by the Wild Colonials. He attempted to link the song to this occasion—something about it being easy to be angry at someone who died but really they don't need to explain—but the logic was tenuous at best. He was credible as far as keeping on-pitch, but his voice was a thin tenor that couldn't begin to capture the dusky undertone the song demanded.

Since it was a memorial, there was no expectation of applause, a lucky thing in this case, because the most Gwen could have mustered was that kind of strained, halfhearted ovation that bespeaks politeness and pity. As his final notes faded in the air, the violet-haired Devon reclaimed his seat in silence and buried his head in the shoulder of the woman with the shaved head. To

Gwen's right, JJ sighed audibly.

Then a familiar, short, round woman from the Labrys group stood and made her way to the front. Even before she began to speak, Gwen recognized her as Peg Morrison, one of her soon-to-be houseguests, and she braced herself for a blast of strident rhetoric. Peg didn't disappoint.

"The patriarchy killed Emma Firestein," the gray-haired woman thundered like a fire-and-brimstone preacher. "The same patriarchy that killed Taya Courtney and D'Nisa Watson and Yolanda Velasquez, three other women under the age of thirty who were killed the same night Emma died."

Her ferocity and vocal projection made her appear to grow larger before the assembly. She paced the entire length of the altar, claiming the space, an old performance trick. Too much movement, however, has the effect of diffusing one's energy, and in Gwen's view, Peg was in danger of crossing that fine line.

"The police," she blazed, "will try to tell us that Emma brought it on herself, that Emma wasn't a 'nice girl,' that she didn't play by the rules."

Gwen felt Howard shift on the pew beside her, saw his fists curl with the effort to control his temper.

"But the police are just the army of the patriarchy whose mission is to enforce the rules of the patriarchy that enslave women. Emma Firestein was not at fault, she did not bring this on herself, and neither did Taya Courtney, D'Nisa Watson, Yolanda Velasquez, and who knows how many others murdered by the patriarchy that night, and every night.

"There's a war being waged against women! Its weapons are pornography, rape, battering, incest, marriage and murder. Patriarchy is our enemy! That's why as feminists we must never give up the fight to take back the night, take back the day, take back the streets, take back our homes, and take back control of our lives from the death-dealing patriarchy!"

Peg concluded at a volume that would not have been out of place a rally. Her face was bright red and her curls shook with each exclamation point. Her explosive energy left an enervated silence when she returned to her seat. There was a lot to be said for understatement, Gwen reflected. If she were Peg's director, she'd judge the performance over the top.

Peg was followed by a young woman whose dark hair was clipped into almost a brush cut. Tight black jeans hugged her stocky frame, her belly bulging over a wide black belt. Her arms were bare beneath a leather vest; tattoos curled on each bicep.

"*Mas macha,*" JJ whispered into Gwen's ear.

Gwen curled her lip. "The more they look like that on the outside, the bigger the baby they are on the inside."

The young woman did not pace, but stood her ground, hand cocked on hip, commanding everyone's attention before she said a word. Her performance power came from focus and concentration.

"I don't know much about 'the patriarchy,'" she began. Her soft voice belied her tough exterior. "But it seems to me we could march our brains out and not do a fucking thing for Emma. Good people get hurt, and the ones who do the hurting never have to pay for it. The world is shit, and if you don't stink of it, someone's gonna come along and rub your face in it until you do. That's just the way it is."

She never did introduce herself, just sat back down when she was finished, but the black-haired girl with the navel ring hooted, "You go, Kick!" The young woman's despair resonated in the atmosphere; one could almost touch its darkness. She couldn't be more than twenty-five. Where was her hope? A long pause followed, no one wanting to step into that gloom.

In the lull, Howard whispered, "So, which of these characters do you know?"

"Just the older feminists," Gwen murmured back. "I'm pretty sure none of them did it. But if *you* turn up dead, I could probably give the investigators a few leads."

When Ayisha stood, she looked oddly small against the backdrop of the altar. She did not cry, but her whole face was compressed with the effort of holding it back. In a voice everyone had to strain to hear, she said, "When my mom died last year, Emma was right there. She moved in with me so I wouldn't feel so alone."

She trailed off for a moment; her eyes seemed to be focused on something in the far distance. Then her concentration returned. "I've known Emma since we were little girls. The first time we ever got our periods, we got them in the same week! Of course, *she* was precocious, only about ten at the time. *I* was the late bloomer.

"We were sisters. I wish..." She paused, and the last words could barely be apprehended, "I wish I coulda looked out for her better." Then she sat.

Of all the speakers today, she was the one who'd put a lump in Gwen's throat. It felt like she might cry, but she knew she wouldn't. She hadn't cried for years. JJ's hand gestured for another tissue.

When at last Dana stood, everyone expected her to deliver the final tribute: the young life lost, the potential wasted, a mother's heart-wrenched search for meaning.

What she said instead was this: "There's gonna be a reception at two o'clock at Gwen Kubacky's loft on the Lower East Side. You're all invited. Gwen's in the back, she'll give you directions."

Gwen shook her head in disbelief as JJ looked at her quizzically. Everything in her longed to stand up and holler, "No fucking way!" but she couldn't do it, not there, not now. Acceptance, she reluctantly admitted, was her only recourse. Emma was dead, and Gwen was hosting a wake. Still, she at least needed to find out what Dana had in mind, so she crawled across JJ's knees to go talk to her.

As if she needed another complication, when she reached the end of the pew she ran smack into none other than Lee Bergman, her old love, her old nemesis, and for a moment she was frozen, as if she'd seen a ghost. "I thought that was you," Lee greeted her, "but I was standing in the back and couldn't be sure."

"I...I never expected to see *you* here," Gwen managed to stammer. Lee had never been political; even twenty years ago she claimed she'd only come to Labrys "to meet girls." It seemed inconceivable that she and Dana would still be in contact.

"I'm in New York on business," Lee explained, "and I ran into Elena who told me about this." Her face twisted in distaste. "It's a goddamn shame. Some sicko bastard gets his jollies killing young girls."

Lee gave her an appraising glance. "You look good, Gwen," she nodded her approval. Still, she couldn't seem to resist a jab. "Even if you do still dress like a kook."

Lee was wearing an expensive man's suit, Armani, Gwen guessed, charcoal gray. Her short hair was still dark, so Gwen decided she must dye it. She'd thickened in the waist, but the lines of the jacket did a good job of masking it. They both used to worry about their weight when they'd lived together, and each had blamed the other for bad eating habits.

"So the party's at your place." Lee grinned; Gwen could have sworn she was licking her chops like a cartoon wolf.

"You'll have to excuse me..." Gwen muttered, and slipped past her up the aisle, trying to intercept Dana. Howard and his partner had made their way over to the small throng of lowlifes with pallid complexions and greasy hair. Dana was trying to fend off her mother while being surrounded by Labrys women. All the while Chi shadowed her like a bodyguard.

"So what are *we* supposed to do," Dana's mother complained, "while you make a party with your friends?"

"Dana, I'm just so sick about this happening to your daughter..."

"Dana, I want you to meet Ruthie..."

"Dana," Gwen called over the clamor.

Dana turned. "Yeah, Gwen, you should probably get on over to your place, because people may start arriving."

Gwen could see she was not inhabiting her body. The brusqueness was simply habit, something to cover the enormous absence. Gwen couldn't take it personally.

"I gave Ayisha money to pick up some takeout," Dana recited like an automaton, "and Peg says she'll stop by the liquor store..."

"Listen, we have to do this without alcohol."

"Huh?"

"I'm sorry, I really need to not have people drinking in my house." Gwen felt a stab of guilt for even taking care of herself to this extent.

Peg overheard this. "I can just get lots of sodas and juices," she offered, and Dana nodded. Clearly, the last thing in the world she cared about was what people ate or drank.

"So, where is it again?" Dana asked, and Gwen dutifully recited the directions to her studio.

"And by the way," she concluded, "although there's an elevator, we can't use it. It's ancient, and it's not safe, and the landlord's freaked about liability, so tell everyone they have to take the stairs. Fifth floor." She inwardly dared someone to give her shit about accessibility for the disabled.

She tried not to think about the clothes and shoes she'd tried on and kicked off to every corner, the army of critics about to invade her life. She especially tried not to think about Lee Bergman, her presence in the place where she lived.

She watched Ayisha watching this exchange, looking relieved that Gwen hadn't made a stink. Now the Labrys women wanted to talk. "Oh, Gwen!" they began, but she extricated herself, saying she needed to get home and get a few things ready for their arrival.

She searched out JJ to tell her the bad news. JJ was talking to Howard, telling him, "Yeah, there's a dude named Jersey who plays sessions for us sometimes. He's a Jamaican dude, or his folks were from there, or something. Plays a pretty good saxophone."

Howard wanted to know how to find him. JJ said when she got to work, she'd ask around.

Gwen had to interrupt then, explaining that the hordes would be descending any minute. JJ put her arm around Gwen, saying, "*Vamanos, papita.*" Howard gave JJ his card, repeating that she should call him the minute she found out anything.

Chapter 5

The soundtrack to *Purple Rain*—no. *Led Zeppelin IV*—no. Chick Corea's *Return to Forever*—no. Cursing under her breath, JJ sorted through the shelf of CDs in Gwen's loft. For months she'd been after Gwen to keep them organized, but "order" wasn't a word in Gwen's vocabulary; the plastic cases were stacked without regard to era, alphabet or musical style.

Finally she stumbled on *Gracias A La Vida*, by Mercedes Sosa. That ought to meet Gwen's rigorous criteria. "Nothing too upbeat or experimental, no hard rock and no men," Gwen fired a reminder as she swept past JJ on the floor next to the CD player.

"How 'bout Madonna?" JJ inquired, deadpan, holding up *Like a Virgin*.

"JJ, use your head! These are *political* women…" Gwen sputtered before she realized that JJ was putting her on. "You're lucky I don't make you play all *wimmin's* music."

"Just try it, *poquetica*, and I'm out the door," JJ rejoined. "Besides, what about Emma's friends? You want them to think you're a fossil?"

"Christ, I'm the same age as their goddamned mothers, so by definition I'm ready for the old folks' home." Gwen feigned a trembling, stooped-over posture as she headed for the stairs with another bulging trash bag.

JJ added the Sosa to a pile of CDs that already included Nenah Cherry, Tori Amos and Abbey Lincoln. Why she was even doing this, she didn't know. She thought she'd made it clear that she wanted nothing to do with the memorial for this girl she'd never met. It messed her up, this grief and shit; she didn't need it.

But Gwen would get this look, helpless and determined, and it was nearly impossible to say no to her. Gwen had a way of drawing people into her projects like a tornado that picked up everything in its path.

"I can't possibly spend one more minute in this outfit!" Gwen announced as she barged back through the door. JJ watched her unbuckle the suede shoes that looked like they belonged to somebody's *abuelita*, and kick them off, sighing with relief.

Then she took off the black uniform and paced the studio in a lime-green satin push-up bra ill-matched to a pair of navy blue underpants that had seen better days. "But what should I wear? People are gonna be here any second!" It was less a request than a demand, punctuated with a whine of panic. JJ knew better than to offer a serious suggestion; Gwen was really talking to herself.

"Just wear that," JJ proposed. "It's sure to snap people right out of their grief!"

Gwen made a face, but JJ knew she loved to be reminded that she was sexy. JJ watched as her lover slid over her shoulders a blouse of antique lace—now dyed a bright magenta—and stepped into a fluorescent yellow spandex miniskirt. JJ's eyes could not escape the way the skirt hugged the curve of Gwen's ass before it ended in a flash of skin.

"Ahh, you're the picture of mourning," JJ joked, to which Gwen replied, "It's fucking hot out, right?" Then she hurried to gather the papers that were strewn across her worktable and began retrieving the dozens of unpaired shoes that were scattered across the floor, throwing them back into their box without bothering to reunite them.

"Hey, Ani DiFranco!" JJ exclaimed. "I didn't even know you had this." She added it to the pile.

"You don't know everything about me," Gwen teased, then

explained, "Emma recommended it to me so I went out and bought it."

JJ returned to searching through the CDs. Tom Waits' *Bone Machine*—no. A *Night in Havana*—great compilation, but it would be wasted on this crowd. But a greatest hits album of the Carpenters—definitely. The day would need that touch of irony.

She added this to the others in the CD changer and programmed it to scramble. Then she poured a cup of the strong coffee Gwen had just brewed, in preparation for a long afternoon.

Watching her lover scurry about the loft, JJ had to admit that the real reason she'd decided to stay was the imminent arrival of Gwen's ex. One look at Lee Bergman and JJ could tell she was going to be trouble. Sure, Gwen said it had been over a long time ago, but the slight color that rose to her cheeks seemed to suggest unfinished business. JJ figured it might be in her best interest to stick around.

Luanne Ingersoll gaped out the dirty window of the taxi as it veered from lane to lane, dodging pedestrians and double-parked cars in its breakneck crosstown rush. She could not shake her suspicion that the driver didn't know where he was going or was perhaps deliberately taking her out of her way in order to overcharge her. She supposed she'd been foolish not to accept a ride with Peg and Ruthie. At first she'd been so happy to see Peg there; Peg was one of the few women at Labrys, aside from Dana, that Luanne had genuinely liked. She was older, motherly, not so likely to get caught in the storms of political controversy that had swamped each day of that summer. And Peg was heterosexual, a distinct minority among the group who'd been drawn to Labrys.

But when Luanne had approached Peg before the service, the large woman had trilled, "Luanne! You've got to meet Ruthie! Ruthie, Luanne and I used to have long heart-to-heart talks late into the night while everybody else was making love like there was no tomorrow! Luanne, this is Ruthie Cowan, the love of my life!"

There'd been no trace of apology in her voice, no hint of acknowledgment that some of those late-night talks at Labrys had been about the isolation they'd felt there as heterosexual women, their resentment at being told they were "sleeping with the enemy." So Peg was a lesbian now, too. Luanne had quickly rearranged her expression to hide her disappointment.

It shouldn't be such a big deal, she supposed. It's not that she hadn't known lesbians in her life. And now, of course, they were everywhere, on television and the covers of magazines. What bothered her was the smugness of lesbians, the assumption that heterosexual women were just too dumb to have figured out a better way, too hopelessly enslaved by the penis. Even Peg, when asked about leaving her husband, had said, "That's why the patriarchy tries to keep lesbianism such a secret—because if women found out what's possible, no one would want to be heterosexual!"

Ruthie, for her part, had been polite, asking her questions about where she lived and what she did. Before Luanne could even answer, Peg had interjected, "Oh, Luanne does union organizing! She's been trying to challenge the sexism of the unions."

And Luanne had to correct her, "I quit doing that a long time ago. I work as a dental hygienist, part-time. I'm married, and my son Ted is seven." She'd cursed the defensiveness in her voice; wasn't the women's movement supposed to be about choices?

The conversation had been mercifully interrupted by the start of the service, and Luanne found a chair a few rows behind them. During the memorial, she'd made an effort to avoid the sight of Peg's chubby hand fingering the wide nape of Ruthie's neck. She'd been further turned off by Peg's harangue about the "patriarchy." So when they offered her a ride, she'd declined.

When at last the cab pulled to the curb, Luanne gazed doubtfully out the dirty windows. "Are you sure this is Rivington Street?" she asked. But the driver merely tapped his thick fingers against the meter indicating her fare. Fumbling with her change purse, she counted out some bills, nervously trying to calculate an appropriate tip. Finally she handed him a wad of bills and told him to keep the change. He did not thank her, but pulled quickly away.

Then she was standing on the pavement with her battered Samsonite suitcase, staring up at the building whose address matched the one on the scrap of paper inside her purse. This handbag was clutched tight against her body, the better to ward off muggers.

She hadn't been expecting the day to turn so hot; she hoped she wouldn't sweat too much in her new Liz Claiborne pantsuit. She'd used the money her mother gave her for her birthday to buy this suit in pale mint green; Mike would have a fit if he knew how much it cost.

Along the block, clusters of boys and men huddled in packs along the sidewalk or leaned in doorways, as if conducting a secretive exchange or commerce. One woman stood dead in the center of the street, defying cars to pass, her dark skin gleaming against the sheen of a cheap red slip, all that she wore. She was howling at the retreating back of a man in a jogging suit, "Come back heah, nigga'—I'ma kill you! You heah me, you heah me!" Salsa blasted out the window of a car double-parked on one side of the street, dueling with the rap that poured from a ghetto blaster stationed on the other side. An indescribable odor seemed to be cooking up from the pavement, some mix of spoiled food, gasoline, and—could it be—blood?

As a shudder of apprehension traveled the length of her spine, Luanne was stunned by the recognition of how sheltered her life had become. She'd grown up in Detroit in the Sixties, and could remember dancing to Motown music in mixed clubs. Later, one of her favorite organizers in the union had been a black woman named Cornelia Watkins. After meetings they used to go out for beers together to a bar where Luanne was often the only white person. Now, in their suburb west of the city, she rarely saw people who weren't white, and Mike wouldn't hear of driving downtown. "Why go all that way just to have your car busted into?" was how he saw it. Standing on the sidewalk of Rivington Street, Luanne couldn't deny that she felt afraid, but it annoyed her and made her ashamed. When had she stopped being one kind of person and become another?

Luanne leaned on the buzzer labeled Kubacky in block letters made with a purple marker. A few minutes later, Gwen appeared and invited her in, slamming the heavy metal door behind them and bolting all three locks.

Having failed to commandeer the sound system—Devon's attempt to play Sleater-Kinney had been met with unanimous rejection by the older women—Emma's contemporaries monopolized the sofa, three of them squirming into its plush embrace. Kick sprawled on the scarred floor, nursing the Corona she'd smuggled in despite Gwen's request for "No alcohol."

Ayisha perched on the arm of the sofa, as if ready to take flight at any moment. She was not entirely comfortable with Emma's friends, but she knew them better than any of the others in the loft.

"So tell me again, what am I doing hanging out here with a bunch of angry women with hairy legs and bad haircuts?" Kendra complained.

"They're friends of Emma's mom. Try to behave yourself, okay?" Ayisha wanted to keep the chastising tone from her voice, but her patience was frayed.

Kendra didn't seem to register the rebuke. "If this is what the Seventies were like, I'm glad I was too young to notice!"

"Speaking of Emma's mom," the bald woman, Darla, interjected, "I can't believe she was such a robot. My mom's pretty fucked up and all, but at least I'm pretty sure she'd cry at my funeral."

"Emma said she was always like that, really shut down. It used to drive her crazy." Kendra reached a languid arm in Kick's direction. "Hey, can I have a sip of that?"

Kick stuck the bottle between her thighs, neck pointed in Kendra's direction. "What'll you give me for it?"

Kendra dropped to her knees and began to suck at the lip of the bottle. Ayisha stood abruptly and walked to the other end of the studio.

"I can't believe I'm never gonna see Emma again. It's so, like, weird." Darla buried her head in Devon's shoulder.

"Somehow I get the feeling that I'm not supposed to be

here. That fat old woman who was raving about the patriarchy keeps giving me dirty looks."

"That's okay, Devon," Darla assured him, "you're as much a woman as any of us."

Luanne had been pleasantly surprised by the arrival of Jolene, who'd come all the way from Tennessee on the bus with her seven-year-old son, Roger. But Peg was bristling at the presence of both Roger and the violet-haired young man who had sung at the funeral. Luanne had to acknowledge a certain guilty pleasure in Peg's upset. Now they and the other Labrys women were clustered around the desk, which Gwen had cleared of her files and computer, and on which were arrayed platters of bread and cheese and cold cuts.

"Dana looked just terrible." Luanne was keeping her voice low, despite the music blasting from the stereo. "And who can blame her, losing her daughter like that."

"You can tell she's really suffering, under that tough façade of hers." Jolene was making short work of a can of Diet Coke.

Elena put down her cell phone long enough to comment, "I'm shocked that no one from the Labrys *collective* showed up." She sipped black coffee from a Styrofoam cup.

Jolene said, "I heard that none of them ever spoke to each other again."

"I ran into Sarah about five years ago at a conference," Peg interjected, spooning coleslaw on two paper plates. "She said Labrys was the worst experience of political organizing she'd ever had. She practically yelled at me just for saying that's where I knew her from."

Luanne marveled at the way these women still kept connected after all these years, the way they traveled and networked and knew about one another. Out of the entire group at Labrys, she had only kept in touch with Dana.

"Gwen, we need some serving spoons for the take-out..."
"Gwen, somebody's on the phone who wants directions..."
"Gwen, do you have any Equal for the coffee?"
"Gwen, where do you keep your extra toilet paper?"

"Gwen, somebody spilled their Coke; do you have any paper towels?"

"Gwen, it's that detective on the phone. He asked for JJ."

"Gwen, somebody said you have Emma's tapes. Can we put them on?"

Ayisha wandered the loft, clinging to its margins, wishing she could lose herself among the giant toy-like set pieces—the enormous clock with bleeding hands or the foil-covered, human-sized coffeepot—and racks of colorful costumes, spangled or sequined or furred. Windows yawned open to the late afternoon, but couldn't manage to snatch a breeze to stir the hot, thick air inside.

The only other person here who seemed as ill at ease was Gwen Kubacky, which was odd because she lived there. From behind her dark lenses Ayisha watched as Gwen too circled the groups warily, never joining in, the crease of her mouth suggesting that she'd rather be anywhere else. But Ayisha did not especially like Gwen, whom she found entirely too extroverted, and so felt no kinship in their isolation.

It wasn't right to leave, she supposed, until Dana arrived, but aside from performing a few hostess tasks she really had no place here. She had nothing to say to the women of her mother's generation, still spouting slogans as dated and empty as TV ads. Nor to Emma's friends, though they were of her own generation; their posing struck her as mannered and brittle, their concerns self-conscious and narrow. Neither group seemed to grasp the particular loss of Emma, to feel the ache of her absence. Emma was as absent from this gathering that was supposedly in her memory as she was from her room in the apartment that once again Ayisha occupied alone.

It had been different with her mother's death. Marilyn's spirit seemed to sing in the bathroom pipes, to cast shadows along the walls. Her mother came to her in dreams, offering advice, once even dancing the Electric Slide.

But Emma had disappeared completely. No hint of her scent remained, no sensation that she was hanging out, watching. Ayisha was finding it hard to remember Emma's face, and the collection of pixels now flickering on the video monitor seemed unrecognizable.

Ayisha was staring, dull-eyed, at the TV screen when she was approached by a small, well-muscled woman whose skin color was rich as bittersweet chocolate. "I can dig the shades," she greeted Ayisha, referring to the sunglasses she still wore. "All this white skin is hard on a sister's eyes."

For a second Ayisha thought the woman was dissing her about her own light complexion, but her shoulders relaxed as she realized she was included in the word "sister." Then her cheeks flushed with pleasure at being identified as a Black woman. She nodded in agreement.

"This sure isn't the way our people do a funeral," the woman continued. Ayisha nodded again, though she'd never been to a funeral in the Black community, and was ashamed of that fact.

The woman wore her hair natural, but tightly cropped around her head. She had wide, quick eyes that appeared to take everything in. "I'm Chi Curtis." She extended a hand that Ayisha gripped shyly. "I dug what you had to say at the service. You were comin' from the heart."

Chafing beneath the compliment, Ayisha changed the subject. "Did you meet Dana at Labrys?"

A barely perceptible wince traveled across Chi's face. "I've known Dana since the mid-sixties. We were both heavy into politics. It's her fault I got roped into Labrys; she was trippin' 'cause the faculty was all white." A short burst of dangerous laughter escaped her throat. "'Course, they had me teachin' self-defense, know what I'm sayin'?"

Then she gave her head a little shake, as if to slough off bad memories, and her mouth relaxed into a wide smile. "And what about you, Miss Ayisha? How'd you get to be so tight with Emma?"

"My mom and Dana used to do political work together. When we were little."

"Who's your mom?"

"She was Marilyn Cain. Marilyn Horton Cain. She died last year. Breast cancer."

Chi's expression turned sorrowful. "That's rough. I'm sorry

to hear it."

"Did you know my mom?" Ayisha looked at her curiously.

"I met her a coupla' times."

"Did you know my dad, then? Lincoln Cain?"

A shadow passed across Chi's face, but she nodded. "Yeah, I knew Linc."

It was as if she had flicked a switch. "My father? You know my father?" the soft-spoken Ayisha practically shrieked. "I'm trying to find him. I've been looking everywhere, especially since my mom died. Do you think you could help me?"

This startled Chi; her eyes snapped and looked hard at Ayisha, as if the younger woman were putting her on. She seemed about to say something, then thought better of it, her shoulders sagging as if the air had been let out of her. She finally mumbled, "Yeah, that's something we could maybe talk about sometime."

Ayisha would not let it go so easily. "Can I call you? Does Dana have your number?"

"Yeah, sure...uh, excuse me for a minute," and with that, Chi headed for the door, escaping the loft. Her behavior puzzled Ayisha, but she was too excited to think much about it. Finally, here was someone who knew her father, who might help her find him. Maybe this was Emma's gift to her.

Lee Bergman stood at the doorway to the address she'd been given on Rivington Street, staring down the block with undisguised contempt. For the third time she leaned on the buzzer, wondering what the hell was taking so long. When finally Gwen threw open the metal door, Lee was ready to ask, "What kept you?" but instead her eyes were caught by the skin that showed through the lace of Gwen's blouse, the mounds of breast rising from the cups of a lime-green bra. Instead a soft leer formed on her lips.

"Well, I guess *that's* worth waiting for!" she announced, then added, "If you didn't feel the need to dress like a clown, no woman in the city would be able to resist you."

"You didn't come all the way from the West Coast to insult me, did you?" The frost in Gwen's tone was long-familiar to

Lee.

"I'm not insulting you, fer Crissakes!" Despite more than a decade in California, Lee's voice had never managed to shed its Brooklyn origins. "Still too fucking sensitive to live, aren't you?"

Gwen made no response as she bolted the three deadbolts.

"I'm sure you need all those in this neighborhood," Lee observed. "What's the idea of living in the slums here?"

"The penthouse on Park Avenue just got to be too much to keep up," Gwen retorted bitterly. She began the long climb up the stairs, leaving Lee no choice but to follow her.

"Listen, baby, I told you when I moved out there you could sublet my place in the Village."

"Lee, I needed a studio for my work. I didn't want to live in your apartment. And I like this neighborhood, okay?"

"Suit yerself, baby." Lee wasn't up for a major argument, especially when her chest was heaving from the long climb. "At least I see how you keep your beautiful shape."

Before they reached the top, Lee began again. "So, baby, I read about you in the newspaper last month. You're ready to give that Senator a heart attack!"

"Everyone thinks that kind of notoriety is glamorous," Gwen complained. "But if the NEA stops funding my work and venues can't get funding to present it because somebody thinks it's obscene, then my career is pretty much over."

"Personally, the obscenity was always my favorite part of your work!" Lee quipped. Gwen merely sighed in response.

Once inside the loft, Lee watched her go to a young Latina in tight black jeans, who caressed her hair with a proprietary hand. Her new squeeze, Lee surmised with a sigh. She posed against an open window, hoping for a breeze. It was insanity to not take off her jacket, an Armani of woven silk, in this heat, but she knew its lines hid the love handles that no amount of effort would eliminate, so she gamely left it on. She had to admit she was still damn well preserved as she approached her fifty-fifth birthday. Her stocky figure was still reasonably in shape, courtesy of Drake, her personal trainer, and, God knows, an Armani suit could camouflage a world of sins. As for the girls—just fuck 'em in the dark, she figured, or in the classic style of by—gone butches, keep *your* clothes on. They rarely minded, and those that did, well, it just gave them something to strive for.

She surveyed the room, looking for something to distract her attention from Gwen, and then she found it: the young woman—*very* young, Lee determined with an expert's eye—who'd spoken earlier at the funeral. Kimba, Kendra, something like that, she recalled. Her lithe body was revealed by the short black top that ended just below her breasts, accented by the gleam of gold in her pierced navel. Her once-blond hair had been dyed obsidian-black, cropped short around her face, then tapering to a skinny braid of jet that snaked her spine.

A pretty girl, masquerading tough, Lee assessed her; underneath the stark haircut there could be found a rather lovely young woman, with pale, delicate features that struggled not to be overwhelmed by the raven-black hair and ebony makeup rimming her eyes like rings on a target.

After a time, the young woman became aware of Lee's gaze and stared back, basking in the attention, an indolent smile on her lips. Probably not twenty-five, Lee marveled, a warmth beginning at the pit of her stomach, soothing the sting of her brief reunion with Gwen. As she sauntered over to introduce herself, Lee caught a glimpse of Gwen, observing her from the other side of the room. Returning her attention to the voluptuous young woman, Lee's smile swelled. The occasion seemed suddenly full of possibilities.

"So, Ayisha, who's the woman with the black braid and the gold ring in her belly button?" Gwen had run out for a twelve-pack of Charmin, and was not the least bit winded from another climb up the stairs.

"That's Kendra DeValle. She and Emma were supposed to do some art piece together, I think, though Emma once told me she thought Kendra's biggest talent was for self-promotion."

"Is there any reason I would know her?"

"I doubt it. I think she's done some writing about art for a couple of magazines or something."

"Mother fuck!" Gwen clapped a theatrical hand to her forehead.

"What?" Ayisha was reluctant to ask.

"*That's* where I know her from. She's the bitch who trashed my last performance piece in the *Voice.*"

"So, Kendra, I haven't lived in New York in a long time. What does a girl do for fun around here these days?" Lee settled in on the couch next to the young woman. Kick had been dispatched for more beer.

"Ohh…things."

"Things, huh? That's a whole lotta mystery for a young kid like you." Lee ran a finger lightly down Kendra's bare arm.

"I'm not such a kid. I've been around the block a few times."

"I bet you have. I'd like to see the neighborhood."

"I think I could arrange a tour. Who knows, you might see some new sights."

"Gwen, it's Dana on the phone."

"Gwen, Peg's all upset that Jolene brought her son. But he's only seven years old."

"Gwen, one of those friends of Emma's just walked in with a six-pack."

"So, that's your ex, huh, *poquetica?*"

"Gwen, I hate to be a narc, but I think one of those kids is smoking pot in your bathroom."

"Gwen, most of us are just in for the weekend. I was thinking how it would be so great if we could get together again here tomorrow, to really talk about what's happened in those years since we were at Labrys. You don't mind, do you?"

JJ was sitting on the top step outside of Gwen's loft, gazing into the dim stairwell, when she heard the door open behind her. A stocky woman in a leather vest emerged. JJ remembered her from the service that morning. The woman offered a beer, but JJ shook her head.

"So, did I get this right? Your name is JJ?"

"Yeah, that's me."

"And you're Gwen's girlfriend, right?"

"That's a part of who I am."

"Right, right. You're a musician too, right?"

"Yeah, so?"

"My name's Kick. I was a friend of Emma's…"

"Yeah, I heard what you said at the service."

"So, they're saying that Emma was on her way to meet someone the night she got whacked?"

JJ shrugged. She wasn't sure what the woman wanted from her.

"Some guy named Jersey?" Kick continued. "I overhead you on the phone. I heard you say you know him."

"I know a guy named Jersey," JJ said carefully. She hated the whole idea of being involved in this in any way. "I'm not even sure it's the same one."

"What's he like?" Kick made herself at home on the step next to JJ.

"He's Jamaican. A musician; plays saxophone."

"So, does he gig around town?"

"Yeah, he's in a band. Lost Midnight."

"Reggae? Ska?" Kick wanted to know.

"Nope." JJ smiled wryly at the assumption. "Fusion jazz."

"So, what kinda guy is he?"

"He's a good guy." JJ grew impatient with talking about this. "*Mira*, he's not my best friend or anything. I dig his chops, okay? Most men in the music business are dickheads; he's not. I don't have any reason to think he killed someone."

"I guess you just never know…"

"*Mira*, I gotta go. I got a gig to get to." With that, JJ stood and clattered down the stairs. She knew she should say goodbye to Gwen, but she'd call her later. In this moment, she just wanted to get away from these people.

Chapter 6

Gwen felt like a hostage in her own home. Her loft, her workspace, her little low-rent sanctuary had been invaded, and the marauders now sprawled on the ravaged ground, dozing after a long day's pillaging.

Peg and Ruthie—whom she couldn't help thinking of as an oversized version of Tweedledum and Tweedledee—were sacked out on air mattresses in the far corner under the giant clock. Even from her bed on the other side of the loft, Gwen could hear them snore. She'd tried to persuade them it wouldn't be safe to leave their van unguarded on the streets of this 'hood, but they wouldn't hear of missing out on the "slumber party." Jolene and her son Roger were on sleeping bags between racks of clothes. The little boy had a bad cough and kept waking up with spasms. Luanne had claimed a dubious respite on the sagging cushions of Gwen's old couch, insisting no one had told her to bring a sleeping bag. Gwen did break down and offer her a spare sheet, which she accepted more for modesty's sake than for warmth, given this freak June heat wave.

Gwen was wide-awake at this weird, post-midnight hour, night's edges just starting to blur. Who wouldn't be insomniac after a day like she'd had? It wasn't unusual to be sleepless at this hour, but tonight she'd been robbed of her usual coping strategies. She couldn't masturbate, for obvious reasons—many a partner had proclaimed her a "noisy fuck." Lee used to put a pillow over Gwen's head when she came so the neighbors wouldn't hear. She couldn't put on the light to read, couldn't turn on the radio, couldn't even make a pot of coffee.

She felt trapped on the island of her bed, sheets rumpled and unfresh, in this studio that used to be hers, on this night that would never end. She couldn't even go to the john for fear she'd trip over the inert body of one of the Last Remaining Feminists.

She could see JJ had been smart to decamp to her folks' house in Queens. She couldn't blame her; she just wished JJ had taken her along. But JJ's mother was not at all fond of Gwen; she thought of her as the aging vampire who'd corrupted her baby girl. Boy, did she have that wrong!

Gwen's head was pounding from too much coffee and too many hours of socializing with people she didn't like. If she'd had any idea the gathering was going to last all night, she might have gone ahead and been a schmuck and just said flat-out no to it. Instead, with every hour that passed—seven, then eight, then nine, then ten—she'd kept thinking *Surely they're gonna leave now.* JJ had departed about ten thirty to play a gig, but everyone else stayed and stayed.

Emma's friends had been the first to split, no doubt in search of more stimulating entertainments. Lee, thank God, had gone with them, and while Gwen would have preferred not to see her sniffing after Kendra DeValle, she'd been grateful to see them go.

There were years when Gwen had fantasized about what it would be like to see Lee again; she'd always imagined herself looking devastatingly sexy, wrapped in a torrid embrace with a handsome butch who adored her beyond reason. Lee would unwittingly stumble upon them and just for a moment Gwen would glimpse regret in her eyes, the recognition of the true worth of what she'd squandered.

Instead, of course, it was just like it had always been between them: Lee flirting and then striking, the velvet glove concealing the steel pipe, and Gwen feeling like a common fly hopelessly stuck in the spider's web. She'd spent years on a therapist's couch trying to get out from under that pattern; it was discouraging after all this time to find herself still susceptible.

And as for the young Miss Kendra—or as Gwen couldn't help thinking of her, the bitch who'd tried to ruin her career— Gwen had had an exchange with her before she departed with Lee in tow.

"Kendra?" Gwen had introduced herself, "Gwen Kubacky. You wrote about my work in the *Voice* last year."

At least Kendra had the grace to blush. "Yeah, that piece," she narrowed her eyes as if trying to recall it. "'Unsafe Sex,' right?"

"That's the one," Gwen confirmed, still pleasant. "You didn't like it much."

Kendra was too young and inexperienced to have mastered the art of looking dead in the eye someone she'd savaged in print. She became intent on studying the chipped paint of the floor. "Yeah, well, you can't like everything."

"Don't you think, though," Gwen had pressed her advantage, "that a reviewer should educate herself about an art movement, say, feminist art of the Seventies, before completely trashing it?"

Kendra had looked at her then as if Gwen were a puke-stained wino accosting her for money on the street, but she'd been spared the necessity of coming up with an answer because just at that minute Gwen had been called to the phone. It was Dana, her third phone call since the start of the reception.

"I'm not going to make it," she'd announced, her voice a blunt instrument through the receiver. No apology, no explanation, no "Gee, I know this must be inconveniencing you."

Gwen should have been furious, but all she'd felt was a dull resignation. Once too many frustrations occurred in a row, she tended to lose the ability to respond to any of them. That had been a few minutes after ten. Gwen realized she must have given up hope of Dana's arrival hours earlier. From across the room she'd watched Kendra whisper something into Lee's ear. They'd both looked at her and laughed.

"Peg mentioned that everyone was coming back tomorrow," Dana said. "I'll be over there in the morning." Gwen heard the click of her hang-up before she could say, "Don't bother."

If only Peg had bothered to mention that to Gwen. And when Gwen confronted Peg, she'd breezily told her, "We just figured we shouldn't waste an opportunity, now that we've all gathered here. We want to talk more about feminism, what our next strategies should be as a movement."

Gwen had been dumbfounded; she'd wanted to say, "I thought we were here to mourn *Emma*?" She'd wanted to say, "*What* movement?" She'd wanted to say, "Get the fuck out of my loft." But the whole experience had become like a speeding train and she saw no point in standing in the middle of the tracks.

From there, the evening had worn down in slow motion, every minute falling like a trip hammer on Gwen's ragged nerves. Chi Curtis came back; Gwen remembered seeing her early in the evening but then she'd disappeared. She'd come looking for Dana, and was distraught not to find her. Gwen always felt like a stupid white girl when she talked to Chi, which meant she talked too much and with too much elaborate politeness and sounded even more like a stupid white girl. This had been true since Gwen took her self-defense class at Labrys. Still, Chi had seemed cheered to hear that everyone was coming back tomorrow including, supposedly, the missing Dana. Elena had departed after that, not that she'd ever seemed really present in the group, one ear glued to her cell phone all day and a distracted, haunted expression. Gwen's encounters with her had never progressed beyond the ritual: "Can I get you something to drink?" "CORR is really impressive; you've hung on in the face of tremendous opposition." "Your best bet is to walk up to Houston to get a cab." Gwen believed Elena viewed her as not political and therefore, no one to take seriously.

Ayisha had at least hung around to help clean up. The women who were staying the night just refilled their glasses and moved to another part of the loft as she and Gwen had loaded up yet another trash bag with abandoned plates and plastic forks, half-filled glasses and take-out cartons that had been picked clean. Ayisha had taken the time to rewind Emma's videos and put them back into their labeled cases.

"Do you want those?" Gwen asked her, thinking to be nice.

"Only if you're going to throw them away," she'd answered. "That's not her, not really, in those tapes. Not like I knew her. She's just trying on attitudes for the camera."

Gwen wondered whether Emma would have agreed, and whether someone might say the same of her and her performances. She didn't think so. Gwen believed she was more herself onstage than anywhere else. Did that make her a better artist or a worse human being? Lee used to complain that Gwen gave everything to art and there was nothing left for her.

Ayisha had been gathering the empty bottles for recycling. "Just go on," Gwen encouraged her, "I'll finish up." She'd seemed relieved, but as she turned to the door, Gwen added, "Are you okay to go home by yourself?"

Ayisha had looked at her curiously. "Sure," she said, like *why wouldn't I be?* Then she'd nodded as if understanding the thought behind Gwen's question. "You think I might be afraid after what happened to Emma."

"It would be only natural," Gwen began, but Ayisha cut her off.

"I'm not, though. I been takin' care of myself a long time." She'd forced a grim imitation of a smile as she disappeared through the door.

It wasn't until the overnight guests had settled down and Gwen was taking her turn at the bathroom sink—scary what twelve hours of sweating had done to her makeup!—that she found someone's silver flask on the floor beside one of the tub's clawed feet.

The vessel felt cool in her hands and fit so well the curve of her grip. Despite her better judgment Gwen unscrewed the cap and held it to her nose, savored the pungent fumes of scotch. She traced the open lip with rueful longing. She could almost taste the bite in the back of her throat, the way it would make her brain float for a while, far away from the heat of the loft and her unwanted houseguests and the whole rotten day.

She thought, *It's fucked up that after twelve years of meetings and twelve steps and the whole shebang, I still long for it. But that's why they say, "Keep coming back."* She didn't want to throw away the flask, but in her present state of mind she couldn't afford to hang onto its contents. She turned the flask on its head and watched the liquor pour down the drain in an amber stream. Then she put herself to bed.

The luminous digits of her clock were flashing 3:15 and she was, as Howard would have said, "NAWW." Not A Well Woman. She could feel herself getting spooked in eighteen different ways: about JJ being gone, Emma being dead, Lee being back, the Labrys women on her floor, and her craving a drink like nothing else would stop the pain in her head or fill the hole in the middle of her chest. Her demons were awake and moving the furniture in her brain. When she got like this there was only one thing to do.

"No matter what time, no matter where you are, call me before you drink." Howard hadn't only meant "before you pour liquor down your throat" but also "before you get yourself so freaked out that you might do something stupid, like drink," and over the years, they'd both held up their ends of the bargain.

She never saw any other tenants on her floor of the building at night, so she wasn't the least concerned about dragging her cordless phone into the hallway dressed in nothing but an old T-shirt that barely covered her ass. The hall was a little cooler, and she could pace it without disturbing The Last Remaining Feminists. Although Howard's number was permanently tattooed in her memory, it was also programmed on her speed dial, so the press of just one button connected them.

On the first ring he answered, "Hey Gwen," in his worn-out Bronx accent. No matter what time Gwen called, he never sounded like she'd woken him up.

"Howard, how can you be so *sure* it's me?" She pronounced it "shu-wah," falling automatically into his speech patterns.

"Gwen, I don't have no girlfriend, I don't have no family, and the crooks are asleep at this hour. Who else is gonna call me at three thirty in the morning—Madonna? It's just you and me, honey, the only ones still alive in this goddamn town."

"Howard, I'm so glad I've got a sponsor who's as cynical as I am." She already felt better, just hearing his voice on the other end of the phone. Her demons were starting to relax.

"Nah, I ain't cynical. I just says it as I sees it. So, come clean—what's a pretty dyke like you doin' alone and awake at this unholy hour?" This was his standard line; he always said he wanted her to be sure he hadn't gone politically correct.

"Trust me," she told him, "alone would be a blessing. What a rotten, shitty day!" Somehow the ache of it felt more acute, now there was someone to tell. "I feel like I want to get loaded so bad tonight."

"Yeah, well, what else is new? I wanna get loaded every day."

In broad strokes, she described the afternoon and evening, the women asleep on her floor, her run-ins with Lee, Kendra and the silver flask. She stretched out on the rough wood floor, hoping not to get a splinter in her ass. As she talked, she studied the pallor of her bare legs; they had a greenish cast under the bare bulb in the hall.

"So you dumped the booze. That's a good thing."

"Yeah, but the sickness is in my head, Howard, y'know what I mean?"

"I sure do, angel. Why do you think they say 'There's no *e-d* on the end of the word *recover?*'"

Cynical though he may be, Howard had always had a fondness for the slogans of AA, while Gwen found them trite and embarrassing. Though he'd never say so, she believed he got a little hurt when she made fun of them, so she tried not to snicker.

"Yeah," she affirmed, "I guess I thought I was recover-*ed* from Lee, but she still knows how to get to me!"

"You used to think that was *love*, Gwen," he reminded her, then pitched another slogan. "Progress, not perfection, right? So be grateful."

But she wasn't ready to be grateful; she needed to dump a little more anxiety. "Howard, did you hear what I said, though? She ends up leaving with this *kid*, this twenty-four-year-old, *less than half her age, Howard*, and worse than that, the kid is someone who wrote one of the worst reviews of my work I've ever received!"

Howard chuckled, though not unsympathetically. "Ya' gotta

admit, Kubacky, God's gotta real sense of humor."

"Oh, I'm laughin', Howard, I'm in stitches over here," she said bitterly. How could he be so cheerful when she was in a crisis?

"Listen, maybe it ain't me you should be talkin' to right now, honey. Maybe you need to be gettin' on your knees and askin' for help."

"Give me a fucking break..." she started to argue. Even after all these years the religion part of the program was the hardest thing for her. Ask any ex-Catholic to pray and see what kind of response you get.

Instead she sighed. "All right, all right, I'll try."

"That'a girl!" He was gracious enough not to lecture her about her resistance.

"You know, Howard, I'm lucky you put up with me."

"Yeah, yeah." That was his way of acknowledging her thanks.

"Before I hang up, can I ask you one more thing? What's happening with the guy who killed Emma? Will you find him?"

"God willing, I hope so."

She heard his exhaustion, his frustration, the rigorously walled-off despair that came from dealing with mayhem on a daily basis. Howard almost never talked about his work but she heard in that moment how it was always there for him. She could see why he was always awake no matter what time she called him.

There was a long pause. She heard him clear his throat. "Gwen, this hasn't really happened before, where any of my sponsees is connected to a case. I don't think it's a good mix, y'know? I shouldn't be talkin' to you about it."

"Howard, she was my student." There was more emotion in her words than she would have expected. Perhaps it was only in that moment, hearing herself implore him, that she realized what Emma meant to her. Yes, her brash innocence, her derivative fearlessness reminded Gwen of herself at that age, but more importantly, she realized, she'd seen her as a link to the future.

Howard sighed, a deep, inexhaustible well of an exhalation. "Tell the truth, Gwen, we don't got much. This guy she was goin' to meet that night, he left on some tour and no one seems to know exactly where he is. JJ thinks he's due in tomorrow. We're definitely gonna talk to him.

"Then over in Brooklyn they're lookin' at a pattern of rape/homicides; this might fit the profile. If that's the guy, then he's moved across the river. And they say he's been strikin' about once a week, so we wanna stop him before another little girl ends up dead. That's about all we've got at the moment. I wish to Christ it was more."

There was more silence, textured with darkness. Gwen asked, "You okay, Howard?"

He offered a dry chuckle. "Yeah, sweetheart, I am. By the grace 'o God, I am. What about you?"

"I should live through the night," she said lightly. The two of them shared a gallows humor. But in truth, Gwen did feel better, more inside herself now. "Thanks," she added, the word layered with meaning.

"Anytime, angel," he assured her. "Now get some sleep, for Crissakes," he couldn't resist adding before he clicked off.

She stayed in the hall for a while, listening to the dial tone pressed to her ear. The humming sound was strangely comforting and helped to clear her mind. Who could say that this wasn't just as good a form of prayer as what the priests taught? She could almost imagine staying there all night, except she promised Howard she'd try to get some sleep.

She made her way through the darkened studio, quiet now except for her footsteps across the floor and the low mumble of Luanne talking in her sleep.

"Find the baby," Gwen heard her say, but the rest of it she couldn't make out.

Chapter 7

"You'll like this club," Kendra had promised in the taxi. "It rocks."

Rock it did. Even the crowded restroom offered no respite from the pounding bass; walls pulsed and the floor beneath her trembled. Lee Bergman stood over a stained sink trying to coax a trickle of water from the ancient plumbing. In the lone stall two women were engaged in noisy, shuddering sex while an impatient throng jostled to gain access to the toilet.

"Hey, d'ya mind?" complained a tall redhead in a leather bustier as she rapped on the locked door of the stall. "Wouldja hurry up and *cum* already so the rest of us can take a piss?"

"Piss in the sink," groaned one of the women from inside the stall.

"Lemme in and I'll piss in your mouth," the redhead retorted.

The door to the stall swung open and an arm reached to pull her in. The redhead disappeared inside and the door latch clicked back into place.

"Hey, what about the rest of us?" grumbled a pretty Puerto Rican who surely must have been underage.

"Wait your turn," giggled the redhead. Through the open space at the bottom of the stall, the waiting women watched as her short Lycra skirt shimmied to the floor.

The moaning intensified.

Lee stared at her reflection in the filmy mirror above the sink. She was a good thirty years older than every other woman in the room, and it showed on her face, in her manner, in the cut of her clothes. She'd been a lesbian since the days of slow dancing at the Sea Colony, the smell of cigarettes and hairspray as you held a girl close while Frankie Laine crooned on the jukebox. The women in this bar didn't know what she knew, didn't want to, why should they? She wondered briefly if Kendra's bringing her here had been to tell her that.

Water dribbled down her arms as she groped in vain for a paper towel, but such amenities were too much to hope for. A chunky blonde with spiked hair and purple lips tried to edge her way to the mirror and noticed Lee's dilemma.

"Here," she offered, turning and bending so her ass was in the air. "Dry 'em off here."

Lee's compliance was diffident; limply she patted her hands over the pockets of the woman's cut-off jeans.

"Whatsamatta? You break yer wrist?" The blonde straightened up, contempt leavening her disappointment.

"Uh… thanks," Lee mumbled, pointing at the door. "I have a date outside."

"I wonder where *her* hands are right now," the pale-haired woman sneered.

"Hey," yelled a voice from inside the stall, "anybody got a dental dam?"

Lee escaped the bathroom, catapulting herself into a huge black expanse where the noise was tactile. The encounter in the bathroom had left her oddly shaken. She was accustomed to making the moves, taking the lead, always being in control. She fancied herself Clark Gable, or Bogart, tough but dapper, knowing how to treat a lady but ready to tame the beast that lurked beneath every ladylike veneer. In search of Rita Hayworth, Ava Gardner, someone with spunk, someone who knew both how to fight and when to surrender gracefully.

The stance had always worked for her—in the Fifties, in the Sixties, even in the Seventies with stalwart feminists like Gwen. But with this Nineties generation of lesbians, their disdain for gender, their aggressive sexual display—even the club was called The G-Spot—where was the room for nuance, for the delicate rhythms of resist-and-relent, the courtship dance? Despite the quantities of flesh on display, it made Lee feel the opposite of sexual, whatever that was. This was a new feeling, unsettling.

Gaping up at a platform on which two women in leather G-strings gyrated to the thumping beat, Lee felt her age, all fifty-five years accumulating like layers of crust upon her back. Trapped in this welter of youth, it was a hell of a sensation. For a moment she thought about Emma; had she too been part of this scene?

She didn't know Dana very well. Devoutly apolitical, she hadn't kept in touch with any of the women from that summer at Labrys. Only Gwen. It was serendipity that she'd run into Elena in an uptown coffee shop yesterday. Lee had recognized her, not from Labrys, but from seeing her picture in the news so many times over the years. Elena had just happened to mention Gwen's name, talking about the memorial, and that's when Lee had decided to pay a call on some unfinished business from the past. Serendipity. Just like ending up here. Life was a serendipity party.

Some minutes passed before she located Kendra, who was leaning against a column animatedly comparing piercings with a young woman with a shaved head. Did women really imagine that was sexy? The hairless woman wore three gold rings dangling from the fleshy swell of her left nostril, and a helix of hoops and stones curling up the pinna of each ear. Lee watched her unbutton the fly of her jeans to display another golden band through the skin of her navel. Lee barely concealed her gawking as Kendra peeled down a cup of her beaded bra and revealed a circle of silver hooked through her right nipple. The two young women admired the ornament as Kendra cradled her breast in one hand. Then she noticed Lee observing and flashed her a challenging smile.

"How d'ya like the tour so far?" she asked, shouting to be heard above the din.

Elena's address book was splayed open on the nightstand,

white pages gleaming in the light cast by the bedside lamp. A file folder marked Illinois and one marked Fund Drive spilled their contents onto the powder blue bedspread. Her leather pumps lay strewn on the plush carpet, her jacket slung on the back of a chair. The meal delivered by room service an hour ago sat cooling, untouched, on the glass-covered table beside the window.

Since returning to her midtown hotel, Elena Martínez had been on the phone with scores of women who were still at their desks Friday evening; none of them had expressed the least surprise to hear from her at this late hour.

Now she squinted at her wristwatch; exhaustion caused the numbers to blur and dance, but with effort she brought them into focus: a few minutes past midnight. Her back muscles were strained from sitting on the soft mattress. She rose and stretched; she longed for a forbidden cigarette.

Lifting the metal dome that surrounded her dinner plate, Elena tried to remember when last she might have eaten. A chorus of voices rose in her ears, white-coated medical men rebuking her neglectful ways: "You've got to take better care of yourself. You're a human being, not a machine. You need food, need rest."

She stared dully into the plate, on which a chicken breast congealed in a puddle of cream sauce, and once more lowered the lid. Listless, she picked at the accompanying salad, but the lettuce had wilted underneath heavy dressing. Her mouth watered suddenly at the remembrance of *chorizo*, savory with spices, and the warm fragrance of fresh tortillas rolled in the fleshy hands of her aunts.

Restless, she turned from the table and padded in stocking feet to the small portable bar and rummaged till she found a tiny bottle of Glenlivet. Peeling the cellophane wrapper from one of the water glasses, Elena poured in the contents of the bottle and returned to bed.

She studied the blank, insipid walls, enclosing her in neutral blues. She'd lived her adult life confined in these kinds of sterile spaces—offices, airports, hotel rooms—spaces devoid of personality, designed to starve the senses. A thick weariness consumed her, though she struggled to resist. When she returned to San Antonio, she promised herself, she would make an appointment for a check-up and this time, she vowed, she would keep it. She couldn't afford to be so tired right now, not with the battle over late-term abortions looming, and the President such an unreliable ally.

The file folders offered up their contents, papers fanned atop the mattress, but she could not bring herself to lift them to the light. She swirled another sip of scotch against her tongue as she idly thumbed the pages of her address book.

Most of the names inked in Elena's deliberate script were contacts related to CORR, women from all fifty states, political contacts, media people, funding sources. A sprinkling of family members, those few who had not disowned her for defying the teachings of the Church. Each year she updated the book, making sure that her contacts were current. Each year, for the last three, she had recopied Kay's name, along with its now useless address, unwilling to let her disappear from these pages too. Elena let her fingertip trace softly over the letters of Kay's name; the touch summoned once more a picture of Kay at the airport, white lilies in her arms. Elena blinked back tears, and scolded herself for being indulgent.

Flipping more pages, her eyes fell on Dana's name. Dana Firestein. How many times over the years had she called on Dana to figure out how to negotiate the power structure? "Use your culture," Dana used to tell her in the early days. "Don't pretend to be white. Drop a little Spanish into the conversation. These guys are liberal enough to feel guilty, or political enough to know they need to act like they are." Dana's radical positions and uncompromising manner excluded her from the mainstream of politics, but she was one of the best strategists Elena had ever known. Unlike most women, Dana was fearless in the face of power.

Dana seemed to be trying to maintain that same ferocity in the face of her daughter's murder, Elena reflected, but it would not serve her now.

She was about to close the brown leather binding when the name Richard Zunaya swam into view. *Ricardo.* Elena heard the name before she knew her lips had formed it. Involuntarily she winced.

If she closed her eyes she could still see him as he'd looked when they first met as law students at Georgetown: strong and dark and always laughing. Dressed in carefully pressed chinos and madras shirts, he would have been the envy of any Mexican boy from the fields of Central California, but he looked all wrong for the gray-flannel world of Georgetown in 1965.

She and Ricardo, the only two "Mexicans" enrolled in the school, both on scholarships, in the days before "Chicano" was a term with any currency. Only to her could he murmur the forbidden words of Spanish; only with him could she share the cups of frothy Mexican hot chocolate her Tia Rosa sent, brewed on an illicit burner in her room.

Elena stopped herself from spiraling into memory. "If you will not work," she sternly lectured herself in the mirror above the dresser, "then you must sleep." She was suddenly too spent to do more than slip out of her suit, draping the skirt and blouse atop the jacket on the back of the chair, and slide between cool sheets. Her body edged the pile of manila folders to the other side of the mattress, her head found the pillow and sank into it, and one arm reached to enfold the leather address book, clutching it to her chest. She left the lights burning.

The Asian woman in the tight red dress had been staring at her for the last hour and despite herself, JJ found that it improved her chops. The band was hot tonight, everyone in sync with everyone else, not seven separate musicians with their instruments, but a single organism producing a complex and intricate sound. At times like this she could lose herself in the notes, her fingers inseparable from the frets and strings, her muscles hard and lean in the smoky light.

This band, Underbrush, was not her ultimate destination; their post-punk stance bored her, and T-Boy, lead singer and songwriter, possessed no real gift for either, in her view. Still, the bass player was killer, and the dude on keyboards was inspired, and whatever T-Boy's failings, he was a great promoter, which meant regular gigs in halfway decent places and most of the time they got paid.

On the next break the Asian woman sent over a beer. Her long black hair was thick and loose on her shoulders and her slender legs ended in a pair of four-inch heels. JJ had never been much of a drinker, even before she met Gwen, but after the miserable day she'd had, a Corona hit the spot. She grinned and waved her appreciation, but didn't go over to make the woman's acquaintance.

T-Boy headed backstage toward the tiny dressing room where the rest of the guys were smoking weed, and JJ stepped out to the alley behind the club; it stank of garbage and piss, but it was quieter. She sucked her beer and tried to imagine what the women she'd met today would make of T-Boy and the rest. Her mind kept returning to Emma, the one she'd never met. It was weird, she mused, the way you could feel close to someone dead, grieve as if she were your best friend, when if they were alive you would pass them on the street without a second thought. The beer tasted bitter on her tongue.

Emma, just a few years younger than she was. Who'd gone out one night to have a good time. To a club not much different than this one. JJ had played a few gigs at the Mercury Lounge, not with Underbrush, but with her old band, Spiteful Virgins.

JJ pictured the woman in the tight red dress who'd bought her this beer. Probably the same age as Emma, just out for a good time on a sultry night. Something hard and white-hot burst in her chest when she thought about what had happened to Emma. Her hands tensed into fists, rubbed at the hot tears that leaked from her eyes.

She had never been embarrassed about her emotions, how they lived so close to the surface, but it did make her a little nervous that Gwen never cried. Didn't, wouldn't, couldn't. "Where do they go," JJ sometimes asked her lover, really wanting to know, "all those tears you never cry?" But Gwen couldn't (wouldn't, didn't) answer.

Gwen had remained dry-eyed at the memorial today, was even sarcastic about the way others expressed their grief. "It's not that I don't feel sad," Gwen had tried to assure her, but sometimes JJ had to wonder how deeply Gwen felt about anything.

Especially about their relationship. Maybe because she was younger, maybe because she was a musician, she just didn't feel like Gwen took her seriously. Or maybe it was because she was Cuban, though she hated to believe that. Something, though. As tight as they were, as torrid as their passion could be, some part of Gwen was always elusive, withheld from her. JJ was beginning to doubt that she would ever fully win her lover's heart.

A siren sped down the street at the end of the alley, its sound slicing the close, hot air. She hoped she'd done the right thing in talking to Howard today. Maybe the Jersey she knew wasn't even the same guy that Emma had gone to meet. He couldn't get in trouble if he was innocent, could he? JJ didn't know him too well, but she recalled the way his fingers, the color of dark sugar, pressed the keys of his horn to release its wails. She couldn't bring herself to imagine those fingers sliding around Emma's neck, squeezing the breath out of her.

Inside the club, she could hear the band members onstage tuning up for the next set. "Hey, Diaz, it's showtime!" At T-Boy's sharp summons, she turned her back on the alley, leaving the bottle, now drained, on the pavement.

She climbed onto the small stage, strapped the guitar around her neck. She tuned reflexively, while her eyes searched the crowded room. The bar stool was empty. The dark-haired woman in the red dress had disappeared.

Kick slid onto the orange vinyl seat of the booth in the all-night coffee shop in Chelsea. Across from her, Devon grinned weakly, red-eyed from the weed they'd smoked on their cross-town walk. He pored over the laminated pages of the menu as if expecting it to reveal holy mysteries.

When the sullen Greek appeared beside their table, Kick mumbled "Coffee, black," but Devon was craving sweets and asked for a banana split. The Greek scowled and disappeared.

The air conditioning was a relief after the heat that continued to press the city long after dark. Kick sank back against the banquette, content not to talk, while Devon tried to braid a hank of his fine, shoulder-length hair. It wasn't until their orders arrived that Devon said, "I can't believe she's dead. I'm gonna show up for class on Monday and she won't be there. I'm gonna finish a rough cut of my tape and won't be able to call her up and say, 'Could you take a look at this for me?'" His hand flailed to grasp at Kick's. "What kind of sense does that make?"

Kick shrugged and shook her head. She'd been listening to variations on this question since they'd left Kendra with her new trick in the East Village.

"What I really regret," he mourned between mouthfuls of ice cream, "is that I didn't make love with her."

Kick raised one eyebrow in surprise.

"She slept with men," Devon argued, his voice a defensive whine.

The eyebrow lifted itself higher. "You and Emma." She paused to let the absurdity of that notion fully sink in. "That wouldn't be heterosexuality; it would be some really twisted kind of lesbianism. Besides," she dismissed him, "it would never work. Emma didn't have a butch bone in her body."

She closed her eyes for just a moment, thinking of Emma's slender bones beneath her own bulk. She'd slept with Emma a few times, a couple of years ago. It had been Kick's opinion that Emma didn't really like sex, no matter how much she engaged in it. Emma had been a strangely abstracted lover, lost in her head. She would submit to anything, Kick remembered, but with more resignation than passion. When she came, *if* she came, her cries were thin and birdlike, like a creature in pain.

"You had sex with her, didn't you?" Devon asked, as if he could read her mind.

Kick nodded. What good was a cup of coffee without a cigarette? That new law about smoking was fucked up. But who was gonna bust her in the middle of the night? She pulled out a slightly bent Camel from her vest pocket and lit up.

"And…?" Devon was leaning toward her, his face eager. He wanted her to let him play voyeur.

"And, shut up!" she barked in response.

He sagged back against the orange vinyl, as if she'd slapped him. She wished she had. Her fist itched.

Devon pretended to be preoccupied with stirring the dregs of his dessert in the bottom of the glass dish. Yellow chunks of pineapple swirled into the unnatural pink of strawberry ice cream. The remains of chocolate sauce were churned into a gray soup.

The Greek slammed out of the kitchen, shambling over to their table. He pointed to her cigarette. "Put it out, or get out," he rasped. Never taking her eyes from his, she doused the cigarette into the bottom of Devon's banana split, the cinders hissing as they met the sweet liquid. The waiter slapped their check on the table and strode away, clicking his teeth in disgust. Kick allowed herself a rude chuckle.

Then she drew from her boot a bone-handled hunting knife in a leather sheath. She removed its protective covering, ran her forefinger lightly over the blade.

"Devon," she said, "you know that guy who Emma was supposed to meet the night she was killed? This Jersey guy?"

He nodded.

"I found out he's in a band, Lost Midnight. I made a few calls, and it turns out they're playing at an after-hours club not too far from here. Whaddaya say we go over and check him out?" She said it casually, as if the idea had just occurred to her.

The boy's pale face grew visibly whiter. "I thought the cops were gonna talk to him," he protested.

"The world is full of men who killed women and the cops let them get away with it!" She gripped the handle of the knife with vehemence and Devon shrank back.

"I know, I know. It's just, I don't think we oughta—"

"We're just gonna look at him," she interrupted. "Check him out. Don't get your pussy in a sling." She returned the blade to its sheath, the weapon to her boot. "Okay?"

"I guess." A line of worry creased his forehead. He pulled some bills from his pocket, left them for the Greek.

"All right, then, let's go." Kick stood and lit another Camel as she strode out, a general leading a most reluctant troop.

§

Howard sat at his kitchen table, red Formica from the Fifties, retrieved from his mother's basement in Queens, God rest her soul. After his last divorce, she'd insisted on furnishing his apartment with the furniture of his childhood, which he found both comforting and disturbing. Since her death a few years back, he'd been too broke or too busy or too lazy—his excuses varied—to refurnish.

His notes on the Emma Firestein rape/homicide were spread over the red surface, already littered with the remains of a salad from the deli around the corner and multiple half-empty bottles of water—his colleagues on the force teased him about being a health nut, but he saw it as part of his recovery. Although he could recite the details of the case in his sleep, he went over them one more time, willing himself to find something he'd missed.

White female. Age twenty-two. Attractive, dressed for a night on the town. Single, no steady relationship, reported to have had multiple partners of both genders. She'd left her apartment at about ten p.m. on the evening of June 11, telling her roommate she was going to meet a man at the Mercury Lounge. Answering machine tape contained a message from "Jersey" confirming this. Whether she made it to the Mercury Lounge was unverified. The bouncer nor the bartender thought they remembered seeing her, but both insisted "It was jammed that night." None of her friends said they were there that night. Whether she actually met Jersey was also unverified.

Her body had been discovered by a patrol officer at 4:17 a.m. under the Houston Street on-ramp to the FDR. No sign of struggle at the crime scene suggested the assault took place elsewhere; the body had been dumped. A canvass of the area had yielded no witnesses; apparently even the homeless were crashed at that hour. Time of death was put between midnight and three a.m.

The ME's report stated she had been raped. Death by strangulation, ligature bruises on her neck. The tox screen had revealed morphine, probably injected heroin, in her bloodstream, though her friends insisted she had no habit of using drugs other than alcohol and marijuana.

The prime suspect was one Jersey Mowatt, twenty-eight. Jamaican, green card, been in the country almost ten years. Sax player for a band called Lost Midnight. They hadn't been able to question him; no one quite seemed to know how to find him. His disappearance from Manhattan "on tour" the day after the murder looked suspicious.

Gwen's girlfriend JJ had described him as a mild guy who played the saxophone and was serious about his music. She'd "gigged with the dude a few times," she had told Howard, and hadn't noticed any temper, drug habit or disrespect to women, which made him, apparently, a rarity among musicians. It didn't add up.

Then there was Bronstein, over in the 78th Precinct. He'd forwarded to Howard some notes on a case he was working in Brooklyn. The perp picked up women in clubs, young women who were there by themselves, and these women turned up raped and dead, with morphine in their bloodstream. The victims in Brooklyn weren't strangled, though; they overdosed. But Emma had fought, maybe that was the difference here.

Johnson had been a good partner on the case; he'd been over all the rape and homicide stats in the precinct, as well as who'd been paroled recently. They'd run down a few leads, but the bastards had solid alibis. Howard threw down the pages he was holding and thumped the table with his fist. The water bottles jumped. He grabbed one and drained it, as if to flush frustration from his system.

Howard had been on the force for thirty-two years, as detective for the last seventeen of them, and for the most part, he found satisfaction in his work. Sometimes it was clear as day who the perp was; the challenge was to build a case with the evidence and do it in a way that was legal.

But cases like the one before him now—no visible suspects, no clear motive—these cases were like unending tunnels, airless and remote, lacking any source of light. He was going to need to catch a break on this one.

Chapter 8

Saturday, June 15, 1996

Predictably, Gwen's houseguests turned out to be early risers. Though it seemed only minutes had passed since her body finally released itself into sleep, it was now slammed once more into wakefulness.

It was Roger she heard first, his congested, high-pitched voice assailing Jolene with an urgent question about breakfast. She had the courtesy to shush him. "People are still sleeping," she explained in a patient drawl. "We have to wait a little while longer."

"Not any more, they're not," Gwen wanted to snarl, but she did appreciate Jolene's attempt to be considerate. Miraculously, the boy complied; he was a scarily well-behaved kid. Still, it was just moments after that Ruthie let loose a vast yawn, and Peg was groaning her girth up from the air mattress and padding toward the toilet.

After that, it was pretty much a free-for-all. Roger could no longer be contained and Jolene had to rouse herself to supervise him. Ruthie was poking around at the coffeepot, Peg had turned on the shower and Luanne was busy putting back together the disassembled sofa.

They kept hurling questions at one another, questions to which none of them could know the answer—"Do you know where she keeps her spoons?" "Any idea where I'd find a clean towel?" "Crap, is she out of milk?"—shouting back and forth across the studio. No doubt they meant to wake Gwen, but she was playing possum, head buried firmly beneath the pillow. Eventually she would need to rise to play the reluctant hostess, but not at seven-goddamn-thirty on a Saturday morning.

She heard a spritz of carbonation as someone knocked back a morning Coke, and the glubbing of water through the Mr. Coffee. There were random clicks as suitcases were opened and closed, and the shuffling sounds of dressing.

Roger was in serious need of breakfast, as he reminded Jolene every ninety seconds or so. There was just the slightest edge to her voice as she told him, "I don't think they have any breakfast here, sugarplum. Just let me get my clothes on, and we'll go out and try to find something, okay? I just hope it's not gonna be too expensive."

Finally Ruthie made a suggestion and became Gwen's hero. "It's been years since I lived in Manhattan, but if I remember right, there oughta be a deli up on Houston not too far from here. Let's go out for breakfast—we can fit everybody into the van."

Peg, who'd finished her shower, protested that with all their stuff, there wouldn't be enough room, but Gwen would have bet money that Peg's real objection was to Roger. *Can't allow a penis*, Gwen imagined her thinking, *to violate our sacred female space.*

"I don't have to go..." Luanne began. It sounded like she was looking for a way out, but Ruthie overruled her, insisting that there was plenty of space for everyone.

You could walk from here, Gwen kept herself from shrieking, because she didn't want to blow her cover. The truth was she didn't care *how* they went, as long as they vacated her space, and the sooner the better.

The worry in Jolene's voice was a little more acute as she asked, "How much do you figure it'll cost to eat there?" Ayisha had told Gwen the day before that Jolene lived on welfare, and was about to lose her benefits under the new law. Apparently Dana had sent her money for the bus ticket up from Tennessee.

Ruthie announced, "Breakfast is on me."

Luanne wondered, "Should we let Gwen know where we're going?" but Jolene said, "Don't wake her. She was up later than all of us."

It was amazing that they really thought she could sleep through their racket, but maybe they were just pretending to believe her slumber, as she was pretending to sleep. An audience-participation performance.

There was more audible fretting about keys and locks, getting out and getting back in, but Roger was persistent with his "Mom, are we gonna eat soon?" and this eventually propelled the group out the door, leaving a merciful quiet in their wake.

Her privacy restored, Gwen stripped off the T-shirt worn for propriety's sake, savored the feel of sheets against bare skin. Even at this hour, the air was heating up, pressing like a damp hand on the city. She fluffed her pillow, sunk her head into its downy embrace. She was just on the verge of drifting back into oblivion when she became aware of a dull ache, a throbbing in her ovaries, a stickiness between her thighs.

This could only mean the onslaught of her period, a whole week early. Her gynecologist had advised her that menstrual irregularity was just one more facet of aging—whenever the doctor referred to her as "peri-menopausal" Gwen had to fight the urge to smack her—but in truth her periods had always timed themselves for the most inopportune occasions: major performances, vacations, romantic trysts. And while the events of this day were none of those, her body seemed to have retained its uncanny instinct for making her vulnerable at a time she least wanted to be.

Her legs reluctantly hauled themselves to standing, carried her to the bathroom. She retrieved a tampon and mopped at the squiggle of red staining her thighs. With the practice of more than thirty years she inserted the spire of cotton into her vagina; thumb and forefinger came away bloody. She sat on the toilet seat to pee, felt the cramp in her lower abdomen intensify.

Her face in the mirror was pallid, the delicate skin around the eyes nearly blue. She calculated she'd have at least an hour and a half before the breakfasters returned, and slogged her way back to bed.

She couldn't have said how long she'd been asleep, a rich, deep satisfying slumber thick as cream, but the next thing she knew she felt a familiar body curled next to her, a warm belly against her aching kidneys, a hand cradling the curve of her breast. She turned to meet JJ's nude body, and for a moment was suspended between dream and wakefulness, consumed in their embrace.

A fine sheen of sweat blossomed in the crevice between bodies, pressed together like hands in prayer, belly to belly on the damp sheets. Daylight spilled into the open window, flooding the room so brightly that even with her eyes closed there was a red glow.

"I missed you," Gwen gasped into her lover's hair.

"You can't say you were lonely," JJ teased back, her eyes half-lidded with lust. Her lips tilted toward Gwen's in sweet expectation.

"We shouldn't get started with this," Gwen said apologetically, kissing the soft skin around, but not directly meeting, JJ's lips. "Everybody went out for breakfast, but they could come back anytime."

JJ adored a challenge. She wrapped an insistent arm around Gwen's waist and held her tight. "I locked all the doors," she confided.

"Up here and downstairs?"

"Upstairs and down," she confirmed.

"That's mean," Gwen giggled. She imagined the whole group of them standing on Rivington Street, leaning on the bell and wondering what to do next.

"You Anglos have no manners," JJ chided. "Didn't your mother ever teach you that when a woman appears in your bed first thing in the morning, it is customary to greet her with a kiss?"

"What she taught me," Gwen whispered, "is how dangerous it can be when *la Cubana* appears in your bed in the morning."

JJ slid her other arm beneath Gwen's ass; her fingers began to lazily knead the mounds of flesh. She scooted closer to catch Gwen's left nipple with her tongue. A shiver raised the fine hairs along Gwen's spine. "JJ, I really shouldn't do this. The whole crew is coming back today and I have to get myself prepared…"

JJ was undeterred, letting her teeth sink lightly into the soft sphere of the nipple, causing it to harden and producing a guttural sigh from the back of Gwen's throat. Cupping a handful of her hair, JJ kissed the hollow of her neck and murmured, "What more preparation could you need?"

"JJ!" It was this kid-like insistence on following her impulses—whatever the consequence—that both delighted and infuriated Gwen, but for the moment, delight won out. Gwen's final protest escaped like a kite into the sky, drifting out of reach. She knew she was lost, could feel the wetness oozing between her thighs, her accelerating heartbeat. With no residue of reluctance, she sank back into the mattress, arms encircling JJ's muscled shoulders.

Returning her attention to Gwen's breasts, JJ feasted, alternately licking and sucking the left nipple, rolling the right one between two fingers, applying and releasing pressure. Heat shimmered from the surface of her dusky skin, as a low song filled the air, a music of moans and gasps and sighs.

When Gwen felt JJ's fingers grab hold of the string of her tampon, she almost stopped her. She had no time to be worrying about laundry. But as JJ's fingers continued to tease and probe her clit, she lost all will to object.

The tampon was discarded hastily onto the floor. Three of JJ's fingers traced the crenulations of Gwen's inner labia, circling and stirring in the fragrant soup that greased their entry. Muscles pulsed to grip her fingers, easing their journey into the canal, pulling them deeper, greedy to keep them there.

"Fill me, honey," Gwen heard myself moan, huskily.

Her eyes closed then and she floated away. A string of syllables began to roll from her tongue, a language without pictures, as if her cells could speak.

"Touch my heart," she pleaded with JJ, because the hand was alive inside her now; there was no place it could not reach.

"*Venga, mi bebé,*" JJ whispered, "*Dame lo todo.*"

Her thumb swam up to greet Gwen's swollen clitoris; her

fingers never lost their rhythm, thrusting in and sliding back. She maneuvered her own body to straddle the jutting bone of Gwen's hip, rubbing her mons across that padded peak. Her thumb grew more insistent as prayers erupted from Gwen's mouth, swirling in the air above them like a summer storm. JJ's petitions were in Spanish, torn from her throat in jagged growls as the room exploded and both dissolved in a shower of sparks.

Afterward they clung together, soaked in sweat, saliva and blood. Gwen listened to the slowing percussion of JJ's heartbeat, felt her own molecules slowly reassemble into human form. She dozed in JJ's arms, the sun warming their skin. Whatever misgivings she had about this relationship, they always deserted her when they made love.

Gwen could have easily drifted away into sleep, but her lover had more on her mind, and in a little while she began to talk. She told Gwen about the gig last night, how fine their playing sounded. Her voice always took on a different timbre when she talked about her music, more resonant, as if her words echoed from some deep place in her core. Then, sheepishly, she mentioned the Asian woman in a red dress who bought her a drink.

"And were you tempted to go home with her?" Gwen pouted. She never doubted JJ's constancy, but it bothered JJ that she wasn't more jealous. JJ believed it meant Gwen didn't care, so every now and then Gwen pretended to be in the grip of the green-eyed monster. "While I was stuck here with the Ghosts of Feminisms Past and Future?"

"*Pepita*, the only one I ever want to come home to is you," JJ vowed.

Such devotion must be rewarded, so Gwen flipped her body over to lie on top of JJ, tracing her lips with her tongue, sucking breath from her mouth, leaving slick red streaks down the length of her thighs. Gwen was just playing around, though, and JJ knew it; from experience she'd learned that Gwen was a woman who needed a lot of down time between orgasms.

Eventually JJ settled Gwen in beside her again, and told her about her talk with Howard. JJ's dark eyes were shot through with trouble as she confided, "You know, cops are no friend of brown people. I worry that this poor dude who just happens to have the same name is gonna get framed, because he's black and because I opened my big mouth. There's gotta be a lotta guys call themselves 'Jersey,' right? Even some other ones who are musicians."

Gwen tried to reassure her that Howard was an honest cop. "He'll be fair. He doesn't just want *some* guy, he wants the right guy. It's not that I have any faith in cops, but I do trust Howard."

"Yeah, he said he just wanted to talk to the guy, find out where he was that night. But still…" JJ spread her palm as if reaching for an answer. "He also said that Jersey screwed himself by leaving town. I told him, 'When a gig comes up, you go. You get a call, somebody's sick, band needs a replacement—boom—you got a paycheck. Damn right, you go.'"

Gwen studied the shape of JJ's long tapering fingers. She wanted to give her the assurance she was seeking.

"JJ, I know you feel loyalty to this guy because you've gigged with him, but you said yourself, you don't know him all that well." Gwen took her hand in both of her hands and held it firmly. "If by some chance he did kill Emma, then you'll have been the one who made sure he won't ever be able to do it to another woman. That's important." The creases in her forehead eased a bit.

The myth of her relationship with JJ was that Gwen was the one who knew things. That was partly because she was older, because she'd been to college (even if she didn't finish), but mostly, she suspected, it was because she was never shy about stating her opinions, often forcefully. Regardless of whether she was right or wrong.

Still, she was constantly reminded that JJ knew things Gwen could only be humbled by. She knew about being born on an island, and about having to leave her home, the red roosters and green banana leaves, stealing away in darkness, soldiers never far behind. She knew about climbing aboard a rough boat to cross endless water, then being washed up on a beach in a new place where the words no longer fit your tongue. That island still lived in the center of her; Gwen could hear it in her music, smell it on her skin. It would have never occurred to Gwen to be concerned for the possible accused, a possible rapist, but then her skin was white and she'd never been in trouble with the law. Who was she to talk JJ out of her misgivings?

"Listen," Gwen told her, "if you're freaked out about this, you should talk to Howard again."

JJ gave her a sharp, surprised look, as if she could read all that had been passing through Gwen's mind. A long moment passed before she nodded and said, "Okay."

JJ kissed her then, and Gwen felt it stir in her cunt and knew she could have her all over again. But her internal alarm clock was screaming; their luck wouldn't hold much longer. She reluctantly broke the embrace.

"We should shower," Gwen suggested, indicating the carnage on the sheets and on their bodies, "before everybody gets back."

"Maybe I want to wear your blood around all day." JJ smiled. "Like a marked woman."

"You'll have rats after you in the subway," Gwen warned. She rose from the bed, and JJ unwillingly followed. The still, hot air of the room smelled unmistakably of sex, and Gwen didn't particularly want her guests to know that much about her. She rummaged in a drawer to find some incense, lit a stick of Blue Nile.

JJ was industriously stripping the sheets from the bed. "The least I can do is take these to the laundromat for you," she offered.

This deserved further reward, but Gwen knew the breakfasters would be back any second, and who knew when the rest were due to show up on her doorstep? Besides, any minute she would start dripping bloodstains on the floor, so she just blew JJ a kiss as she scurried into the bathroom.

Before she could get into the shower, she heard the buzzer from the street. "JJ?" she called, grabbing a washcloth and scouring at her cunt, thighs and underarms—*a whore's bath*, the gay boys called it. As she inserted a fresh tampon, JJ joined her behind the curtain, swabbing away at her own stains, then hurled herself into her jeans and shirt and clattered barefoot down the steps.

Gwen raced to grab underwear, and pull a sundress off the nearest rack. It was strapless, white, circa 1950, sporting huge red poinsettias on its full skirt. Frantic, she tugged the zipper up the back and jammed her feet into scarlet, high-heeled mules. She barely had time to run a brush through her hair and pile it on top of her head with a clip. In the mirror, she noticed her face was reddened and blotchy, her post-orgasm face. There was nothing to be done, though; in the last seconds of privacy she spied the discarded tampon on the floor by the bed and scooped it into the trash. Then the studio door opened.

She expected to see JJ followed by Peg and Ruthie, et al., but it was Lee who swung open the door, trailed by a glum-faced JJ. Gwen's face reddened, a detail obvious to both women.

"I hope I'm not interrupting anything," Lee gloated, taking in JJ's bare feet, the air of haste in the room. "Somebody told me I was supposed to come back in the morning." Unlike Gwen and JJ, Lee looked cool and well-groomed in a short-sleeved linen shirt the color of celadon and pressed beige linen trousers. Her tone was a bit too innocent not to be calculated.

"Surely you didn't think that meant nine a.m.?" Gwen challenged her, but she shrugged it off.

"I didn't want to miss anything." Then, as if elaborately concerned about them, she offered, "I can leave and come back if this is a bad time."

"Nah, I was just going," JJ growled, and jammed her feet into her boots. She was clenching and unclenching her jaw, an unmistakable signal she was working on a slow burn.

Gwen walked her to the door. "Hey, don't let her get to you, okay?" She murmured into JJ's shoulder.

Her lover looked at her with eyes that were molten. "Don't let her get to you, *nena*, that's what I ask."

She turned to go and Gwen said, "Oops, don't forget this," and clattered back across the studio to pick up the pillowcase stuffed with bloodied sheets. She took it, and Gwen made a show of kissing her slowly and with passion, although some of her fervency was for Lee's benefit.

They slipped into the hallway. "Come back and get me this

evening," Gwen said, "I think I ought to go to a meeting, and maybe we can get some dinner. Okay?"

JJ's gaze continued to smolder. "So, did you ask her to come at this time? Was *I* the inconvenient surprise this morning?"

Gwen grew very calm, the way she'd learned to, a better strategy than vehemence to combat JJ's fits of jealousy. "JJ, I swear to you, I'm even less happy to see her here than you are, if that's possible."

JJ's expression was split in two, as if her rational brain accepted the words, as did the part of her that hungered to believe. Still, there was another aspect, perhaps the young one whose island had been irretrievably taken from her, who was certain it was foolish to trust.

"Look at what you're wearing," she accused. "You didn't dress that way for your feminists."

In a quiet tone, Gwen insisted, "JJ, I didn't dress this way for anyone. I was naked and I grabbed the first thing in sight." This sounded lame even to her own ears, so she tried again. "And besides, if I wanted to look sexy, it would be because of the way you made me feel this morning."

The memory tugged at JJ, softening the corners of her mouth.

"Okay, *bebe*," she said softly. "Sorry I flew off the handle."

"It's okay," Gwen soothed. "Just don't tell yourself bad stories about me."

As JJ disappeared down the stairs with her bulging pillowcase, Gwen called, "I love you." She listened as it echoed in the stairwell. It occurred to her that she didn't tell JJ that nearly enough. She stood at the top until she could no longer hear her lover's footsteps on the stairs.

Howard always told her that God had a sense of humor. That must be why she was now praying for the return of her houseguests, the more the merrier, anything to keep from having to be alone with Lee Bergman.

She could just follow JJ down the stairs, out into the street, keep walking and not look back, an enormous temptation, but if she ran from Lee it would make her old adversary victorious yet again. To be unaffected was what Gwen wanted, to not crave

Lee's approval or flinch under her criticism or compete with her for control of their interaction. This was the measurement of her mental health, and she'd settle for being able to pull off even a semblance of it.

So Gwen squared her jaw and returned to the room, where Lee leaned against the wall next to an open window. Her eyes traveled the length of Gwen's body, lingering on her bare shoulders, the slight cleavage created by the tight bodice of the dress, the shape of her legs in heels.

Lee's grin was appreciative. "So," she said, "you got the maid to do the laundry."

Lee's racism was one of her least attractive features. "Fuck you," Gwen snapped, chiding herself for unoriginality.

"Well, if she's not the maid, she must be your girlfriend." Lee lit a Marlboro with a slim gold lighter, blew the smoke out the window. "Except I'm thinking, why wouldn't she introduce me to her girlfriend?"

"I figured you two had already dealt with the hello-how-are-you's," Gwen lied sweetly. She headed for the coffeepot, poured a cup that looked suspiciously pale. One swig of the weak brew and she spat it back into the mug. "Tastes like piss! Excuse me a minute, I gotta get rid of this."

Which gave her the opportunity to disappear, dump the contents of the pot and the mug into the bathroom sink, rinse them out, and swipe some lipstick across her mouth. Hollywood Red, to match the poinsettias on her dress. She also swabbed a little blush across her cheeks, the better to counteract her menstrual pallor. She returned to the main room and busied herself with measuring spoonfuls of ground French roast, pouring bottled water into the coffeemaker.

Lee had finished her cigarette, and was grinding it out on the window ledge. "So, how long?" she wanted to know.

"How long, what?"

"How long have you and the Chiquita Banana been seeing each other?"

Gwen turned to face her, gripping the bag of coffee as if she might throw it at Lee's head. "Either cut that shit out or get the hell out of my sight."

"Calm down, Gwen, it's just a joke."

Her standard defense. Gwen was always the one who was crazy, whose reactions were extreme, the one who couldn't take a joke. She gave Lee the look she knew so well, the look that said, I'm not laughing.

Lee was persistent. "C'mon. How long have you and the lovely Latin been an item?"

"About two years."

"So, it's a serious thing?" She raised her eyebrows in surprise. "And you used to call *me* a cradle-robber."

Gwen knew better, but she rose to the bait. "She's not that much younger," she defended herself. "She'll be thirty her next birthday..."

"Thirteen years. The exact difference between your age and mine." Lee beamed as if she'd made a profound discovery.

Gwen decided she couldn't wait for the whole pot to brew. She yanked the glass container out of the way and stuck her cup beneath the spout. She got a good half-cup before returning the pot to its receiving platform. The coffee was scalding when she gulped it, but she wouldn't let Lee see that. She turned away as she blinked back the tears that sprang to her eyes.

When the shock of the burn had finished coursing through her body, she turned back. "Now *that's* a cup of coffee," she proclaimed.

"So, two years," Lee was still musing, "and the sex is still good."

She caught Gwen's "what business is it of yours" frown and purred, "You know, when I walked in this morning and saw you, I said to myself, 'There's a woman who just got laid'."

Despite herself, Gwen's cheeks caught flame again. Lee continued, "Do you think I could forget that look you get after sex? Your whole body relaxes. It's the only time you ever really look happy."

The color in her face deepened but this time it was fueled by rage at the presumption of familiarity and the implicit criticism lurking just beneath the surface of Lee's words. Gwen had promised herself to remain detached, free of the snares of the past, but the ire was like a hook in her heart. This was how she'd get herself caught if she wasn't careful.

"Want some coffee?" she asked, intending to deflect the conversation.

"I'll wait till it's ready," Lee replied, amused, pointing to the half-full coffeepot. She enjoyed this cat-and-mouse game, especially when the mice got nervous. She was getting ready to pounce.

"Hey," she crooned, inching closer, easing a deft paw onto Gwen's bare shoulder. All on its own, the shoulder twitched as if stung by an electrical charge, dislodging her hand.

"What's the matter with you?" Lee demanded. "You treat me like I'm a fucking stranger."

"I guess I'm not comfortable with you touching me." Even to her own ears she sounded uptight and prissy.

"Do me a favor, cookie, hey? Lighten up, okay?" Lee lifted her hands like a convict under arrest. "I'm not trying ta put the moves on ya or anything."

She continued, her voice a satisfied growl. "It's been a long time since we've seen each other. We used to be so close. There's no reason we can't be friends. I was hoping you'd have lunch with me today."

Gwen could feel hot breath on the back of her neck. "I don't think that's such a great idea."

"So, why not?"

She turned to face her and planted her tottering heels more firmly on the floor. "Lee, it's like this: my friends are people who *like* me, who respect me, people I trust. You've never been my friend."

Lee's forehead pleated in disgust. "This isn't some scene from one of your performances. I asked you to lunch, right? You don't have to turn it into some big drama."

How many years, Gwen wondered, and how many thousands of dollars had she spent in therapy trying to spin her way out of this particular web? If she said no, she was being dramatic, or neurotic, and if she said yes...

"Come on, baby," Lee urged into her left ear. "For old time's sake."

Chapter 9

"The cause of violence against women is patriarchal power."
Peg was thrusting her finger at the air. "Rape asserts that
women are property, that a man can do what he wants with his
property."

It was nearly eleven in the morning and the group was only
now settling in on the ragtag furniture Gwen had none-too-
happily shoved into a loose approximation of an oval in the
center of the loft. The last thing she was in the mood for was a
massive talk-a-thon, which was how she remembered this kind
of meeting from the old days. *Then* she'd believed that this
group of women held the key that would unlock the revolution.
Looking around the room now, Gwen thought everyone looked
as played out as she felt, including Emma's friends. *We all
underestimated*, she thought, *the power of the system to co-opt us.*
Even this language harkened back to twenty years earlier.

She'd also set up a couple of fans to stir the stagnant air; the
whir of their blades produced a screen of white noise over which
Peg, and in fact everyone, had to strain to be heard.

"You say that like it's all men," Luanne contested.

Peg whirled around to face her. "It may not be all men, but
it could be *any* man."

"Word!" Kick signaled her agreement.

"It's bullshit to act like it's only men who are violent," Kendra lobbed from across the room. Lee was sitting beside her, one arm draped casually across the back of the younger woman's chair. Kendra was wearing a tube top, its puckers stretched taut over her breasts, revealing the outline of her nipple ring.

Ayisha broke in. "I can't believe we're supposed to sit here and talk about some abstract, theoretical ideas. Emma is dead, remember? What good was your feminism to her?" She turned to Dana for her reaction, but Dana was staring into space, abstracted, as if something else absorbed her attention.

"She's right," Kick growled. "We can't sit here and talk this shit to death. We need to get off our butts and do something."

"That's the spirit." Peg beamed her approval.

Dana's long-delayed arrival at the loft had brought a welcome end to Gwen's sparring with Lee. At the sound of the buzzer, Gwen had clattered down the four flights of stairs and released the locks with an eagerness she wouldn't have predicted even an hour before.

Dana looked as if she hadn't slept at all. She still sported the Stop Violence Against Women T-shirt she'd worn at the memorial, and her hair, always disheveled, looked as if it had been caught in a particularly severe storm. The thick glasses that so magnified her blue eyes also deepened the shadows beneath them.

For a moment, Gwen had squirmed under Dana's harsh scowl. *Here I am in this dress*, Gwen scolded herself, *these shoes, she thinks I'm completely frivolous, totally without substance or worse, that I have no respect for her daughter's death.* But these thoughts extinguished themselves as she realized that Dana wasn't even looking at her. Instead, Dana was staring at a point just over Gwen's left shoulder, but when Gwen tried to follow the line of sight, she found just sheets of bare drywall.

"Dana," Gwen said gently, and the woman's face grew momentarily disoriented, as if she couldn't imagine where she'd been or how she arrived here.

"They said I should come this morning," Dana snapped, as if Gwen had questioned her presence. Whatever had been on Dana's mind, it had not softened her truculence.

"Peg and Luanne and all have gone to breakfast," Gwen explained as she led Dana into the building and up the stairs, "but they should be back any minute." Her efforts at small talk capsized under Dana's unresponsiveness.

Lee remained by the windows, staring out at the hazy sky, while Gwen got Dana a cup of coffee and showed her where the bathroom was located.

Finally Lee had approached and murmured, "I don't know if you remember me—Lee Bergman? I was at Labrys. I'm sorry about your daughter."

Without indicating whether or not she remembered her, Dana asked, "So what kind of organizing have you been doing since Labrys?" Although an odd response for a grieving mother, it was pure Dana.

Lee rejoined quickly, "Same kind I've always done—trying to organize the cute girls into bed with me!" She gave Gwen a broad wink.

Dana had never been known for her sense of humor. With a withering look at Lee, she turned to Gwen. "Surely you didn't bring me here for *this*."

I didn't bring you here at all. Gwen bit back the retort, but Dana had simply turned her back on Lee and walked to the other end of the studio, where she sat in a folding chair, from which she did not move the whole time the others were assembling.

"How are we supposed to have a meaningful discussion about feminism with men here?" Peg protested.

Jolene shot up from her metal folding chair. "Jesus, Peg, he's a seven-year-old boy! He hasn't had time to commit any crimes against women."

"Jolene, you know my position on boy children," Peg insisted. She had written several articles in the feminist press in the late Seventies about the need to preserve "wimmin-only space" by leaving boy children at home. "But that issue aside, what about *him?*" She stabbed her index finger in the direction of Devon, whose violet hair was today pulled into a high chignon, skewered and held in place by an X of chopsticks. His thin frame was covered by a loose shift of pink flowered cotton; the thrift store dress ended just above his knobby knees.

"Get serious, Peg," Lee snorted. "*I'm* more of a man than that kid!"

"I wouldn't brag about that," Peg retorted, her face reddening.

"It's more complicated than that," Kick protested on Devon's behalf. "She's taking hormones."

"I can't believe you're all, like, still trippin' on this gender thing," Kendra sneered from her seat beside Lee. "It's, like, so retro. As if there's only two genders, and *as if* those categories defined anything!"

Peg gaped at her, incredulous. "If gender doesn't define anything," she demanded, "then what's the point of feminism?"

Kendra snickered and shrugged one shoulder, as if the question provided its own answer.

"It's too fucking hot to bicker," Gwen interrupted before Peg could launch her rebuttal. "Everybody's here because someone invited them, so could we please just leave it at that and get on with whatever it is we're supposed to do here? Which, by the way, is exactly what?" Her eyes cast about the room, seeking clarification from any quarter.

"Labrys was one of the great feminist think tanks of the Nineteen seventies," Peg explained in a tone that made it clear that she felt this point was obvious. Perspiration had studded her forehead, and ran in rivulets down her ample neck. Her fair skin was reddened with heat. "And *we're* the ones from that gathering who are still active. Or at least most of us are," she qualified the assertion with a sour glance toward Lee and Luanne. "So it makes sense that we should be the ones to wrestle with the question of feminism's future, especially in light of what happened to Emma. What has our work meant if young women are still not safe, and what is the appropriate response?"

"Why do men rape women? Because they think they can get away with it. The appropriate response is to make men *pay* for what they do," Kick declared.

"That's right," Peg agreed. "They have to be held accountable."

With a sigh, Gwen nodded and left the circle to pour herself another cup of coffee. It was going to be a long morning.

She'd wanted witnesses. She hadn't been able to live with the idea that her daughter's death might go unnoticed, unmourned, that Emma might pass from the world as if she'd never been. *That's why*, Dana reminded herself, she'd invited all these people. That's why she found herself sitting with them after all these years in a loft on the Lower East Side.

The Lower East Side, where her parents had lived when they were first married, in a railroad apartment over her grandfather's store on Orchard Street. She had lived there, above the shelves crammed with bolts of fabric, until she was eight, when her parents moved to Scarsdale. Now they hated to even come into the city, and had been scandalized when she'd invited them to the reception here yesterday.

"Why would we want to go back there?" her father had argued. "Your grandfather's store, what he spent his whole life building—now it's owned by Koreans. And the streets full of drug dealers, who needs to see that?"

When she left home at eighteen, Dana had intended to never see her parents again. She'd turned her back on their life—their underpaid Puerto Rican cleaning lady, the new-every-three-years Cadillac, their winter vacations in the Caribbean, their backyard swimming pool. She had hitched her way to Alabama to work on voter registration for blacks. 1965. That was the summer she lost her virginity to a sandy-haired, uncircumcised boy from Illinois. Mark. It was odd to remember his name all these years later. His mouth had tasted like the Juicy Fruit gum he was never without.

It was that same summer she'd met Marilyn and Lincoln Cain. They'd seemed in love then, although years later Marilyn would wonder aloud whether it had just been the thrill they'd felt at crossing the color line. A dangerous transgression in those days, north or south.

Dana caught a glimpse of Ayisha across the circle. At a certain angle Dana could always see Marilyn in the girl's face—the round cheeks, slightly jutted chin—but there was a stubborn set to her mouth that was pure Lincoln.

Dana felt a sigh blow through her body like the hot, exhausted air through a subway grate. She should have done more for Ayisha after Marilyn died, or even before, those years Marilyn was so sick. She'd been furious with Marilyn for giving up on politics; it had been easy to stay away. And after, she'd relied on Emma to care for Ayisha, so that Dana could go on with her work. Central America, it had been then, El Salvador, Nicaragua. And of course, Palestine.

Kendra was still challenging Peg. "It's just that kind of judgmental crap—telling people what they can and can't wear, how they're supposed to look, what they're allowed to say, even how to *fuck*—that made the women's movement irrelevant."

"I resented everyone telling me I was supposed to be a lesbian," Luanne said.

"Hardly irrelevant! The women's movement has done more to change our society than any other social movement in our lifetime." Peg always talked with her hands; now she was sweeping them into broad circles in front of her body.

Unable to contain it, Chi expelled a breath of pure disgust, and for a moment everyone was silent, looking at her. She was gripping the arms of her wooden chair as if she might tear them off, but she just shook her head.

"Well, of course," Peg amended, "the civil rights movement..." Her voice trailed off, before rebounding, "But a political movement has to have discipline, that's my point."

"I've always said a little discipline is a very good thing," Lee quipped, her tone insinuating.

Peg ignored her. "It's not just about everyone doing what they feel like. Dana, didn't you always tell us that?"

All eyes turned toward Dana who'd said nothing since she sat down in the circle, allowing the words to swirl around her without reaching out to catch any of them. It took her a moment to even register the silence, the expectant gazes trained on her. She blinked behind her thick glasses, as if trying to remember where she was or what was being asked of her.

It was painful to witness her hesitancy, her disorientation, this woman who'd always been as relentless as a bullet. Those who knew her slid their eyes away, embarrassed to have intruded on what they assumed was her private grief.

"Emma thought that was all a bunch of crap, all those rules about what you could and couldn't wear," Kick volunteered, and the conversation resumed its swirling.

"The degree of backlash only proves it," Ruthie was saying. "If feminism had been no threat, it would have just been ignored."

"That's right! Think of how the FBI crushed the Black Panthers—" Peg directed this comment toward Chi, as if she'd chosen the example expressly for Chi's benefit, "—because they were so powerful."

"Panthers were assassinated, or thrown in jail for life. I didn't see that happen to any feminists, so what'chu talkin' 'bout *backlash?*" Chi ground the muscles of her jaw.

"Backlash like people saying feminism is dead," Peg sputtered, "or irrelevant! Or like the media making us into jokes!"

"Or the people who want women to go back to having dangerous, illegal abortions," Elena added, briefly dipping into the conversation. She'd spent most of the morning on her cell phone, calling senators, the murmur of her conversations blending with the whir of the fans. Although Elena respected Dana for her ongoing activism, for the most part she saw the other women were on the sidelines now, spouting opinions instead of doing the often dirty work of making real change.

"And feminists *did* go to jail—" Ruthie began.

But Gwen interrupted, "Not for being feminists, though. They went to jail for what they'd done in the Left, *before* they became feminists. The Panthers had guns; they were in the streets. Nobody bombed any buildings for feminism."

"And thank the Goddess it's true. We're a non-violent movement," Peg declared in reverent tones.

"That's a big part of the problem," Kick asserted. "If women don't stand up for ourselves, nobody takes us seriously."

"There are other ways of being powerful besides violence," Ruthie told her.

"Personally, I think a little violence can be, like, pretty

exciting," Kendra interjected with a salacious grin, but only Lee grinned back.

"Yeah," Kick responded to Ruthie, "and the other way is money. But we don't have billions of dollars, right?"

"Those aren't the only ways," Peg insisted. "There's the power of knowing who you are, acting with integrity—"

"That's total bullshit!" Kick stomped her boot on the wooden floor. "The moral high ground, that's the wet dream of the powerless. Look, if a man was about to rape you, or rape Ruthie, and you had a gun, wouldn't you use it? If someone was gonna rape your kid?"

And Peg had to admit, "I'd blow his fucking head off."

The conversation eddied in the space defined by the circle of chairs, but Dana watched it all as if from behind thick glass. The cops had tried to make her look at Emma's body through such a barrier but she'd refused, and argued till they let her see her daughter. *This* glass, though, was for protection. It muted the vehemence of everyone's opinions, reduced them to dull murmurs that couldn't pierce her with meanings.

Had it always been like this—words wielded as weapons, the skirmishes between allies more bitter than battles against adversaries? It hadn't been like this in Alabama, that summer of 1965. She remembered meetings in small Black churches, worn pews crowded with sharecroppers and domestic workers and black and white college kids from up north, planning a common strategy to outwit the sheriff, the police dogs, or the governor himself. Then, their differences had seemed to symbolize the strength of their cause.

Even that hadn't lasted, she reminded herself. By the time Lincoln and Marilyn came to New York, in the fall of 1967, Watts and Newark and Detroit had gone up in flames, and black berets and clenched fist salutes had supplanted sit-ins and prayer vigils.

The anti-war movement was riddled with factions, but it was in the women's movement that she'd seen hand-to-hand combat. Down south, in that summer of 1965, no one had called her racist, because the pernicious face of racism had been only too clear, but at Labrys, white women who'd organized nothing more than their plane trips to get there felt free to level that charge against her. "Racist" because there were so few women of color at Labrys; "classist" because it cost money to go there; "anti-mother," because the childcare facilities were seen as inadequate; "exploitative," because the childcare workers felt underpaid; "oppressive" whenever she took a stand that someone didn't like. It wasn't that she hadn't agreed with some of the charges; there was no more unanimity within the organizing collective than outside it. But how had the original purpose of Labrys—to train women in the skills of political organizing—become obliterated by the expectation that in the span of eight weeks Labrys would create a feminist utopia?

Dana looked at the women who sat around the circle. They were, except for a sprinkling of Emma's friends, women she had known at Labrys. Of more than a hundred women who'd attended, she'd kept in touch with only a handful, those who seemed most likely to continue their political work: Elena, who worked harder than any of them; Peg, who traveled now like an old-time revivalist, spreading the gospel of feminism. Her contacts were invaluable, even if her message was outmoded. Jolene, still scrappy, organizing welfare mothers as the whole country lined up against them, and Luanne, once the toughest negotiator Dana had been privileged to know, who'd succumbed to her own anger, the way fire eats up all the available oxygen. And Chi.

Somehow they'd picked up a few more—Gwen and Lee and Ruthie. Dana had needed help remembering who any of them were.

Now she had to struggle to recall what she was doing here with them. *Witnesses*, she reminded herself once more, *she'd wanted witnesses.*

"Look, it's over," Kendra was saying. "Okay, maybe things were bad for women, but they're better now. Nobody discriminates against me for having a clit."

"Wouldn't dream of it," Lee murmured beside her.

"How can you say that," Gwen demanded, "in the face of

what happened to Emma?"

"Rape is a crime against women," Peg intoned.

"Men get raped too," Devon insisted. "And gay-bashed. And AIDS."

"Women get AIDS," Chi asserted, never taking her eyes off Dana.

"I'm just sayin'—" Kendra uncrossed her long legs that were barely concealed by her miniskirt, "It's time to move on."

"You ungrateful little..." Peg's face seemed to compress into a whorl of pure hatred. Fury propelled her forward, a towering, red-faced mass, until she stood, quivering, just feet from where the young woman sat.

"Chill out, *bitch*—" Kendra began, but Peg overran her.

"You think because you're twenty-four years old you know everything?" Peg spat the words into the girl's sneer. "What do you know? Nothing! Your generation got liberation handed to you on a platter—choices, opportunities, *lifestyles*. When I was your age there was just one choice—marriage and motherhood, that was it. And if you didn't want that, if you had a brain and wanted your independence, you were a freak, and it was too damn bad."

Pouches of flesh swayed beneath her arms as she translated her rage into gesture. "The happiest day of my life was the day I threw away my girdle. Twenty years I wore it, every day, even if all I was doing was cleaning the house. My mother told me it was *indecent* not to wear it. And now I open up the pages of the newspaper, and once again they're being sold to women. 'Body-shapers!' It's like we're going back in time!"

She hovered in front of Kendra's chair, commanding the young woman's eyes to meet hers. "And your generation says, 'What's the big deal? If we wanna wear girdles or push-up bras or lipstick—we're free to choose.' How am I supposed to feel when you celebrate things that kept me in slavery? You spit on the symbols of my liberation! And then you tell me I'm *humorless*."

As determined as Kendra had been to keep the defiant smirk plastered to her lips, she could no longer maintain it in the face of Peg's outraged lamentation. She could not recall ever having felt so fervently about anything, and she felt a bit embarrassed for the older woman at the same time as she envied that intensity. Emma had been impassioned in this way, Kendra reflected, and in that moment, a sliver of grief wedged itself into her throat, the first she had allowed herself since hearing about her friend's death.

The combustion drained from Peg's eyes then, replaced by a vast gray sorrow. She turned and lumbered back to her seat beside Ruthie, who grabbed for her hand and clutched it tight as soft sobs began to burble from deep in Peg's chest.

Startled, Dana looked up to see where the disturbance was coming from. As if an invisible switch had been turned on, she stood then, and began to speak in the voice of her old, vehement, political self. "I no longer think that women can assume a shared context," she began.

Dana put her large red hands together and, in a single reflexive gesture, cracked all the knuckles of both hands. The older women were reminded of Dana's blunt, acerbic style; like a sudden slap across the cheek, it could seem insulting and yet bracing at the same time, the way the truth can be a welcome, if painful, relief.

Devon whispered to Ayisha, "What a *bitch!* Poor Emma."

But Ayisha whispered back, "She wasn't like that with Emma."

"Labrys is as good an example as any," Dana continued. "No two women there—*including* the members of the collective—had the same idea about what Labrys was supposed to be. A school? A think tank? Feminist boot camp? A dyke version of summer in the Catskills?"

Dana Firestein had always possessed a sultry voice, deep and smoldering, which she offset with clipped, unsmiling delivery. Hearing once more those throaty intonations, Chi Curtis was reminded of the contradiction between the extravagant promise of that voice and Dana's tough, unsparing attitude. Observing the speaker's fists planted firmly on her narrow hips, Chi wondered too if Dana was still in the habit of forgetting to eat more often than not. It had once been she who reminded her.

"Based on the debacle of Labrys," Dana went on, "as well as

the decimation of progressive politics in this country over the last twenty-five years, I've come to believe that identity politics just don't work in the United States, and for two reasons. First, because capitalism has assured that, above all, *individualism* is the cornerstone of identity in this country, which means that nobody really identifies with anybody else.

"Second, because of the multiple intersections of oppression. Race and class divide women as a group; class and gender fragment people of color. You say 'woman' or 'feminist' and everybody has a different idea about what that means, let alone what we're supposed to do about it." Her tone was cut-and-dried, her view presented as fact, not inviting contradiction or debate. It was this, as much as anything, Chi thought, that had pissed off the women at Labrys, who'd accused her of *acting like a man*. This was the worst sin one could commit in 1976.

"Issue politics can be effective," Dana continued. "We can mobilize men and women to fight for reproductive freedom; or pay equity; or family leave. But the women's movement as some once imagined it, the great uprising of women united by shared biology or monolithic oppression—I'm sorry Peg, but I no longer believe in the women's movement as a vehicle for political change."

Then just as suddenly as she had begun, she stopped, the switch turned off. Dana seemed to sink into the chair, as if her legs had forgotten how to hold her up. Her eyes behind thick lenses grew blank once more; her face lost all expression. Although the room erupted in response to her provocation, she retreated once more behind the glass, ears roaring with the white noise of the aged fans.

Chapter 10

What the fuck is my karma? Gwen had to wonder as she stood on the curb at First Street waiting for a cab with Lee. The almost twenty years since they'd last done this threatened to melt away, as if Gwen's whole life, everything she'd done, all those years of therapy and recovery, had boomeranged to return her to this exact place.

Come on, baby, Lee had sighed into her ear, *for old time's sake.* That was all it took. Sometimes you just did things you shouldn't do, and you *knew* damn well you shouldn't, but you did them anyway. What was that, denial? Death wish? Gwen's therapist had talked and talked to her about a certain recklessness, the refusal to act in her own self-interest. Howard had said this was just another hallmark of the addict personality.

If someone were to ask just what it was she was afraid of, she would have a hard time answering precisely. Perhaps it was less an apprehension over what might realistically occur—it was, after all, only lunch—and more like the reawakening of memory, some ancient trepidation wired into her nervous system.

She remembered a performance she'd toured in the Eighties, a piece called "Phobophobia"—the fear of fear. Her research had led her deep into the vast array of human dread; beyond the realm of commonplace anxieties lurked a universe of inexplicable terrors, and its lexicon was still embedded in her brain. Sometimes at night when she couldn't get to sleep, she would lull herself with the recitation of phobias, the string of Latin syllables producing a strangely narcotic effect on her insomnia.

Stasophobia, the fear of standing. Aulophobia, a fear of flutes. She had to count herself among the sufferers of papaphobia (the Pope), kenophobia (the void), and—lesbian to the core— spermophobia. Now as a coil of alarm snaked through her small intestine, Gwen wondered if it was the pangs of katagelophobia (fear of ridicule) that had surfaced with this proximity to Lee. Or tyrannophobia, the fear of tyrants?

Lee appeared unfazed by the heat, her short hair freshly combed and slicked into place, her skin exuding a citrusy aura of expensive aftershave. Gwen felt grubby and disheveled in comparison, and when Lee threaded her arm around her waist, she snarled "Cut it out."

"Aw, come on," Lee began a whine that crackled into anger when Gwen didn't relent. "Jesus fucking Christ, Gwen, you act like we were never close."

"Look, you're the one who wanted to go to lunch. If I'm gonna go along with it, then it's gotta be on *my* terms."

She knew Lee Bergman had never been a fan of open conflict. She remembered all too well that Lee liked to fight dirty, win through trickery and wit, and always keep the upper hand. Instead of contradicting Gwen, Lee allowed her face to slide into a smirk and let loose a sinister chuckle.

"You're not turning butch on me, now, are you baby? That'll be sad news for that Chiquita Banana I saw you with this morning." She fixed her with a knowing grin.

"Lee, I *hate* that shit!"

Lee retained her customary nonchalance. "Relax, okay? It was a joke, you know—as in ha-ha."

"Racism is not a joke to me." Gwen stared down the street, but there wasn't a cab in sight.

Lee held up her hands in surrender. "Baby, let's start over. Believe it or not, I didn't ask you out to fight with you. The truth is…" Her tone slipped into a deeper register, almost husky as if with real emotion, "I've really missed you. I just want to spend a little time with you, okay?"

Red flags swooped before Gwen's eyes. Lee was only that much more dangerous when she was being nice. Sweat seeped in the nests of her armpits; tiny hairs rose on the back of her neck.

Luckily, a cab cruised by then, and Lee hailed it like a pro. "See, I haven't lost my touch!" she announced, triumphant, then ordered the driver to take them to the Village. Gwen looked at her with a question mark.

"We have to go to John's!" Lee proclaimed.

In the cab, Gwen leaned her head against the worn plush of the ancient upholstery and tried her best to tune out Lee's animated tirade. She was thinking instead about time, how the passage of years could mean everything and nothing; here she was, after all this time, riding in a cab bound for Greenwich Village with Lee Bergman. Her first lover.

She thought about Labrys, remembering the night of the big blow-up between the Collective and the women attending, the night the Collective had walked out. The beginning of the end of Labrys. Fragments of the group's argument had filtered through the open window of Gwen's dorm room, where she lay panting on the narrow bed as Lee coaxed her to accommodate the length of a large dildo. It had been absurdly pink and spongy to the touch, and it had been partly the thrill of transgression—engaging in politically incorrect sex in that temple of political correctness—as much as any physical sensation that had aroused her. She'd kept imagining some of the more dogmatic women bursting in to find the two engaged in what some would have no doubt considered flagrant hetero-sex.

For a moment Gwen couldn't tell what decade it was, couldn't seem to identify the changes in the skyline that signified *now* instead of *then*. All that had been good and all that had been wretched in their connection seemed to converge on her at once. Perhaps their relationship had never really ended, but had continued all these years. Perhaps they still lived in a fifth-floor walk-up on Bank Street; perhaps even now they were on their way home.

Her musings were jarred by a sharp tug at her elbow.

"Couldn't you at least *pretend* to pay attention when I'm talking to you?" Lee demanded, but Gwen had no chance to respond because at that moment the taxi careened to the curb in front of John's.

John's had been the very first place Lee had taken Gwen after picking her up at Penn Station when she'd moved to New York right after Labrys. Lee never tired of extolling the virtues of their brick ovens, their perfect crust, the rich legacy of jazz tunes to be mined from their jukebox. The place was stinking with memories of their time together, and Gwen couldn't help wondering: what was signified in this particular choice? But of course, she couldn't ask. If she were to ask, Lee would deny any significance—*Just lookin' for a decent pizza*—and project onto Gwen the fact that she found meaning in the choice.

"After eight years in L.A.," Lee declared ruefully, "I still miss this place."

"I'm surprised you've stayed this long in California." Gwen could remember a time when leaving New York would have been unthinkable to Lee, but all it had taken was an affair with a young actress with dreams of Hollywood. The actress was long gone, but Lee had never moved back.

"I guess you never know what's in the cards." Lee shrugged with her usual bluster, but the offhandedness was tinged with unmistakable regret.

"I started my business out there," she continued. "I'm, like, the Real Estate Queen of West Hollywood; I couldn't leave it. Besides—" She jerked her head in the direction of Bleecker Street, beyond the grimy windowpane, "New York is finished. Really, it's terrible now. I don't know how you can live here."

Gwen ignored the jab of criticism. A white-shirted waiter greeted Lee with the enthusiasm of a long-lost relative. "Where you been?" he demanded to know. "I no see you inna long, long time."

They sat in a wooden booth, where Gwen remembered them sitting many times before. She couldn't help but eye with something like envy the glass of Chianti from which Lee was taking satisfied sips. The past was opening up like a giant hole beneath her feet, threatening to suck her in.

Once they'd ordered their old stand-by—a large pizza, extra garlic, pepperoni on Lee's half, anchovies on Gwen's—Lee excused herself to go plunk quarters in the jukebox. "That's better," she insisted, resuming her place in the booth. "What could be more perfect than sharing the best pizza on the planet with a beautiful girl, drinking good *vino* to the strains of King Moody's trumpet?" Her sigh was a parody of contentment.

"So tell me," she clamored, "how the hell are you? You look more beautiful than ever, do you know that? I never thought I'd find a woman prettier at forty-... what is it?"

"Forty-*two*."

"Prettier at forty-*two* than I did at twenty-two! My tastes must be changing," she chuckled to herself.

Gwen shirred her lips together to refrain from pointing out that the business with Kendra would seem to dispute that contention. She was well acquainted with Lee's style of flirtation and flattery; now she was waiting for the knife.

"You're skinnier," Lee continued. "Your body's more muscular. You still have those delicious-looking breasts." She rolled her tongue across her lips in appreciation. "You could be such a knockout. I don't know why the hell you have to dress the way you do."

There it was; the blade slid easily between her ribs. "Spare me the critique, okay?" Gwen snapped. "I like the way I look, and I don't care whether you do or not. When we were together, I let you dress me up like a Barbie Doll. Now I dress to amuse myself."

"Damn it! You're just too pretty to look so kooky!" Lee shook her head. "So how come a beautiful, sexy girl like you isn't married yet? Or is there something you haven't told me about that Chiquita–I mean," she corrected herself before Gwen could make good on her threatening look, "that tall, dark handsome woman of Latin persuasion?"

Gwen rolled her eyes. The last thing she wanted was to subject JJ to Lee's scrutiny, so she answered Lee's first question instead. "You know the answer to that better than anyone. As you used to say, with distressing frequency as I remember: I'm already married. To my work."

Lee nodded with an expression of bitter recognition. It had always been a sore topic between them, the cause of a thousand skirmishes. Lee had wanted a lover for whom a relationship—specifically, a relationship with *her*—was the most important thing in life. But for Gwen, art would always come first; it was something Lee had never gotten used to. "I guess it's paid off. You're a famous artist now, huh?"

Gwen shrugged.

"You know, I saw that piece you did when you were out in L.A. a few years ago," Lee continued.

"You did?" Gwen's face rounded with surprise.

"Yeah, that thing about angels. But I thought you told me you were afraid of heights."

"I am," Gwen admitted, "I sweat bullets every night when they hooked me up to those wires." She gave a wry grin. "What I did for *art*."

Lee couldn't fail to recognize the lyric parody; she grimaced. The hush that followed was thick with old recriminations and the seepage of reopened wounds.

Into that silence, finally, a pizza was set down, fragrant with garlic and yeast and spicy pepperoni. Its aromas filtered into the stagnant air between them and, at least temporarily, broke the spell of the past.

Lee offered extravagant praise to the beaming waiter, and allowed him to serve her the first steaming wedge. A little groan of pleasure erupted from her mouth as the baked cheese oozed between her teeth.

"Damn!" she exclaimed. "That's almost better than sex." Then she added, "Almost," with a dark twinkle in her eye.

"But speaking of your art, what about this thing with the arts endowment? Do you think this asshole from North Carolina is in a position to hurt your career?"

Gwen set down her slice of pizza and rubbed a worried hand across her temple. "I don't fucking know. I haven't even had much chance to think about it."

Lee nodded. "Kendra filled me in a little bit on some of the history—that whole Mapplethorpe fiasco and those four artists who got their grants denied."

A sour taste invaded her mouth, imagining Lee and Kendra talking about her work. A picture flared in her mind—the two of them in bed, laughing at her while they made riotous love— but she quickly doused it.

"What worries me," Gwen answered, "is that I just don't know how far the right-wing is prepared to take this. It could just be a cheap shot to pacify the fundamentalists, but then it could be the start of some big crusade, like the McCarthy Era. I can live without another NEA grant," she assured Lee. "They're not usually that much money to begin with. But are galleries and theaters gonna be pressured to stop booking me? Or universities made to stop hiring me to teach?"

"Don't you think that's getting a little paranoid?" Lee suggested.

"Maybe." Gwen was willing to consider it. "But maybe it's not. I remember in the Seventies we used to say about the government, 'No matter what you think they're doing, they're always doing something even worse than that'."

"I say, if you're pissing off the Republicans, you know you're on the right track."

Gwen picked at a sliver of anchovy and popped it in her mouth, feeling a rush of saliva greet its salty presence. "You know what's the worst? Last year I got a terrible review on a piece I did." She was careful not to mention Kendra's name. "The reviewer thought my work was really old-style feminism, out of touch with the times. It hurt, right?"

"Well, you've always been so damn thin-skinned when it comes to anybody saying the least little thing to you."

Gwen had to marvel; Lee never missed an opportunity.

"No, it's more than that," Gwen insisted. "It made me really question what I'm doing as an artist. Do I have anything more to say? Does anybody care? What good does my work do? It doesn't keep someone like Emma from being raped and killed."

Lee shook her head. "That's really bad business," she agreed, "I keep thinkin' about my niece. I don't know what I'd do if something like that happened to her." She could never dwell for long on bad feelings; she brought herself back with a grin. "But your art..." Her tone encouraged Gwen to continue.

"Really, I haven't been able to make any new work in months. At night I dream about deserts—dry, desiccated landscapes, empty. That's *me*! I've been paralyzed. And now with this NEA thing, I'm being attacked from the other direction, for going too far." Gwen rested her head across the back of the wooden booth, even though the hard, narrow ledge cut into nape of her neck. "Maybe I should just fucking give it up, just quit being an artist. Maybe it's time I tried to do something else with my life."

It was the first time she'd said this out loud, this thought she'd been harboring for the last year. She stared up at the ceiling, its tiles of pressed tin; self-pity and defeat swamped her muscles, leaving them slack as a leaky balloon.

"But then you'd let them win."

Gwen jerked up in surprise. The sardonic edge was gone from Lee's voice.

"The one thing I know about you for sure, Ms. Kubacky, is that you are a goddamned artist, and no young punk reviewer or Bible-thumping senator can take that away from you. That angel piece you did was beautiful; it made me cry, if you wanna know the truth.

"And the desert—you've never even been! What do you know from the desert?" Her voice was filled with wonder. "In the spring the desert is full of flowers, strange exotic stuff like you've never seen before! It might look like it's all dried up and dead, but it's full of life!

"Listen to me, Gwen, I want you to fight this NEA thing. If you have to take it to court, if you need money for legal fees, I'll help you, I swear. Now don't look at me that way; it's an offer with no strings attached."

Gwen clung to her wedge of cooling pizza as if it were the only thing that could keep her from sinking. Praise for her work? From Lee? Encouragement to keep doing it?

She felt her heart stir, its armor sag, but her guts still clenched in suspicion, leaving her misty-eyed and tight-jawed in the same moment. She couldn't trust herself to make a direct response, fearing what promises her tongue might knit, so she asked instead, "How did you know that reviewer was a young punk?"

Lee winked, flashing a crafty grin. "Let's just say she's mortified to meet you in the flesh and find she likes you."

"*Likes me?*" Gwen raised an eyebrow in disbelief.

Lee polished off the final crust of her half of the pizza before she qualified, "Well, she thinks you're not as bad as the rest of them. And I think she's probably impressed with your new 'outlaw' status at the NEA."

For a moment, Gwen pressed her eyes shut against the mounting irony. "Lee, can I ask you a question?"

"Anything, doll, I'm an open book."

Gwen sought her eyes and held them for a long moment before she asked, "I always thought that what you wanted more than anything in the world was to settle down and find a woman to be with for the rest of your life..."

"Yeah, that's what I want!" Lee interrupted, the defensive edge restored to the Brooklyn cadence. "So? You volunteering?"

Gwen disregarded this and grabbed Lee's hand across the table. "Then why do you always go after the kind of women with whom that's out of the question?"

On the jukebox Ella was singing "I Can't Get Started," filling the room with luxurious notes that belied the song's sad sentiment. Lee sat back heavily against the wooden booth, her face crumpling. There was a long pause before she spoke, and the answer was as much in the tightening grip on Gwen's fingers as in the actual words, "I wish I knew, doll. I wish to God I knew."

Chapter 11

Chi Curtis had sat through the entire morning's discussion—which had contained more than a few opportunities for serious aggravation—just to arrive at this moment when she could be alone with Dana. Her former lover seemed tense to the point of shattering, and Chi longed to rest a soothing hand against Dana's heart. She knew better.

For now she tugged impatiently at the sleeve of the "Stop Violence" T-shirt. "Can we get outta here now?"

Dana peered distractedly through her thick lenses, as if aware that Chi had spoken to her, but unable to track the meaning of the words.

"Come on." Chi extended a hand and Dana obediently grabbed it. *A first*, Chi observed.

Outside the loft, a knot of women still debated their lunch plans. Chi steered Dana past them toward the stairs.

Without warning, Dana hollered, "I'll race you!" and began hurtling down the stairs in her shiny boots.

"You'll be sorry!" Chi shot back, taking the steps two at a time to catch up. She passed Dana before they reached the fourth floor landing, and was calmly waiting on the sidewalk whistling a blues riff when Dana burst through the door into the hot sun.

She was gasping. "All right, all right," she conceded, "so

you're still in better shape than I am."

Sweat matted the wild hair against her neck, and it was all Chi could do to keep from reaching for a strand, tasting the salty skin beneath. Instead she teased, with grim amusement, "As I recall, your idea of staying in shape is to sleep three hours a night—whether you need it or not—and supplement that with about ten cups of coffee a day. Is that still your health and beauty regimen?"

For a moment, it was like everything was normal, walking crosstown with the woman she loved, their banter contentious yet suffused with tenderness.

"I haven't quite been keeping up with the three hours this week." Dana kept her tone light, yet beneath sliced the blade of her loss.

Of course, Chi realized; nothing was normal; nothing would ever be the same. "Hey, sorry, I..." Chi stuttered, but Dana stopped her with a raised hand.

"No need."

They walked on in silence, Dana swept once more into the abstracted state she'd been in most of the morning. Chi wasn't sure of the best course of action: give her space? Try to get her to talk? Distract her?

Finally they reached the destination Chi had in mind, a cheery open restaurant that served health food cafeteria style.

"I know, I know," Chi defended herself against the protest Dana would have lobbed at another time. "You'd be happier if we just got something off a cart on the street, dined with the proletariat, the more fat-filled and vitamin-deficient the better. Me, I'm trying to eat healthy these days." She patted her washboard stomach.

Was it in poor taste, she wondered, to gloat about health when Emma was dead?

But Dana was back with her now, playing along. "My own strategy is mind over body," she smirked.

"Mind over body?" Chi feigned horror. "That's the White Girl's Disease!"

"And just when did you start calling women 'girls,' Ms. Curtis? Or is it only *white* girls?" Dana poked her in the ribs with a swift elbow.

Chi held up both hands, her face a study in contrition. "Busted, *Ms*. Firestein. Thanks for raising my consciousness once again."

They began pushing their trays down the line. Chi picked out salad, baked tofu, brown rice. Dana's tray remained bare until they reached the beverage section, where she gratefully grasped a mug of coffee.

"How about pie?" Chi offered a wedge dripping with cherries. "Have you eaten since Monday?"

Dana offered a bemused smile; she was wise to Chi's caretaking strategies, and skilled at eluding them. She waved the pie away, dismissing it, but Chi added it to her tray anyway.

She led the way to a small table by the window, over which a robust fern twirled from the low ceiling, fronds grazing the tangles of Dana's hair when she sat.

"It feels good to be away from that room, doesn't it?" Chi asked when they were settled.

Dana began loading three packets of sugar into the coffee and noticed Chi's gaze following her actions. "I still like it sweet and black," she said, then ducked her head, as if embarrassed by the subtext of her words. It had been an old joke between them, so long ago.

They'd met in 1971, one of those early meetings of the women's movement, high voltage with the sense that *this* was the revolution that would shake the world to its foundations. Dana had been less naïve than most; she'd studied history and believed she understood the lengths to which power will go to maintain itself. This refusal to romanticize the struggle was something she and Chi had shared.

Chi had come by her realism the hard way, watching the FBI decimate the Panthers. She'd been especially skeptical of the absence of black and brown and working-class women within feminism. But Dana had struck her with the force of dynamite—her intellect, her fearlessness, her complete commitment to resisting injustice.

"So how did you hear about..." It was unlike Dana to leave a sentence unfinished, but Chi knew what she was asking.

"Olivia told me about the memorial." Olivia had worked with Dana on the Nicaraguan campaign in the Eighties. She now volunteered at the AIDS clinic where Chi spent her spare time. "She knew I'd want to know."

An unspoken rebuke lay coiled beneath these words. Chi had been hurt that Dana had not called herself. She would have wanted to be the person to whom Dana would have turned at this time, but Chi understood she'd forfeited that position twenty years earlier. Dana, for her part, was no more willing to apologize for or explain her actions now than she had been then.

It had been this quality, Dana's absolute refusal to consider the feelings of others, that Chi had been unable to reconcile in her lover.

Chi reached for the plate of pie and scooted it across the table in Dana's direction. "Just have a bite," she suggested. Dana used her coffee spoon to carve through the flaky crust. A small, distracted smile bent the corners of her mouth as her taste buds registered the mouthful.

"So what kind of work are you doing these days?" Chi asked.

She expected Dana to talk about her political work and was surprised when she answered, "I'm finally back at the print shop."

At Chi's questioning look, Dana explained, "About three years ago I had an accident on the press; I was out of work for eighteen months. The doctors kept telling me I'd never use this hand again."

Dana extended her left hand. It was slightly misshapen and etched with a long, jagged scar, pale, like a fossil in stone. Chi marveled that she hadn't noticed it until now, then realized that Dana had kept it close to her side, subtly out of sight.

"Those doctors obviously had no idea how stubborn you are." Chi took the hand in both of hers and studied the fingertips, a little discolored from all the inks, as if each were a deep and permanent bruise. Three fingers stuck out at an odd angle from the thumb and index finger. Without thinking she brought the damaged hand to her lips and bestowed a light kiss.

"Can't feel a thing," Dana mocked. She extricated her hand from Chi's grasp. "There's some nerve damage."

Chi frowned and started stabbing salad greens with her fork. The kiss still burned on her lips. She was suddenly called to question her own agenda here; could she be so sure it was merely to provide comfort to a bereaved mother? As if to reground herself in this intention, she ventured, "If you don't wanna talk about this, just say the word, but...would you tell me about Emma?"

She'd been disapproving when Dana had first announced her pregnancy. They'd been together a couple of years, and Chi couldn't tell if she was more hurt by Dana's having slept with a man or by her making a major life decision without ever discussing it with her. "Don't you think this is something the two of us should have decided together?" she'd blustered.

Dana had appeared genuinely mystified. "Why?" It was *her* body, *her* pregnancy, *her* life. She could not even conceive of another way to think.

Still, Chi had been there the night Dana delivered Emma, in a hospital against her wishes because there were complications. August 9, 1974. The night that Nixon had resigned the presidency. Dana had insisted on keeping the radio on in the delivery room to hear his speech. Later the nurse had asked, "Emma? Is that your grandmother's name?" and had been treated to a passionate discourse on Emma Goldman.

Chi had been the primary caretaker while Dana continued to attend endless rounds of political meetings. She had powdered Emma's heat rash, had sung her to sleep with tunes like "Mercy, Mercy Me."

Chi remembered Emma at Labrys, nearly two, refusing to keep her diaper on, refusing to stay in childcare, instead padding around after Dana or Chi, watching the often contentious meetings with wide eyes.

Dana raised her gaze from the bright cherry she was pushing around on the plate. "She was a great kid, Chi. Complicated as hell. She did everything I didn't want her to do. I was so goddamned proud of her."

A wash of tears surged into Chi's vision, blurring the face

across from her, but Dana's armor did not crack. Nor did she reach to comfort Chi. Instead she continued, "The hardest thing when I went to prison was being away from her. Marilyn took care of her—Ayisha's mom."

"You know I would have…" Chi began, but Dana stopped her with a wave of her misshapen left hand.

"I was in Alderson for thirteen months after the grand jury investigation."

In the late sixties, a few years before she'd met Chi, Dana had been involved with a woman named Quimetta, who'd gone underground in 1970 after helping to plant a pipe bomb in the offices of Dow Chemical. Chi had known Dana a couple of years before she learned of Quimetta's existence or that Dana still kept in touch with her through an elaborate network of pay phones, code words and safe houses.

The grand jury had begun calling witnesses the summer Labrys was in session, the summer Chi and Dana had abruptly severed their connection.

"I knew they'd call me, and I knew I wouldn't testify." Dana signaled a circulating busboy to refill her coffee. "They granted me immunity and I still refused. I got three years for contempt."

"And how was it?" Chi worked to banish the anxiety from her voice, to match the cold matter-of-factness in Dana's.

Dana responded with a grim chuckle. "All that prison organizing we did paid off."

It was in '71 that they'd begun to do prison advocacy work, the prisons full of political prisoners—Black Panthers, SDS— the justice system propping up a criminal government. After Attica, a massacre in which they'd both lost people they were trying to save, Chi and Dana had become lovers.

"I raised some hell inside, so I spent a lot of time in solitary." Dana shrugged, her face blank as slate.

"And what about Quimetta? Weren't you a pretty important part of her support network?"

Again the shrug. "Not as important as I once thought. She surfaced about ten months after I got sent up. Turned herself in. Imagine my surprise—she came up with a husband and a kid.

The word on the street is that she *cooperated* with the FBI. She ended up doing less time than I did."

Because Chi had loved this woman once, because she loved her still, she could see beyond the brusque syllables, the guarded eyes, could see the pain so fiercely dammed inside her. She longed to reach into that place, but knew from harsh experience that with Dana, one had to wait to be invited in, and even then, to mind one's manners, never snoop, and not outstay the welcome. Chi hoped that twenty years had taught her that kind of patience.

"And Emma?"

"Marilyn did a great job. She always made sure to tell Emma, 'Dana's away doing very important work and she misses you like crazy.' She used to show Emma my picture every day, so she didn't forget me. But I missed a year of her life, and no one can ever give that back to me."

She looked almost about to break down then, and Chi watched her refortify herself, the steeling of the jaw, the clenched hands and shoulders. "Still, thirteen months was nothing. I met women whose babies were taken from them in prison, who won't get out until their kids have babies of their own."

"Speaking of Marilyn...I met Ayisha yesterday."

Dana nodded, as if she'd just been reminded of something.

"She asked me about Lincoln," Chi persisted.

Dana gave a sharp intake of breath, and nodded again. It frustrated Chi.

"How come you never told that girl about her daddy?"

Dana returned Chi's gaze evenly. "Marilyn didn't want her to know."

"Since when do you not do the right thing," Chi demanded, "just because somebody doesn't want you to?"

Dana took off her glasses, rubbed both fists against her eye sockets. Then she looked at Chi once more. "I wasn't a very good friend to Marilyn when she got sick. I was mad at her for getting cancer. It doesn't make sense, I knew it even then, but it was like I felt like if she were just tough enough, she would beat it."

She put her glasses back on, as if for shielding, her naked eyes too defenseless. "I stayed away; I was *so busy with Nicaragua*." Her voice was caustic with irony.

"Before she died she asked me for two things: keep an eye out for Ayisha, and never tell her about Lincoln. I guess I felt like at least I owed her that."

Now it was Chi's turn to nod. Dana didn't need her judgments right now.

"So what about you?" Dana signaled the end of that topic. Then she whacked impatiently at the fern above her head. "This damn thing's driving me nuts."

"Ever the nature-lover." Chi grinned softly. "I went back to school. Got my certification. Now I teach high school."

"Public school?"

"What else? South Bronx. Right down in the trenches."

"So you teach P.E.?" Dana pressed.

"Your racism is showing, Ms. Firestein," Chi gently chided. "As a matter of fact, I teach geometry."

"You're right, Ms. Curtis," Dana admitted levelly. "That *was* racist. I forgot you were a math whiz. So what about political work?"

Chi cleared her throat, knowing in advance that her answer would be found wanting. "Up in the 'hood, I put in time at an AIDS clinic."

Dana narrowed her eyes, a frown stretching her mouth. "But that's more like social service work, isn't it? What about political organizing?"

Chi snorted. "Can't organize nuthin' if everybody's dead. Don't try to pull that white leftist crap on me. Brothers and sisters are dyin' out there—white community won't share their resources, black community's hidin' behind the church. That ain't political enough for you?"

Dana had the grace to blush. "Well, so now you know I can still be an asshole."

"You said it," Chi sulked.

She was never able to stay mad at Dana, though, and especially not now. "So, what will you do?"

Dana looked up, her face completely naked. "For the first time in my life, I don't have any idea." There was a vulnerability in her eyes that was almost unbearable. "I can't organize, agitate, or protest my way out. I've exhausted my repertoire."

She cracked her knuckles again, as she had before the group earlier that morning. "And the thing is, I'm supposed to be all gung-ho about catching the man who did this to my daughter, and I'm supposed to rely on the cops and on the tragically misnamed criminal justice system to help me do it, or I'm supposed to get all vigilante like some female action hero and go out and grab him up myself."

Her fingers tore through her wild crop of hair. "And you know what? I don't believe in any of it. I don't believe in justice or punishment or redemption or any goddamn thing. *I'm* supposed to work to put another man in prison? Or on death row? I'm just fresh out of things to believe in right now."

"You don't have to know anything today," Chi assured her. "You just have to get through one day, then the next."

"I've never lived that way."

"I know." Chi decided to take a risk. "Do you need to go back to the group this afternoon?"

For a moment, Dana seemed not to understand the question. Then she said, "Oh, *that* group. I don't know what I was thinking, asking people to come all this way. I don't know what I thought anyone could do."

"So," Chi forged ahead before she lost her nerve, "what if I were to take you away for the afternoon?"

A tense quiet swept the table, the lull between thunder and lightning. It thickened to a palpable charge. Dana stared into her coffee cup for a long moment, then removed her glasses and looked up, turning the full force of those blue eyes onto Chi.

"Do it," she said simply, never dropping her gaze.

Out on the street, Chi insisted on hailing a cab. "I don't care how bourgeois you think it is, I don't want to share you with anyone right now."

Inside the taxi, bound for 123rd Street, she reached for Dana's mangled hand and held it all the way uptown.

"Who's got a match?" Kendra extracted a joint from the pocket of her short skirt. She held it poised between index and middle fingers like a Forties starlet until Kick touched the flame of her lighter to its end. Kendra pursed her lips to draw the smoke deep into her lungs, then held it while she passed the joint to Kick. Exhaling finally, she said, "Nimo scored this stuff. It's bomb."

"My brain cells could use a rest," Kick agreed, expelling smoke. "Fuck, those women can talk!"

"Mmm, tasty." Devon grinned appreciatively as he finished his turn and passed the hand-rolled cigarette to Kendra. The three lounged on a park bench in the noon sun. The rays burned them, but they didn't care, so happy were they to have escaped the loft.

"So has anybody seen *I Shot Andy Warhol* yet?" Kendra wanted to know.

"Yeah, I did." Kick took another toke. "It was all right, but they made her seem so crazy. It's like, any time a woman stands up against a man, she must be fuckin' insane."

"Lee says she used to know Valerie Solanis, back in the old days, and that she was completely nuts."

"So what's the deal with your new squeeze?" Devon arched his eyebrows meaningfully.

For a moment, Kendra looked perplexed. "Oh, you mean Lee?" She chuckled at the absurdity of the notion.

"Yeah, well, she's certainly been squeezin' you," Kick observed.

"Hey," Kendra dismissed her, "my *grandmother* is only a coupl'a years older than she is."

"Now, would that be ageism?" Kick's voice a parody of political correctness. "And the vibe between you is not exactly grandmotherly, I might add."

"Yeah, I know, it's just..." Kendra paused to take a long toke, "she's all *curious* about me, and you *know* how I love to satisfy a woman's curiosity."

Kick waved the fingers of one hand as if they'd once been burned by that particular flame.

"And besides..." Kendra hugged her knees with childlike excitement, "I think she could be a little *mean*."

"Ooh. Ooh. Ooh. You. Go. Girl." Devon punctuated

each syllable like a torch song.

Kendra finished the roach and let it fall to the pavement. She lifted both arms overhead to arch her back against the wrought iron bench. "So, what about you, Kick? You gettin' any action these days?"

"No, I'm sublimating my drives," she responded dryly, scooping up a rock to throw at a nearby tree. "It's all going into my paintings."

"I never did figure out why you went into painting," Kendra said. "It's like, so, eighteenth century."

"You should see this new series she's working on," Devon rose to Kick's defense. "She works from these stills from porn videos and then paints them, like, hyper-realistically. And really huge."

"Oh, sublimating, I get it," Kendra teased.

"No, but she makes them look like video, the kind of texture of that medium," Devon explained, "except in paint."

Kendra considered this, closing her eyes as if to conjure the vision. "Are you gonna have a show of them? Maybe I could get assigned to review it."

"Uh, that's okay." Kick pressed both palms forward to stave off the suggestion.

"What?" Kendra couldn't understand the reluctance. "Why not?"

Kick and Devon exchanged a look. Then Devon explained, "It's just that you've never exactly *liked* anything you've reviewed."

"That's not true!"

"Really?" Devon challenged. "Name one thing you've reviewed positively."

"Oh come on, nobody wants to just read that a work is good. It's not about stroking the artist's ego. People are looking for something more from criticism, some deeper analysis."

"Kendra," Kick interjected, "attacking a work in print does not in-depth analysis make."

"Even Emma felt that way," Devon added. "One time she said, 'I wouldn't want Kendra doing a hatchet job on my work.'"

Kendra jumped off the bench. "Oh, that's nice. Hide behind a dead girl who isn't here to speak for herself! Fuck you, then. I gotta go make a phone call." She started off in a huff, but couldn't resist spinning around to boast, "I think the *Voice* might be interested in this little feminist reunion," over one shoulder before she turned again and left the park.

"Only she could make a career opportunity out of a wake," Kick observed dolefully as Kendra's back disappeared toward Houston.

Kick slid closer to Devon on the bench. "So, did you look for it?"

Reluctantly, Devon nodded. "Yeah, my mom keeps it next to her bed."

"That's great." Kick launched her body from the wrought iron seat. "I found out he got back today. From his *tour*," she spat derisively.

"I've got it all worked out. This afternoon we'll get my van out of the garage. We'll drop by your mom's tonight, and then we'll go pay him a little visit."

Elena Martínez spent her lunch hour on her cell phone, dialing coast-to-coast. In her opinion, the entire morning had been wasted on trivialities. She despised wasted time; the sole remedy was to immerse herself in work. She perched on a stool, her appointment calendar precarious atop a sheaf of files in her lap, just outside the small kitchen area.

Around her swirled Jolene and Luanne, with some assistance from Roger, unpacking groceries, clattering dishes out of makeshift cupboards, opening cans and jars and cellophane wrappers of bread.

"Tell him that's too late!" Elena barked into the mouthpiece that was clipped to her lapel. "The article's got to run Monday; they're taking the vote Tuesday morning."

Without being asked, the voluble pair of cooks tried their best to keep their voices down, but Elena appeared to be utterly unmindful of their presence

"Don't forget," she admonished on another call, "to stress the economic impact. Loss of reproductive freedoms means more unwanted babies; more babies means more money for social services now, more crime and more prisons down the road. It's a Republican state," she emphasized. "People are very responsive to that angle. They may not like abortion, but they *hate* welfare."

Jolene thumped a jar of mayonnaise on the countertop, loud enough that Roger came over to grab the hem of her shirt, but Elena was too absorbed to register the protest. Jolene ruffled her son's hair in reassurance, but hissed, "Can you beat that? We're supposed to fight for abortion rights so poor women like me don't have more kids for the state to support with their crummy five hundred a month?"

Luanne was dishing up bowls of Campbell's Chicken with Stars, but Elena's comment so infuriated her that she dropped the big spoon to the bottom of the pot, and had to go fishing around in the hot liquid to retrieve it. What was the difference, she wondered as the soup scalded her fingertips, between Elena and any man, any politician so driven that he would adopt any strategy just to get his way?

Luanne hastily carried the soup bowls over to the table where Jolene and Roger waited; three bologna sandwiches on white bread occupied the three place settings.

"Eat up," she recommended, plunking the bowls on the table. "If this morning is any indication, we'll need to keep up our strength!" She didn't dare say what she was really thinking; Jolene would never agree with her views and she didn't want to risk ostracism by this potential friend.

Instead, Luanne turned an approving gaze on Roger, who was cautiously spooning broth and stars into his mouth, careful not to spill a drop.

"I can't believe how good he is," she marveled. "My son Ted would have torn apart the entire place by now. I never could have brought him here—talk about male energy!"

Roger said nothing, didn't even look up. Veins glowed blue beneath his pale, translucent skin. His face remained impassive as he took a bite from his sandwich, leaving the shape of a perfect half-circle in the bread.

"So what didja do with him?" Jolene wanted to know. "Is he

with his dad?"

"God, no," Luanne exhaled. She briefly summarized the ruse that had gotten her to the reunion.

"I left Ted with my mother, but the thing is—" Her tone grew more confiding, "she's seventy-six and she's getting pretty senile. I'm scared that Ted's just running all over her. I feel kind of guilty about it."

Jolene patted her hand in a comforting way. "Don't you worry," she advised. "They act way different around Grandma than they do around you. He's probably helpin' out more than you'd ever believe, and she's spoilin' him to death, and they're both havin' a grand ol' time and hopin' you'll never come home."

Luanne leaned back in her chair, relaxing finally for the first time since she'd arrived in New York, or perhaps it had been even longer than that. She basked in the simple reciprocity of the exchange.

Roger finished his lunch, carried his dishes to the bathroom sink, then asked, "Mommy, can I go read my book now?"

Jolene nodded and the two women watched him toddle to his sleeping bag in a corner and lower himself down to read.

"Does it ever scare you, having a son?" Luanne wanted to know.

"Scare me?" Jolene seemed puzzled.

"Yeah, I mean, raising a boy."

"Naw." Jolene grinned. "My ex-boyfriend accused me of raisin' him too much like a girl, anyway." She began stacking the used dishes on the table.

"It terrifies me," Luanne admitted. "There are so many messages from the culture, all kinds of things working on him— including his own father—about how to be a man, what kind of man to be. And I feel like those things have so much more power over him, so much more influence than I do."

"Maybe bein' poor is an advantage," Jolene considered. "We don't have TV and we live out in the middle of nowhere. I'm home schoolin' him. I feel like I'm still the biggest influence in his life. Even though *that's* a little scary sometimes, like, there'll be no one else to blame!"

"I don't know," Luanne sighed. "I always wanted to have a girl. And when Ted was born... I don't know—do you think it's possible to love your kid even if you don't really like him?"

Jolene slipped an arm around Luanne's shoulder. "I think every mother has days like that."

Luanne wanted to argue that it wasn't just a day or a passing mood. Instead she picked up the stack of dirty dishes and stood. Before she turned to go wash them she said, "It's just that I get afraid of what kind of man Ted will grow up to be. Could he turn out to be the kind who would do what some man did to Emma? That man was some woman's son, too."

Chapter 12

As they stepped from the dim coolness of John's into the blast furnace of Bleecker Street, Gwen knew there was no way she could go right back to the loft. Her time with Lee had left her insides roiling, and she needed to walk and clear her head. She needed to figure out what she was feeling besides drunk on adrenaline.

She'd given her spare key to Luanne, so people could get in and out of the loft without her. Now her only problem was to figure out how to get away from Lee.

They stood on the sidewalk scanning the traffic, waiting to hail a cab. Gwen let the car pull to the curb, swung the back door open before she said, as if the impulse had just overtaken her, "You go ahead. I need to run a couple of errands before I go back." She didn't give Lee the chance to argue her out of it, but turned and began to power walk down Bleecker, a challenging feat in the red, high-heeled mules.

Lee sputtered for a second, but her objections were lost to street noise, so she got in; the cab passed Gwen before she'd reached West Tenth. *She probably can't wait to get back to Kendra,* Gwen fumed to herself, suddenly disappointed by Lee's lack of protest. Although undoubtedly she would have gotten steamed if Lee *had* chased after her. God, she really *was* a freaking handful sometimes!

Instinct guided her west, then south along the river, though its rancid waters were now obscured by high-rise developments, wide swathes of concrete jutting into its listless flow. For a long time she just walked. Sun baked her shoulders and blistered her nose, and tonight JJ would look at her with sorrowful reproach and wonder aloud why a girl whose ancestors come from Poland would think she didn't need sunscreen. None of that mattered in the moment. There was solace in motion, relief from her crackling nerves and churning ovaries.

Her emotions were heightened, she reminded herself. By her hormones. By the death of Emma. By this uninvited visitation from the past. Lee's presence pulsed like neon on a dark street, like the sign on some bar Gwen knew she didn't dare enter. Howard's voice flitted into her head, a graveled Bronx rendition of *Feelings Aren't Facts*, another fucking AA slogan.

Gwen tried to imagine what her life would have been like had she never gone to Labrys. If she had stayed in school at the Art Institute. If she'd never met Lee. She'd never have become an artist, she was pretty sure. There'd been no support at school for her "crackpot" vision. But would she even have become a lesbian? For some lesbians it seemed like there was no choice. Lee was like that; no one would ever imagine her with a man. But with femmes, sometimes it was more ambiguous. It wasn't that she liked men; she'd always seemed to find the mean ones, the ones who were just on the verge of spiraling out of control. But she could have stayed a drunk and continued that pattern, she supposed, squandering her youth and her health.

Her heels clicked along the pavement; she mesmerized herself with the sound, small and particular amidst the din of the street. Then her brain seemed to split in two like an apple, its seeds revealed, each facet a mirror of itself. There'd been another walk along the Hudson, she remembered now, another sultry summer day, the wind electric. Suddenly it was as if she were walking in two lifetimes, then and now.

After eight weeks in the vortex of Labrys, Gwen had felt she couldn't go home, couldn't return to the clean dark rooms of her parents' house, the orderly routine of classes at the Art Institute. Something in her had broken free, and she couldn't fold herself up again to fit into the constriction of who she'd been. She'd emerged from Labrys a lesbian, an artist, a revolutionary—three facets of the same transformation. When Lee had asked her to come to New York, live with her in the Village, she'd felt this glittering island open to her, an outstretched hand.

"New York, New York, so nice they named it twice," Lee would enthuse as she squired Gwen around town, showing her off in the dyke bars, introducing her to Soho, Staten Island, Little Italy, unlocking the city as if with a golden key.

Gwen had been eager to stride through every door, each step carrying her further from her past—the sting of her father's belt, her mother's incessant prayers. She was twenty-two years old, a dyke now. She was an artist in New York. She wanted to walk every block of her new city, memorize its vistas.

With what had she fallen in love? With Lee, her first woman lover, or with the life she offered? Or with the promise of her own possibilities?

They'd walked along the Hudson one August day that first year, giddy with rum and dope and passion, locked in the sun's blazing grasp. Lee had caught her by the waist, pulled her close. "Marry me," she'd whispered. "You're all I want."

But, although her words caught Gwen's heart and made her gasp, although she felt she owed so much to her, Lee was not "all" she wanted. Art was more important to her than love, even then, and Lee's bitterness at this discrepancy between them began to seep through all their days...

A horn blast slammed Gwen back to the present. In a daze she'd stepped from the curb into the path of a panel truck. Even as she jumped, she shot the driver the finger and shrieked, "Watch it, asshole!" while he bellowed, "Stupid cunt!" before zooming away. No one could say she hadn't adapted to the environment.

Suddenly she was livid. There was no shortage of possible targets—the driver who cut off a Toyota and careened around a corner, the women who'd taken over her loft, the sick bastard who murdered Emma, Lee with her smarmy arrogance. No lack of targets, but it was JJ on whom she focused this fury. If JJ had stuck around this morning like she'd asked her to, she wouldn't have even gone to lunch with Lee. If JJ weren't fucking twenty-nine-years-old, Gwen wouldn't feel so ridiculous introducing her as her girlfriend. How could she possibly see this as a serious relationship with a thirteen-year age gap?

Even Gwen knew none of this was rational. No one could help what age they were, and if she was so tripped out on the age gap, what the hell was she doing with JJ? But damn it, if JJ weren't so into her own career, she might be more helpful to Gwen in figuring out her own.

Had she really said out loud that she was thinking of giving up performance? And to Lee, of all people? Gwen would have thought she'd stand up and cheer, but she hadn't. *She hadn't.* And who the fuck would Gwen be if she didn't perform? A grant writer? A musician's girlfriend? On the other hand, she hadn't made a new piece in over a year, and the phone had not exactly been ringing off the hook with offers to commission something. Maybe she'd already given it up and was just too stupid to know it.

She was bored with the river now, with its sludgy indifference. She was bored with the office workers and old men hoping for a breeze on this hot day, so she began to wander into TriBeCa. She felt like such an asshole to be whining over her career doldrums when Emma would never have the chance to pursue her calling.

She remembered the day Emma came to her loft—had it really only been six days ago?—the way she'd been shy and cocky at the same time. "Before I'm twenty-five," she'd announced, "I want a solo show at BAM."

You and me both, sister, Gwen had thought at the time. The performance series at Brooklyn Academy of Music was one of the highest profile venues for performance art in the country. Laurie performed there, Meredith. Gwen never had. She should have been nicer to Emma. She shouldn't have been so critical. What Emma probably needed most was encouragement, positive reflection from someone she admired.

Insecure as she was right now, all she could do was see Emma as competition, the next generation trying to push her out of the way.

She thought about the gathering that morning at her loft, old farts bickering with young whippersnappers. Were the women of her generation all so frustrated that they couldn't cede ground to their generational daughters?

And suddenly it dawned on her—she hadn't let herself realize until just this moment—that Emma had come to Gwen's studio on the morning of the day she died. She'd walked around Gwen's loft, taking in the neon cross, the giant clock face. She'd been itching to browse through the costume racks, but politeness had restrained her. She'd worn jeans a million sizes too large, impossibly baggy waist cinched on her tiny hips with a man's wide belt. She'd worn a tight black T-shirt that bared her belly. She'd worn patchouli oil, a scent Gwen had hated ever since the Sixties.

The young woman had refused coffee, instead drank tap water out of an old, chipped mug. Her lipstick had left a vermilion smear on its rim, and after she left Gwen had washed the cup in a desultory fashion, never imagining that lip print might be precious to her now.

Abruptly Gwen felt like throwing up; the acid of tomato sauce and anchovy stung the back of her throat. She was damned if she was going to upchuck right there on Church Street. She took deep breaths of stagnant air and forced herself to focus on controlling her reflexes.

Sheathed in sweat, she began to walk more purposefully. She could feel the blisters on both feet where the leather mules chafed them, but she welcomed this distraction from the overwhelming ache of loss of this young woman with her appropriated hip-hop clothes and her giant ambition. Gone. Poof. Snuffed out. *God fucking damn it.*

Whatever shield had been keeping this knowledge at bay dissolved, and Gwen found herself practically running—hobbling, actually—across Canal and over on Grand and up Allen. She tried not to imagine the sight she made, dashing through SoHo in her vintage dress and sweat-matted hair; she didn't care, because everything in her was willing her to East Houston, to the Mercury Lounge.

She only knew this club because JJ had played it. She didn't go to every gig but did when JJ asked her, unless she had a gig of her own. She'd been in more straight clubs in the two years she'd been seeing JJ than in the whole rest of her life. At first JJ had been very cautious, like, "Do you think you'll be okay to be in a...you know, in, like, a bar...?" Gwen had never really talked to JJ about the struggle to not drink; she believed it was not JJ's weight to carry.

Howard always told her, "Be careful, honey, when you take the tiger for a walk."

But if she wanted to drink, she figured she wouldn't need a bar for an excuse and, because she wanted JJ to come to her shows, she practiced the Golden Rule by going to JJ's. Not to mention, JJ really rocked, and there was nothing Gwen found sexier than talent.

There was no one on the door at the Mercury Lounge at three in the afternoon, and Gwen slipped into the dark coolness, gulping breath to calm the heaving in her chest. She tried to gather herself, fluff her hair, wipe the sweat off her forehead, reposition her breasts in their push-up bra. She took a moment to swipe lipstick over her mouth. She wanted to appear as if she'd just sauntered in on a whim, not like she'd sprinted all the way from the Holland Tunnel. She needed some water to cool herself down.

She was in luck. She spotted a woman she vaguely recognized setting up behind the bar. The woman's short, disheveled hair was the same color as the ultra-black liner around her eyes, and her nipples protruded through a skin-tight tank. She glanced at Gwen in annoyance and barked, "We don't open till nine tonight."

"Yeah," Gwen nodded in acknowledgment. She moved closer to the bar, scrambling to remember her name and then it came to her. "Luce?"

The barkeep looked at her a little more sharply, sizing her up.

"It's Gwen. I'm with JJ, you know, Underbrush?"

The pieces were falling together for her then; her face relaxed. "Sure," she said, and inclined her head like Gwen could take a seat. She slid onto a barstool.

"Ya' want anything?" Luce asked.

There was just a moment when a song of scotch insinuated itself in Gwen's brain, but she answered, "Just some water would be great. It's hot out there."

Luce squirted a wedge of lime into it before she set it in front of Gwen on a square of paper, then leaned her elbows on the bar. "What can I do for ya'?"

Gwen took a long, long swallow from the glass, and left her lip print on its rim. She offered a quick prayer for help from the universe. She'd come this far on pure, unexamined impulse, and now she had to improvise. "You've heard about that young girl that got killed this week? They found her body under the FDR?"

"I ain't worked since Monday night. I guess that's the night it happened, right? Buzz says the cops have been all over this place all week." From the hardness in her face, it was impossible to tell if Luce was twenty or thirty or forty.

"You worked Monday night?" Gwen felt a stirring of hope.

"Yeah, I came ta' work high last week so the boss tried to punish me by giving me all the shit shifts. So I went onna little strike f'the rest 'o the week. Turned my phone off so I wouldn't hear that moron tryin' ta' order me around. Fuck that shit." She grinned, revealing perfectly straight teeth; she had not always been who she was now.

"This girl, Emma, I knew her. She was a student of mine, a really talented young artist." She needed to establish the reason she was asking questions; she needed to make Luce care. "And her roommate says she went out that night, she was supposed to meet somebody here. But nobody knows whether she got here or not, whether she met who she was supposed to meet. We wanna find the guy who did this."

"Asshole bouncer," Luce snorted, "he wouldn't remember if a tornado hit the place the night before." She shook her head at his uselessness. "But, truth, there's a fuckin' lotta people in here *every* night. You gotta picture of her, or somethin'?"

It was Gwen's turn to shake her head. "No. But she's about twenty-two, natural blond hair, with studs in her nose and eyebrows, and a tattoo on her neck. A hexagram from the *I*

Ching," she finished weakly.

Luce cocked one hand to her hip, the better to telegraph her skepticism. "Okay, you've just described the female half of our clientele, except not everybody's blond with Hebrew whatever... Wait a minute," she shook a finger at Gwen. "I'm tryin' ta' remember somethin'. Monday, Monday...yeah. It was early, I think. The main band wasn't on yet. Some group was on...The Floating Heads, I think their name was. They're a buncha headbangers, so it was rowdier here than usual on a Monday."

She paused to draw herself a beer and chugged half of it. "You sure you don' want anything? On the house!" she offered but Gwen assured her she was fine. Wordlessly she urged her to continue.

"Yeah, I didn't start thinkin' about this until just now. You reminded me. So this chick comes up to the bar. She's kinda cute, y'know, and dressed to advertise it. But she's a little freaked, tells me this guy is hittin' on her and she can't shake him. Keno was on with me that night, but he was in the back takin' a smoke break or gettin' a blow job or whatever the hell he does when he wanders away in the middle of a shift, so I couldn't leave. I told her to tell the bouncer. At the time I thought she was just a cute little chickie who got in over her head, y'know, but now I think about it, she seemed kinda scared."

"Did you see the guy?" It was all Gwen could do not to climb across the bar and grab her by the front of her sleazy tank top.

"I can't tell for sure if he was the guy, but there was this old dude, like forty or somethin', all decked out in leather pants or some shit, who seemed to be hangin' pretty tight with her."

"And did he follow her?"

"Like I'd know that, with about fifty other people screamin' at me for their drinks?"

"So you don't know if she ever talked to the bouncer?"

Luce didn't even bother to respond, just threw her hands up in frustration with the pressures of her job.

Adrenaline shooting through her system, Gwen had to remind herself to stay cool. "Listen," she told Luce, "the detective on this case is a friend of mine." Luce's face screwed up again, disbelieving this. "It's a long story. It's not from bein' a cop that I know him. He's a good guy, really. Anyway, he's gonna need to talk to you."

Anticipating her protest, Gwen continued, "We gotta stop this guy. He's gonna kill somebody else," she pleaded with her.

Luce drank the other half of the beer, wiped her mouth on the back of her wrist. A sigh that was half a curse exploded from her mouth, but her shoulders gave in.

"Tell him I ain't testifyin'. *If* I talk to him, that's it. I'm not goin' to court."

"I'm sure that's fine," Gwen assured her, not that she had the faintest idea if it was or not. "Hey, do you think I could use your phone?"

Reluctantly, Luce beckoned Gwen behind the bar. "You are one pushy cunt, do you know that?" she griped. Still, Luce handed her the receiver. Then she lit a cigarette, apparently her last refuge from this turn of events.

The acrid fumes made Gwen's nostrils burn, but she felt so grateful to this woman, she didn't even care. She punched in the familiar number, heard Howard's voice crackle at the other end. She made her report. He sounded more pained than grateful.

"Okay, that's great," he said gruffly. "I'll take it from here."

"Are you gonna come over now? It might be better before they get busy." There was a momentum, and she didn't want to lose it.

"Yeah, I'm on my way." He sounded like he was swallowing the last bite of a sandwich; sliced turkey was his staple.

Gwen felt a small twinge of guilt for disrupting his lunch, late as it was. "Okay, I'll see you when you get here."

"Gwen, go home. Let me do my job."

"Howard, she's not gonna talk to you without me here..." she protested, but he'd already hung up.

Luce had disappeared into the back, and Gwen let her head rest on her arms on top of the bar. There was always that sour smell in bars, sweat and fermentation.

Howard barged in before Luce returned up front. His limp was more pronounced than usual; that happened when he got tired. He glowered. "Gwen, what did I tell you?"

She saw him eye the liquid in her glass, as if to assess its contents. She wasn't sure which made her madder—his trying to get rid of her or not trusting her not to drink.

"It's water," she told him flatly. "And this woman won't talk to you without me here." That might be a slight overstatement, but she felt the need to stand her ground.

Luce came behind the bar with a case of something, the biceps in her thin arms bulging. She set the carton on the floor and began unpacking bottles, not acknowledging the two of them.

"Luce, this is Detective O'Hara."

"I already told her I ain't testifyin'," she snarled.

Howard kept his expression level. "I just need to talk to you about what you might have seen on Monday night." Turning to Gwen he added, "For the last time, you gotta go." His tone was not friendly.

In her direction, Luce cracked, "Oh, yeah, he's a peach."

"He's okay," Gwen assured her with more equanimity than she felt. "He's just got a job to do. Listen, thanks, Luce, I mean it." She said nothing to Howard as she left the bar.

Back out on Houston, the afternoon had a used-up feeling, the sun already dipping below the outline of the tall buildings, though the sky would still be light for hours. It was in the faces of the people on the street; those who had evening plans were already rushing toward the night, watching the lengthening shadows, hungry for darkness, while the others seemed resigned that nothing more can be wrested from the day.

Chapter 13

Blinds shuttered to the afternoon sun cast the hot tiny room into twilight. An occasional breeze lifted the shade and flung fleeting streaks of brightness over the rose-colored walls and across the soft brown sheets where Chi dozed against Dana's sleeping, sweat-moistened back.

Outside on the stoop, one floor below, a cluster of girls were jumping rope; their sassy rhymes and the steady slap of clothesline on pavement provided the accompaniment to Dana's gurgled breath, her throat still clogged with the tears that had come, finally, when she'd released into orgasm. Somewhere in the building a neighbor was baking despite the heat of the day, and the aroma of melting chocolate rose in the sweltering air like sweet, beckoning smoke, curling its tendrils into Chi's waking dreams.

Lying there, one hand cupped around Dana's small, slack breast, she was happier than she could remember being. She lay there and tried to think of Emma, tried to summon sorrow and outrage to balance the delight that kept breaking through. But she could evoke only the infant, the toddler, the loss of whom had broken her heart so many years ago. Ever since she'd heard about Emma she had only been able to think about Dana. It was human nature to think about the living rather than the dead. The dead didn't need us; the living did.

And was it predatory to hope in the face of this tragedy that Dana would finally need her again? Chi could not believe this, not after feeling Dana relax, release, open herself to touch, allow the storm of emotion to find expression under Chi's fingertips.

Satisfaction hummed in her chest. She inched her knees closer to contain more completely the swell of Dana's ass in the hollow of her own curved lap and was just about to let herself drop fully into sleep when the phone shrieked from the bedside table.

Chi bolted up, desperate to silence the phone before it woke her lover. Dana, however, did not stir, just clutched her hands between her thighs and slumbered on. Chi summoned a harsh whisper to snarl hello in the direction of the receiver.

"Chi, are you okay? Were you sleeping? Oh, Chi, I'm sorry."

The youthful voice sounded out-of-breath, chagrined. To Chi it sounded familiar, yet she could not place it.

"Who is this?" she demanded, keeping her voice low.

"It's Ayisha. You know, Emma's friend? Look, I don't mean to be a drag, okay? I just really need to talk to you."

Chi fell back against the headboard with a thump; the pillows had somehow found their way to the foot of the bed. She glanced at the pale skin of Dana's legs, untangled from the sheets, white as pearls and gently furred from knee to ankle with light brown hair. Chi ran a hand through the dense brush of her own tight curls and wondered what the hell she was supposed to do.

"How'd you get my number?" she asked, stalling for time.

Ayisha paused, perplexed, as if the question had disrupted her momentum. Then she took a deep breath and re-gathered her resolve. "Chi, last night you said you know my father."

A pool of dread opened in the older woman's belly. "I *knew* your father, Ayisha. It was a long time ago."

The remark did not deflect Ayisha. "Whenever it was, it was a hell of a lot more recently than I've seen him," she argued. "*Please*, Chi, you've got to help me find him!" Her voice bloomed with hope.

The air in Chi's bedroom grew so close that it seemed

impossible to breathe. Never in her life had she felt so tired, so old. "This isn't a good time, Ayisha," Chi muttered dully.

"Then when?" the young woman demanded.

Chi stared into the dim light of the room, seeking some avenue of escape from this spot where fate had cornered her. Her restless eyes lit on a framed photo of her grandmother—dead now nearly twenty years—hung above a battered chest of drawers. It was her grandmother who used to say, when confronted with any adversity, "Only way *out* is *through*."

"Chi?" The utterance was soft and urgent as a child awakened in the night by bad dreams.

"I'm here," Chi answered.

There was no exit from this circumstance, she knew, except to fulfill her part in it. Her grandmother had been right. "Later, Ayisha. I'll meet you at the loft this evening."

"You promise?" the young woman asked, her voice plaintive with hope and doubt.

"Six o'clock. I'll be there. I promise."

Chi replaced the receiver and reached for a pillow to clutch at her aching chest. Arms wrapped around it, she remembered something else her grandmother used to say, something about, "Fools'll do anything to find out what they don't really want to know."

Before Gwen had turned the key in the deadbolt, she could already hear contentious voices spilling from the loft. So charged was the confrontation, no one bothered to turn around as she entered. The circle had shrunk since this morning, and she took a quick inventory: Chi was gone, Dana, gone. Ayisha and Kendra were all that remained of the younger generation. Where was Lee? Gwen had expected her to be glued to Kendra.

Gwen slipped into the bathroom area, woefully shook her head at the state of her face and hair. She took a few minutes with her comb and a cold washcloth, then moved to take a chair in the circle, trying to force her attention toward the discussion at hand. Her thoughts, though, were full of her conversation with Luce at the Mercury. She was still miffed at Howard for making her leave; she ought to get some credit, she felt, for turning up what might be an important lead. She deserved to know how it panned out. Instead, Howard had dismissed her like a child. Gwen wished JJ were around, or even Dana; she was dying to tell someone.

Kendra and Peg were arguing about AIDS. The older woman insisted that here was one more case of women being asked to put men's needs first—"You don't see men rallying around the epidemic of breast cancer," she thundered—while Kendra shrieked, "Don't you think women get AIDS too?" What marked this exchange as different was that each evinced a new respect for her adversary; they fought as equals now, each determined to sway the other.

It was no surprise to anyone when Elena Martínez steered the conversation to the issue of abortion rights. "We have reached a critical juncture," she cautioned as she stood before the group, still in her dark suit, despite the heat. "It is only a matter of time before the Court overturns its 1973 ruling. We must be ready."

Luanne had deliberately seated herself across from the giant clock face; it had watched over her as she slept the night before and she had come to identify it as a kind of guardian. She felt her heart quicken as she raised her hand to speak. "Don't you think it's dangerous," she asked Elena, "the way the movement's come to be defined by this single issue?"

It had been years since she'd stood before a union hall to speak to rank and file, but she could still remember the way her heart would pound, her extremities turn to ice.

The gaze Elena fixed on her was cold as obsidian. "The danger," she rejoined in a tight, brusque voice, "is in failing to understand the true intentions of the so-called 'pro-life' agenda. We've infiltrated these groups and believe me, their long-term goal is nothing less than to return women to a state of total subjugation."

Luanne sunk lower in her chair, feeling chastised and intimidated. She'd never be able to find the words to say what she felt, and even if she did, who would listen to her? What, after all, had *she* ever infiltrated?

Peg was quick to agree with Elena. "Those fundamentalists

have made an easy alliance with the old guard Republican elite who have a stake in keeping women's labor underpaid."

"You mean *un*paid," Jolene interjected.

Ruthie added, "And having a Democrat in the White House doesn't make a damn bit of difference."

"Amen to that," Jolene agreed. "He's ready to sell welfare mothers down the river."

"They're keeping him so tied up in lawsuits that he can't advance his own agenda," Peg complained.

Dismissing Luanne altogether, Elena's face warmed with a triumphal glow. "My organization is working to drive a wedge into that unholy alliance between the fundamentalists and the country club Republicans. We're drafting legislation that says if a state forces a woman to bear a child against her will, then the state must assume financial responsibility for its care." Her grin was calculated. "The last thing those fiscal conservatives want is more government spending for social programs. They're going to run to the pro-choice camp so fast it will make your head spin."

"But wait a minute," Jolene interrupted. "As feminists, don't we believe that government *should* provide for social needs, including infant and child care for those who can't afford it? Usin' that as some kinda scare tactic seems cynical, if not downright self-defeating! And what kind of message are you sending to poor women—that we're the sacrificial lambs?"

Elena threw an impatient hand in the air. "We're never going to achieve some perfect vision of socialist utopia. Not in my lifetime, not in yours. The message we're sending is that we are going to do whatever it takes to preserve women's reproductive rights."

The words flowed, eloquent and imperious as ever, that same forceful articulation that had signaled to senators and justices alike that they would find in Elena Martínez a formidable adversary. Still, even as she spoke, Elena knew that she was not herself. A buzzing in her ears obscured her hearing; it seemed connected to the pressure building in her head.

"Isn't that the problem with single-issue politics?" Ruthie was asking, but the drone in Elena's ears eclipsed the question.

Luanne still watched the giant clock; its encouraging grin made her rise from her chair, twisting the tail of her blouse with nervous fingers. "I know I'm gonna get blasted for this, but I have to say it: I think this movement has made a huge mistake by focusing on abortion as a right. Women have a right to control their own bodies; I don't argue with that. But we'd be much further along and we wouldn't have alienated so many women if we weren't out there advocating the legalization of murder."

The word hit the group like a shock wave, provoking howls of protest around the circle. "That's bullshit!" Kendra bellowed, while Jolene cast worried glances at her friend. But Luanne stood her ground, refusing to yield the floor. She stole a glimpse at the clock face, seeking the courage to continue.

"I know I'm speaking feminist heresy," she went on, "but it's time somebody said it. It's like Orwell's *1984*, it's doublespeak to say abortion isn't murder, that the fetus inside us isn't life. Any woman in this room who's ever been pregnant knows the truth." She looked hard into Jolene's eyes, forcing a grudging acknowledgment. She turned to stare at Peg, who looked at the floor.

Elena tried to concentrate, but something in her attention had slipped just for a moment, a cog disengaged from its wheel. An image of Kay rose before her eyes, Kay with her armload of flowers. White flowers. Kay had been murdered, and all of Elena's work had done nothing to prevent it.

Seconds later her focus was restored, the wheel turning smoothly once again. "What about the murder of innocent women who die during self-inflicted or back-alley abortions?" Her voice lashed like a whip. The words came easily; she had used them hundreds of times. But now she was angry, and that was unusual. The noise in her head was building to a roar, and her vision was full of blood. "Are you saying their lives don't count?"

Luanne plodded on as nearly every pair of eyes in the room riddled her with accusation. "It's not that I want to see anyone return to the days of back-alley abortions."

She turned a pleading look toward the clock, but its face was once more flat, expressionless, merely a disk of numbers.

"Sometimes I guess it's necessary to kill in self-defense. But what kind of world is it that pits the life of a mother against the life of her child? We've spent twenty years fighting for something that at best is a last-ditch desperate solution. We could have used that energy working on positive options—new birth control methods, better education—so that women aren't forced by circumstance into killing their babies!"

Rage was swirling in Elena's head, stealing her equilibrium. "Who do you think you are?" She was screaming at Luanne, scarcely aware that she was doing so. The noise in her brain was so loud, her vision clotted with red. "What have you fought for in your life? What have you risked?"

"Elena, calm down," Gwen rose to intervene. "She's just expressing her opinion—"

"Goddamn her opinion!" Elena howled.

The room fell away like the shucked skin of an animal and she was suddenly nine years old. She could feel the heat of the Texas summer pressing around her in the tiny room, scorching the air; light slivered through cracks in the wood-slat walls. Her mother lay on the bed, shivering, rocking in pain as sweat drenched the sheets, trying to stifle her cries so as not to frighten the younger ones.

Elena drew the sheet across the door to keep the little ones out. Her mother's dusky face was nearly gray, and her dark hair plastered her forehead.

"¿Que pasa, Mama?" Elena had asked, her voice cracking with fear.

Reluctantly her mother pulled aside the bed sheets to reveal the creeping pool of blood that oozed from between her legs. Throughout the endless afternoon Elena had held her mother's hand, sponged her forehead, gotten her ladles of water to sip. She'd pleaded to be allowed to go to a neighbor's for help, or run to the fields to find her father, but her mother insisted that no one must know. Instead she held tight to Elena's small hand, staring into the eyes of her eldest daughter, repeating, "*Lamento mucho. Perdóneme.*"

Toward evening, as the sun dropped low in the sky, her mother had started to pray, begging forgiveness in a tight, quiet voice. A while later she was still, and the grip on Elena's hand relaxed. Elena continued to sit with her until it grew light again, until her father finally came home.

At last the memory released her, but she could not return to the present. Elena felt herself falling, hurtling through a dark space that had no boundaries. She was barely aware that she had begun to weep, her wails rising, rolling, one over the other, as though they too were now part of the wheel, nearly obscuring the words wrenched from deep in her throat, "*Mi madre, mi madre.*"

Gwen stepped forward and gently led Elena to a seat, guiding her down until the chair supported her. The rest of the group sat in stunned silence, uncertain what to do as they gawked at this normally steely woman now hunched over, dissolved in private anguish.

"Could we give her some privacy?" Ayisha suggested, and the women were grateful to comply. Everyone moved toward the makeshift kitchen, where Jolene started a pot of coffee no one wanted to drink. They clustered at the table, picking at remnants of leftover bagels, pretending not to watch Elena and Gwen.

Elena had stopped crying. She huddled in her chair like an accident victim, her stare vacant, a polite smile plastered to her face. Seated beside her, Gwen clung to her hand and murmured, "Elena, Elena," until a glimmer of consciousness flared in her eyes. "Elena, are you all right?"

The older woman nodded absently, whispered, "*Sí, sí.*"

"Elena," Gwen tried again with more urgency, "You seem very upset. Is there anyone you'd like me to call?"

Elena Martínez considered the question. "Kay," she answered softly. "*Quiero llamarse. Quiero llamarse.*" Elena, who never spoke anything other than perfectly articulated English around Anglos.

"Who?" Gwen rested a hand on Elena's back; it was rigid, a ramrod of iron, unreceptive to comfort. "Who is it I should call?"

Elena shook her head to clear it. She couldn't call Kay now. Kay was...somewhere else. Florida?

Slowly she rose from her seat and picked up her purse and briefcase. *"Necesito salir ahora,"* she muttered. *"Soy arrepentido."*

Ruthie stepped forward then. "Would you like me to drive you somewhere?" she offered.

A few moments passed before Elena seemed to register the question, as if her mind were elsewhere. Once she did, her response was firm. *"No, no es necesario. Yo lo puedo hacer."*

Ruthie tried to persuade her, but Elena was insistent.

"I'll walk down with her, make sure she gets a cab," Gwen promised.

"Maybe you should go with her to the hotel," Ruthie suggested. Gwen nodded as she followed Elena out of the loft.

She was tempted to use the elevator just this once, but someone had left it on the ground floor and she thought maybe the walk down would help restore Elena's equilibrium. They descended the four floors in silence.

Out on Rivington Street, they were in luck: A skinny man pulled an enormous oil painting out of the backseat of a taxi right in front of them. Gwen commandeered the back door and gestured for Elena to slide in. One hand on the door she offered, "Do you want me to ride along with you?"

"No, no, estoy bien," Elena patted the hand Gwen rested on the open window.

Although relieved, Gwen persisted. "Are you sure?"

Elena told the driver the name of her hotel.

"That's up on Forty-seventh, isn't it?" Another stroke of luck: the driver spoke English and seemed to know his way around the city.

Gwen swung the back door closed. "Elena, call me when you get there, okay? You have the number here, right?" The cab began to pull away. "I mean it, Elena, call me!" Gwen hollered toward its departing taillights.

Chapter 14

It seemed millennia ago that Gwen had awoken to JJ's naked body pressed against hers in bed. Her feet ached and her back was sore from her sprint through SoHo in heels; sometimes she forgot she wasn't twenty anymore. Her ovaries were still throwing a tantrum. Her shoulders were sunburned, and her nerves felt stretched and thready from an overabundance of stressors.

As if lunch with Lee and chasing down a murderer/rapist and dealing with Elena's nervous breakdown hadn't been enough, once the meeting broke up there was Kendra in her face, asking could she "interview" Gwen for some article.

"Sorry," Gwen told her, "you already had your crack at me," and walked away. That felt good, until Lee came in with Roger, all chipper like some Father-Figure-of-the-Year—she'd taken him for a walk in Central Park. This had been another sore point between them: Lee had always wanted kids; Gwen absolutely had not—yet another way she'd let Lee down. So Gwen was already feeling sour when Lee sidled up to her, cooing that she "oughta give the girl another chance."

"What girl?" Gwen was confused until she realized Lee meant Kendra, and then she exploded.

"Don't," she warned her. "Don't try to play *me* just because you want to get in that girl's snatch."

"Calm down, Jesus, calm down," Lee insisted, which only made Gwen more livid. Lee could do the most outrageous thing, but Gwen was always the one who was being hysterical.

Gwen retained enough of her dignity to say, "I am *not* going to talk about this with you," and walked away from Lee. But of course, there was no place to go, with women still all over her loft. That was when she snapped.

"Okay, everybody, listen up," she boomed in her best "make-sure-they-can-hear-me-in-the-back-of-the-auditorium" voice. "I know some of you are staying here and all, but I am five minutes from having a meltdown and I need to do it in private. So I need everybody to clear out of here *now* for at least an hour. I know, I know, it's rude, it's inconvenient, but really, if you don't, it's not going to be pretty for any of us."

"But it's raining," Luanne protested.

Gwen raced to a corner of the studio and dragged one of the storage bins to the center of the room. Then she began to toss umbrellas onto the floor: one was neon yellow with a smiley face at its crown; one was Day-Glo orange. One was pink with black Scottie dogs; another was resplendent with van Gogh's irises. Several years ago she'd done a performance about birth control in which she'd included about thirty women dancing with umbrellas (their shields against sperm). Strewing them at the feet of her dumbfounded guests, Gwen didn't mind if she appeared crazy. In fact, she hoped her lunacy would seem just menacing enough to buy her an hour of peace and quiet.

It didn't work quite as smoothly as she'd hoped. There were plans to reconnoiter and keys to negotiate. Luanne and Jolene wanted to go out, but what to do with Roger? Lee couldn't take him because she was departing with Kendra. Ruthie would take Roger, it was decided; she was going to visit her sister for the night and her sister had grandkids. Ayisha was supposed to meet Chi there in a little while. Peg wanted to just stay in. But she would go out for an hour and then come back. So she needed to be trained in the use of the keys.

By the time they were all gone, Gwen had just enough time to call Elena's hotel to make sure she'd arrived safely. Elena assured her she was resting and was sorry to have caused any concern. She was, she insisted, "just tired."

Gwen set the phone down and futilely dragged a brush through her hair. Then she had maybe five minutes to sit stupefied, staring into space, before she heard the signal of JJ's horn from below.

Still dressed in her now-less-than-perky strapless poinsettia print dress and mules, she limped down the stairs to her front door. The rain that had started an hour earlier had become a deluge, complete with thunder and lightning; sheets of water poured onto the sidewalks. She thought of the scattering of unclaimed umbrellas on the floor upstairs, but knew they'd be useless against this water.

She was drenched before she even reached the van. Her hair was dripping and her shoes squished water onto the floor mats. JJ looked at Gwen with alarm, and that was all the mirror she needed.

"¡Cosita!" JJ exclaimed, and reached behind her for a towel, in which she enfolded Gwen. Ordinarily Gwen would have melted at her consideration, but she was long past reason.

"I'll do it," she snapped, and yanked the towel from JJ's hands. Pressed against the passenger door, as far from her as she could get, Gwen sat sulking, squeezing water from her hair. No warm hello, no kiss in greeting.

JJ registered all of this, but she shifted gears and pulled away from the curb into the downpour. One thing Gwen loved about JJ, she was not a drama queen. She didn't speed or tailgate or act out her hurt and anger behind the wheel the way Gwen would have done at her age, the way she might have done even now. JJ wouldn't take shit, but she almost never overreacted. She drove in silence up First Avenue, cutting across town on Fourteenth. There was no need to discuss the destination; she was headed toward the AA meeting they went to most Saturday evenings.

Why JJ went to Alcoholics Anonymous meetings, Gwen couldn't say. JJ was not a big drinker; she seemed to be one of the lucky ones who could have a beer and walk away from it. Gwen had never seen her drunk, which was a good thing because she couldn't bear to be with people when they were intoxicated. But ever since Gwen had told JJ about her recovery, she'd been going to meetings with Gwen when her schedule allowed it. Gwen wasn't sure what she got out of it, but it made her feel like JJ understood what she went through, and she appreciated that.

Gwen was still too cranky to apologize, but their silence gave her time to take a quick personal inventory. When she managed to slice through her irritation with JJ, what she found at the core was guilt. She realized she didn't want JJ to ask, "How was lunch?" Lee had gotten Gwen all stirred up; something she'd thought long dead had been reactivated, and she felt divided, disloyal, deceitful. Some part of her was held back from JJ in order to nurture this secret, and it was with some horror that she realized she must have been withholding it the whole time they'd been together. Without even knowing it, there's been some piece of herself she hadn't been willing to give.

Gwen turned to watch JJ's profile, her cheek shadowed by the streak of the windshield wipers. JJ didn't take her eyes from the road, but Gwen could tell she was aware of Gwen looking at her; she could feel the shift in JJ's energy.

In the program they said, "You're as sick as your secrets," and Gwen had the urge to unburden herself of this one. But therapy had taught her to choose carefully whom she picked to receive this kind of revelation. It wouldn't do JJ any good to hear what was roiling inside her. Lee had always been an addiction for her, and if she felt herself in danger of a slip, surely it couldn't be JJ's job to keep her clean and sober.

When they reached the church on Waverly, JJ broke her silence to offer gallantly, "You go ahead and get us seats while I park."

Then Gwen wanted to fall into her arms, but that would be drama, too. She softly said, "Okay," and flung herself from the van, holding the towel above her head, even though she was already soaked. In four strides she was through the door, turning to watch JJ pull into traffic.

One hundred voices were already midway through the Serenity Prayer as she clattered down the steps into the musty basement that housed the AA meeting. A cluttered room crowded with folding chairs under the greenish glare of fluorescent bulbs:

it felt like home. Gwen was grateful to plop onto a battered metal chair on the far side of the room; the middle section was entirely filled. She lay her sodden towel onto the chair next to her, to indicate the seat was saved.

The room held an assortment of people who would come together for no other reason: men in exquisitely tailored suits sat elbow to elbow with punk girls in skull earrings and black tights full of runs. Women with elaborate coiffures and perfect aerobicized figures applauded the stories of grizzled guys with trembling hands.

There, no one cared what she looked like, if her hair was lank with rain, her shoes waterlogged. No one judged if her politics were imperfect, or what the Senator from North Carolina thought about her artwork. No one minded how crazy or scared she felt—they'd all been there.

JJ came through the door; her eyes found Gwen and noted the chair beside her. Before coming over, she went first to the refreshment table and filled a Styrofoam cup with coffee. She brought it over and put it into Gwen's hands. Then she wrapped her leather jacket around Gwen's shoulders as she sat. The jacket was warm from her body, and for a minute Gwen collapsed her head onto JJ's shoulder, breathed in the musk oil that wreathed her neck.

Gwen took a sip of coffee, savoring its bracing effect, and squeezed JJ's hand in gratitude. Then she turned her attention to the front of the room, where an overweight woman in a flame red pantsuit stood at the podium reading aloud the Twelve Steps. "We admitted we were powerless..." Her voice was clotted with fear, yet she looked straight ahead as she recited the familiar words.

When Gwen had first come into these rooms, she'd fought so hard against the notion of being "powerless." She had already been a feminist for a decade, had dedicated herself to overturning women's conditioned and enforced passivity and helplessness. She remembered speaking up at one meeting early on, "I am goddamn well *not* going to admit that I am powerless. And don't even get me started on that God 'he' thing!" She'd had enough youth and enough arrogance to think she would bring the feminist revolution to AA. Everyone had just smiled and urged her to "keep coming back," which only pissed Gwen off more.

But she had kept coming back because she'd grown tired of waking up every morning with her eyeballs aching; she didn't know how else to stop drinking. It took her more than a year to understand that "powerless" didn't mean defenseless and victimized, but was a recognition that there were things that she could not control or will away.

The red-clad woman at the podium was talking about her drinking days, how many mornings she found herself waking up next to strangers. "It's a miracle none of them ever hurt my kids," she told the group. "God looked out for them when I couldn't," she began to cry, "and I am so grateful for that."

Gwen noticed JJ wipe a tear from her cheek. She was so tenderhearted. Sometimes Gwen thought JJ came to AA for the stories. She grabbed her hand and squeezed it again.

Before she'd come to AA, Gwen had renounced her belief in God, the punitive Catholic God of her family, the God who monitored her every move, ready to give demerits on her soul. She couldn't say for sure if her mother had been more upset when she'd declared herself a lesbian or an atheist. Once she'd grown to embrace the decidedly non-denominational concept of a "Higher Power," she'd told her mother she could stop praying for her, but Wanda Kubacky didn't buy it. It was God the Father or nothing in her book.

People in AA talked about "God's will," and Gwen tried to come to terms with that. But she couldn't understand why God would will Emma to die, and in that way. When she asked Howard, he'd admitted he wrestled with that all the time in his work. "In the end," he said, "I just hafta accept that there are mysteries I don't understand and trust that there's a purpose beyond what I can see."

Faith, that's what he was talking about. She'd heard people speak in meetings—people who'd lost their jobs or their homes, people who'd been in prison or gotten divorced or had their kids taken away, people who had AIDS or cancer. And what they talked about was faith, the knowledge that their Higher Power would carry them through. And Gwen could see it worked for them; she'd watched them walk through whatever disaster they were facing and somehow endure. So who was she to knock that, even though she couldn't seem to muster it herself?

She thought of Dana. What was going to sustain her now? She thought of Elena, her armor shattered. Or Kick, so angry she wanted to destroy something. Gwen thought of the fact that she felt so much more at home here, in this room crowded with secretaries and bikers and aspiring actors and accountants, people whose politics she might be likely to abhor, than in her own loft with the women who should be her compatriots. Was that just buried remnants of misogyny, a failure to identify with her own kind? Or was it evidence that what Dana said this morning was right—identity politics had no basis anymore? Or was it easier to find solace among people who accepted their character defects and clung to faith in something more than their own anger, their own self-righteousness?

The woman at the podium had finished; the group applauded her. Someone was bringing forward a cake with three candles blazing. Everyone celebrated this woman's third year of sobriety, singing happy birthday.

At the break, as alcoholics rushed to refill coffee cups and some lined up for a chunk of the white-frosted cake, Gwen sidled up to JJ. "Sorry I was a butthead before." She wrapped an arm around her girlfriend's waist.

"I'm used to it," JJ joked it off, but Gwen heard something else in her tone—hurt, discouragement, resignation; she couldn't tell exactly what.

"No, really, I'm on my last nerve, and it isn't about you." Gwen was determined not to unload on JJ everything that was churning in her overtaxed brain, and JJ asked no questions. Still, Gwen could feel a distance in her, and she wondered if this time she'd pushed her too far.

"I have other news, though," Gwen remembered, and told JJ about her visit to the Mercury Lounge. "I don't know where it will lead, but it's another possible scenario for what happened. Maybe Jersey had nothing to do with it."

"Yeah, that'd be good." Even that didn't seem to cheer her

up. Gwen's worry index rose.

Then Howard lumbered through the door, wearing a shapeless tan raincoat, looking at his watch. What was left of his hair was plastered to his scalp and his shoulders were dotted with rain.

Before he could take a seat, Gwen dragged JJ over and besieged him, "Howard, were you able to track down that guy from the Mercury Lounge?"

She saw him make an effort to contain his temper and he raised both hands to fend her off. "Whoa! First off, I'm not here on duty. I came here for the meeting, late as I am, and I need you to respect that. Second, Gwen, and for the last time, I cannot talk to you about this case."

A look was exchanged between Howard and JJ, a "How do you solve a problem like Maria?" kind of look. It would have made Gwen mad if she weren't so rattled. *This is just great,* she thought, *now I've managed to alienate my girlfriend AND my sponsor in under an hour. A new record.*

Howard moved closer, so as not to make the conversation public. "Gwen, like I told you the other night, I'm in a tough spot here. I am your sponsor and I wanna do right by you with that. It's my worst nightmare that you would have any kind of connection to one of my cases. If I lose my head and confuse the two, it could not only fuck up my sponsorship of you; worst case, it could compromise my whole investigation. Please, sweetheart, hear this in the right way: I need you to stay out of this."

"Yeah, okay, I get it." She walked away from both of them, crossed the room and pretended to read the bulletin board. She was sulking, hurt, but underneath she was embarrassed by her own bad behavior and being called on it. An unnaturally thin man who was obviously living with AIDS called the meeting back together.

For the remaining half-hour, Gwen stewed, unable to concentrate on the parade of speakers who shared their experience, strength and hope. Gone was her solace, her comfort at being in that room. Now she was locked inside her brain, which had become a place in which JJ was going to break up with her and Howard was going to drop her as a sponsee. "Sometimes the mind is a bad neighborhood," Howard had often warned Gwen, "It's not safe to wander around there by yourself."

At meeting's end, she stood for The Lord's Prayer with the rest of the group, but she mumbled the syllables on autopilot. She offered a curt, "Sorry," to Howard on the way out, and he said, "Hey, me too," as she escaped the room.

The rain had stopped, leaving the air just as hot but a whole lot stickier than before. When they reached the van, Gwen handed JJ back her jacket, "Thanks for this."

"No problem."

It was their custom to eat Indian food together after the Saturday night meeting, even when JJ had a gig, which she did again that night. But as she opened the passenger door, Gwen said, "You know, I'm in a bad place, and we're in a bad place, and I haven't been to the gym since Monday, so I think I'm just gonna walk home and do that. Maybe we can hook up later."

Surely JJ could see through the idiocy of this plan. Gwen was wearing a limp, strapless flowered dress and wet high-heeled mules. She looked more like she was on her way to Bellevue than like she was headed for the gym. Ordinarily Gwen loved it that JJ never pressured her about whatever she wanted to do, but tonight Gwen took it as a bad sign when JJ said, "Okay." Gwen couldn't tell if she was disappointed or relieved.

"But I probably won't see you till tomorrow, *chica*, because don't you still have company?"

A man in an Eldorado was waiting for JJ's parking space, and she moved to go, but Gwen was hit with a surge of desperation and grabbed her elbow. She waved the Eldorado on. "Honey, this is fucked up. What's going on with us?"

JJ shrugged. "I don't know, *poquita*. Maybe I'm just tense about Emma's death and all. But it really feels like you don't ever take this seriously between us, like you don't take *me* seriously, and sometimes it makes me tired." Her voice was so gentle as she said this; it cut deeper than if she'd screamed it.

"We're both tense, baby," Gwen tried to reassure her. She was trying to keep this from spiraling out of control. "Let's talk about it when we can be in bed together, naked, okay?" Gwen cajoled.

JJ couldn't be reached, though. She didn't even smile at this image. She just said, "Yeah, we'll talk about it later." Ever courtly, she added, "Are you sure you don't want a lift home?"

Of course Gwen wanted a lift home. Her feet feel like bloody stumps after a day in these shoes, and the cloud-filled sky promised it would rain again tonight. But she had set this thing in motion and didn't know how to stop it.

"I'm good," Gwen told her, and JJ didn't insist.

"Play good tonight," Gwen called, as JJ climbed into the van. Then she was gone and Gwen was standing on the sidewalk on Waverly, not at all sure of where to go next.

Chapter 15

It could have been any time at all. Drawn curtains obscured all clue of daylight, and when Elena first opened her eyes she did not know where she was. She blinked and turned her gaze in each direction, as pieces of her surroundings came into focus.

She was stretched atop the blue bedspread, still dressed, though her shoes lay neatly at the side of the bed. There was a dull ache in the back of her head, and her eyes stung like raw sores. She felt as if a giant hand had crushed her, reduced her to fine, dry powder; she was more tired than she could ever remember. Squinting in the semi-darkness, she looked at the tiny face of her gold watch. Six thirty.

A.m. or p.m., she wondered, but she didn't really care. No doubt there were things she was supposed to be doing, but her brain was dead to function, like a factory shut down. She could only lie there in the artificially chilled air, vacant and limp.

She stirred just enough to fold back the sheet and roll her body under it, pulling the blanket under her chin. Curling to one side, she wrapped her arms around the extra pillow, cradling it to her chest. Then she slipped once more beneath the surface of the dark.

She was getting off a plane at one of those small airports, the kind where they roll a staircase up to the door of the plane and you step outside and down the stairs, hurry across the tarmac to a spare, squat terminal building. While the plane was in the air the day had been sunny, but as she disembarked, the sky darkened and big drops of rain began to fall. A wind blew up, swaying the palms on the distant horizon. Then she knew she was in Florida.

Down on the tarmac someone was waiting for her. As she descended the stairs she saw that it was Kay! Kay held a huge bouquet of white calla lilies in one hand. Inexplicably, no rain fell on her.

Elena embraced Kay with fervor; she was so happy to see her again! "How is it you're alive?" she asked, and Kay gave her a radiant smile. She brushed back her silver hair to reveal the smooth pearl of a scar on her forehead, where the bullet had entered her skull.

Elena grabbed her friend's arm and they walked into the terminal. She remembered that her luggage was full of presents for Kay. Joy welled inside her, but also immense relief; Kay's death could not have been her fault, because Kay wasn't dead!

When they reached the baggage claim area, Kay announced that she would bring the car around. Elena begged her to wait, they'd go together, but Kay insisted it would be faster.

Elena stood alone in front of the moving conveyor. Suitcase after suitcase tumbled down the chute; hers did not arrive. Beyond the automatic doors, Elena could see the clouds grow blacker as the rain's velocity increased. No red station wagon waited at the curb. Kay had instructed her to look for that.

Time stretched like a slender thread, began to fray. The airport was emptying, preparing to close. All the baggage from her flight had been unloaded, but Elena's suitcase was gone. Kay was gone. Elena was not able to stifle the feeling that something terrible had happened to her friend, that she was not coming back.

Just then the conveyor started up again, and slowly a long black box thudded down the chute. It came to rest right in front of Elena and the conveyor stopped. Trembling, Elena approached it and carefully lifted the lid. It was heavy and she struggled to set it aside.

Inside the box, draped in red satin, lay her mother, stiff hands folded across her breast, dark hair wreathed by a ring of calla lilies.

Elena woke up screaming.

Chi Curtis bounded up the steps from the subway, struggling to open her umbrella as she elbowed her way past slower-paced workers in uniforms or jean-clad artists. Both the storm and guilt at her lateness fueled her haste, but her thoughts kept returning to the empty bed where she'd awakened, the imprint of Dana's body pressed into the bedclothes.

Sometime in the late afternoon, Ms. Firestein had slipped away; an old trick, Chi recalled. Dana never let herself stay the entire night in someone else's bed, said it made her feel *colonized*, yes, that was the word she'd always used.

Arriving at the street door to the loft, Chi buzzed, then pounded until Ayisha swung it open. She appeared to Chi a brittle figure, forlorn and fragile, her slender body clothed simply in a sleeveless black T-shirt under loose black overalls, cut inches above the knee. As Chi entered the building, she noticed drops of rain in Ayisha's hair, worn loose for once across her shoulders, and thought she could detect a hint of tell-tale kink in the mass of tawny curls.

Gazing into Chi's face, the girl looked younger, even, than she was, and Chi cursed the task that lay before her. Beneath her breath she called upon the spirit of her grandmother: *Help me to inflict a healing wound*, she prayed, *show me how to cut without killing*.

"Hey, there," she growled, "sorry I'm late."

"You came!" Ayisha exclaimed, her eyes so naked with relief, it hurt Chi to look at them.

"Where shall we go?" Chi asked quickly, to cover her discomfort.

"We can just stay here. I found a place." Ayisha guided her down a hallway to the back of the building and into an enclosed stairwell. They ascended a flight before Chi parked herself on the cement landing between floors and gestured for Ayisha to join her. The walls rose high around them, gray and dismal, windowless.

Once seated face to face, a sudden shyness overtook them. Their silence echoed in the stairwell, along with a fluorescent hum, until finally broken by Chi's blunt query: "So, how much do you know about your dad?" She could see no point in beating around the bush.

Ayisha responded by unbuttoning the large pocket in the

flap of her overalls and extracting an envelope. Slitting its seal with one long fingernail, she produced a folded square of cardboard, protective covering for the two documents inside. These she handed to Chi with the solemnity of a priest offering the Eucharist.

The first was a black-and-white snapshot, its scalloped edges dating to the late fifties. Within its borders grinned a shy Black man, his tall, skinny frame dressed in a dark suit, a thin tie hanging from his long neck, hair cropped close against his head. Handsome, with an easy smile. He stood posing on the porch of a small wood frame house, which looked old but in good repair; someone had taken pride in its upkeep.

"When he left, my mother threw out all his stuff," Ayisha explained. "But I found this when I was a kid, stuck behind a dresser drawer. I never let her know I had it."

"So you don't know where this place is?" Chi asked as she studied the photograph, trying to measure it against the image of the man she remembered. But Chi had met him more than a decade after this picture was taken, and in another world altogether. She wondered if Dana knew where Linc had grown up.

Ayisha shook her head. "Down south somewhere I guess."

"Is that where he was from?"

Poised on the top step, Ayisha wrapped her arms around her bare knees. "I don't know much of anything. My mother wouldn't talk about him. Except in generalities, in political terms—'He fought for civil rights, he went to jail'—like those corny radio spots for Black History Month. It was almost like...."

She paused to search for words to fit the thought. "Like she could accept him as a representation, you know? But she hated him as a real human being."

Pulling herself up by the handrail, she turned to Chi, demanding, "Tell me how you know him."

Before answering, Chi unfolded the second document, a yellowed clipping from an unidentified newspaper. Judging from the hyperbolic headline—"Comrades Fight On to End Racism, Imperialism"—Chi guessed it to be from one of the underground tabloids of the late Sixties, *The Militant* or *Revolution Now*.

This photo showed another Lincoln Cain, an enormous Afro circling his head. A beard obscured the bottom of his face, but not the twisted, snarling mouth, nor the eyes hooded with bitterness. He was dressed in fatigues, fist raised in furious salute.

The picture made Chi ache inside, something sharp and vicious tearing at her ribs. It wasn't only Lincoln Cain, his transformation from somebody's son into guerilla warrior, but all the wasted young men lost to crack or bullets, their manhood in collision with their outcast state. At least Lincoln had had an image of the enemy, a vision of the world for which he fought.

When Chi finally spoke, she stood too, leaning against the opposite side of the staircase. Her voice was raspy, strained, the sound squeezed out through shards of feeling, "I met Lincoln in early Nineteen Seventy-one, when I started doin' some prison advocacy work."

"Did he work with you?" Ayisha interrupted.

"You could say that," Chi answered cautiously, wishing she could stop there, that her brain would empty like a cage opening, the past escaping into a boundless sky. She knew she would not be delivered; fate had picked her for this task and would not relieve her till the job was done. Steely-eyed with resolution, she paced the landing as she continued.

"Both Dana and I started working up at Attica that winter. There was a whole team of us, mostly lawyers, but a lot of activists too, trying to pressure prison authorities to conform to legal guidelines. The place was a hellhole—six men crowded into cells meant for two; people had to sleep in shifts. Food that nobody should be forced to eat; no medical care."

"So Lincoln was part of that team?" Ayisha stopped Chi's pacing, pressed for eye contact.

Chi looked at her sharply. "Lincoln was doin' *time* inside that prison."

The young woman blinked, too stunned to register surprise. Without intending it she began to climb the stairs, constructing a story as she went.

"So he was jailed for some political act," she stated, her face rigid with vehemence. "What did he do—blow something up, or kill a cop, or what?"

Chi felt something bubbling inside her, the urge to climb up to this pale-skinned girl, wrap her arms around her, sit and rock her like an infant. Ayisha stood ramrod-straight, deflecting such intentions; she looked as if a touch might shatter her.

"He would'a been put in federal prison for something like that," Chi explained as gently as she could. She ascended the stairs, coming as close as she dared, pausing on the step just below Ayisha. "Lincoln was sent up for rape."

"Rape?" On Ayisha's tongue the word seemed foreign, a syllable bereft of meaning. Then as if language had been restored to her, the term regained significance, and she queried simply, "Who?"

Chi gazed up at the dust motes in the air. "A white woman," she answered in a voice without inflection. "A college student he met at some rally where he spoke."

Ayisha scurried to the next landing, as if to escape Chi's words, then turned and sneered in disbelief. "Black men are always accused of going after white women. If Lincoln wanted a white woman he could've stayed with my mother. It's gotta be a bogus charge." Her eyes glittered with conviction.

Chi stayed where she was and nodded carefully. "It could be. A lot of political people got set up for various things. Drugs was always a big one; cops plant the dope on you, then bust you for it. My brother got sent up that way; he was stopped for speeding.

"On the other hand, those were crazy times. Eldridge Cleaver wrote that Black men raping white women was an act of political resistance, a revolutionary act. Too many brothers bought into that, I'm afraid."

"Lincoln was set up," Ayisha yelled, and her voice echoed off the concrete in the open shaft of the stairwell.

"It's possible. It's hard to say." Chi shrugged. "In jail, everybody's innocent. You'd meet some nice people, remind you of the brothers you grew up with, then you find out they're convicted of doin' terrible things. You never know."

Ayisha came flying down then, grabbed Chi by the shoulders, her nails biting into the dark flesh. "*I know,*" she insisted, snarling. Her eyes sought those of the older woman and held them, searching for corroboration. "I know he didn't do it."

"Okay, okay." Chi forced herself to relax her posture. She could have broken the young woman's grip, but she had no desire to fight her.

Mollified, Ayisha released her arm. She watched as Chi massaged the little moons indented in her skin. "I'm sorry," she began, but Chi waved away the penitence.

"So then what happened?" Ayisha had to know. "He can't still be in prison after all this time. Do you have any idea where I can start to look for him?"

Chi wished she could avoid the verdant eyes that swam with hope. In a hushed tone she asked, "Do you know what happened at Attica?"

The green eyes dimmed and Ayisha shook her head. Chi slumped onto a step and Ayisha apprehensively sat too.

"In September that same year there was a riot at the prison. The inmates finally had enough and the place just exploded. Guards were taken hostage; it was a big mess. After five days the governor called in the state troopers. We begged him not to; we were sure we could negotiate a solution, but they wouldn't let us near the place. They accused us of fomenting discontent.

The troopers stormed the prison. Thirty-nine people died. Including Lincoln."

She flicked a glance at the young woman's face, but nothing could be read there. "Later there was talk that certain inmates had been targeted to be taken out, you know, executed; that it was a big government conspiracy. But I've also heard it was a war zone inside, bullets flyin' every which way, so we'll never know."

She couldn't tell if Ayisha had heard the last; she was staring straight ahead, focused on nothing in particular. Finally her lips moved, "He's dead."

Chi nodded but the young woman seemed scarcely aware of her presence. "HE'S DEAD," she bellowed upward, the sound striking the cement and steel on all five floors. Chi thought that in her crouched position, Ayisha resembled a gray wolf howling at the moon.

Abruptly though, the girl began to laugh, a helpless, frenzied cackle that bounced off the ceiling and fell back down, a relentless rain of laughter. Between chokes and gasps, she stammered out, "He's been… dead… ah, ah, ah… since I was… huh… two years old! Eeeyay! … And my mother… ah, ah… my mother… never told me."

The thought sobered her and she seemed then to deflate, collapsing against her knees like a rag doll. When she spoke again, her voice seemed to come from the concrete steps, a flat, colorless voice.

"She had to know, didn't she? All those years I used to ask her why he never came to see me, why he wasn't even curious… She knew all the time, didn't she?"

"I don't know what she knew," Chi answered. She inched closer and placed her broad palm on the girl's back, between her slender shoulder blades. She expected Ayisha to cry and wanted to encourage it, to provide the place for grief to be released, at least a beginning.

But the young woman let that feeling harden inside her, and when she straightened her posture, shucking Chi's hand from her spine, her eyes were dry, her expression flat and calm.

"And Dana had to know, right? She was there. And probably even Emma knew. All these *white* women lookin' out for me, tryin' to protect me from my blackass dead rapist father." Her bitterness radiated off her skin.

"I guess it don' make no difference." She attempted a caustic smile. "Can't be missin' whatcha never did have."

She rose to her feet with a swagger of bravado. "Thanks for givin' me the four-one-one. I appreciate someone finally tellin' me the truth."

"Ayisha!" Chi felt the pain in every bone as she stood, as if her own body had absorbed all that Ayisha had refused to. "I only talked to him a couple of times; it wasn't easy for us to get in to see the prisoners. I liked him though. He had a good mind and a big heart. He was tryin' to organize on the inside, and he took a lot of heat for it.

"You're his daughter, Ayisha. It don't matter what color you are."

Something yielded in the stiffness of the young woman's features; her lips parted and the question formed before she could think to stop it. "Did he ever, you know, talk to you about me? Did he say he had a little girl?"

Chi Curtis did not have the heart to tell the truth. She had to give the girl something to carry with her, some shred of something that would feed her spirit.

"Sure he did," she answered, not quite looking Ayisha in the eyes. "He felt real bad about bein' away from you; he said when he got out, he was gonna come see you. I believe he woulda done just that."

Some small light was reborn in the young woman's eyes then. She said, "Thanks," and scurried down the stairs. When she reached the bottom, Chi could hear the bang of the front door.

Surely no harm could come from giving an orphaned girl a crumb of faith that she'd been loved. Chi trusted that her grandmother would have understood.

As they rode up in the elevator, Kick grumbled, "What about that doorman? Are you sure he's cool?" The elevator had mirrors on the side walls; she scowled at her reflection.

"I bring my friends here all the time. He's used to it," Devon assured her.

"How come you never brought me here before?"

Hands on his narrow hips, Devon struck a pose. "Usually I have *gentlemen* callers," he vamped.

Kick ignored the attempt at levity. "And you're sure your mom's not home?"

"I told you, she's with her boyfriend in East Hampton all weekend."

The elevator stopped on the twelfth floor; the two stepped out into a carpeted hallway. Fresh flowers sprouted from a tall vase across from the elevator doors.

"This is some ritzy titsy place," Kick scoffed.

"Two lawyers, what can I say? They needed to keep up

appearances." Devon did not sound defensive. He pulled a key from the small, embroidered bag he carried, and opened number 1207. They stepped into the foyer of a spacious apartment.

"So what about your dad? Do you see him?"

"Not so much. When they first divorced I did every other weekend with him, but once I began to wear dresses in public, that pretty much stopped." He led the way across champagne-colored carpeting to the kitchen, where he pulled open the door to the refrigerator. "Want some chicken?" he offered, pulling foil-wrapped drumsticks from the shelf.

"Okay." The immaculate kitchen featured a black marble countertop in front of which tall-legged stools were lined up. Kick swung herself onto one and began to attack the chicken leg, still in its foil.

Devon was playing hostess, pulling out take-out containers of potato salad and coleslaw. He patiently slid a plate in front of Kick, lifting the drumstick, and placed a knife and fork at either side.

"Let's not make a fucking production of this, okay," Kick growled. "We gotta be back downtown in an hour."

Chastised, Devon stopped fussing and sat down. "What about your folks?"

"Still together, go figure. They live in Bay City, Michigan, which is pretty much a fuckin' timewarp. My dad sells fuckin' Buicks and plays golf. My mom went back to work when I was about ten—she does accounting for the local department store. It's a big snooze."

"So how'd you get to art school?"

Kick slammed down her fork. "What is this, fuckin' *Biography?* Let's just get the gun and get out of here."

Without a word, Devon began to gather the leftovers and put them back in the refrigerator. He loaded their dishes into the dishwasher and washed his hands. "It's in here," he said.

He led the way into his mother's bedroom, a decorator's fantasy in beige and copper and mauve. To the right of the king-size bed, Devon slid open a drawer in the nightstand and pulled out a .22 Magnum pistol.

Nodding her approval, Kick said, "That oughta do the job.

Is it loaded?"

"I don't know how to check, but I'm pretty sure it is," Devon presented it awkwardly by the handle.

"Careful with that," Kick snapped, "you'll shoot your dick off."

Luanne stared through bottles of colored liquor into the mirror behind the bar. In the dim, reddish light, her face looked unrecognizable to her. She couldn't remember the last time she'd had more than a few sips of beer, but tonight she'd lost count of how many bottles she and Jolene had drunk.

They'd had a couple at the bar over on First Avenue where they'd started out. Then they'd gone to dinner—Indian food, something Luanne couldn't remember ever having eaten—and had one or two more with their spicy meals.

Now they'd landed in a bar on Prince Street, a little neighborhood kind of joint where the crowd was not as young as it had been on First Avenue. Jolene was flirting with some guys over by the jukebox, into which she'd been plunking quarters since they'd arrived, favoring a mix of country western and head-banging rock 'n roll. Both men were in jeans; the tall, balding one wore a T-shirt that nicely fit his lanky frame while his shorter buddy, whose dark blond hair grazed the collar of his sport shirt, was wearing cowboy boots. Jolene was laughing with them, dancing a little to a song Luanne didn't recognize, even though there was no dance floor.

In her woefully optimistic pastel pantsuit, Luanne felt overdressed, ridiculous, years older than Jolene and the two men she'd managed to attract. Luanne stared into the mirror at her graying hair, her mouth without lipstick, the shadows that circled her eyes. Clearly, drinking was improving neither her mood nor her appearance.

Jolene came over then, dragging the men after her. "Eddie, Joe, this is my friend Luanne." She grinned tremendously, as if she'd done a wonderful thing to bring them together.

From this introduction, Luanne was unable to determine which man was who. But Jolene had clearly latched onto the taller of the two—why do the most diminutive women always snag the tall men, Luanne wondered. The blond, whatever his name, was just about Luanne's own height. He bought the next round of drinks.

As she reached for the bottle that was set before her, Luanne tried to determine whether she found him attractive or not. Just then, she caught sight of her wedding ring, and the image sobered her.

"Jolene, why don't you come to the restroom with me?" she announced in a tone that didn't offer the option to decline.

"Why is it that women can't go to the can by themselves?" the tall man complained good-naturedly.

His friend winked. "Oh, they gotta go talk about what they think of us." Then he looked at Luanne and said, "Don't be too long in there. You don't want a beer to get warm or a man to get cold."

Luanne grabbed Jolene by the wrist and hurried her to the back of the bar, where three other women waited outside the door labeled with a skirted stick figure. "I'm not doing this, Jolene."

"Doing what?" Jolene was still moving her hips to the music.

"I'm married." Luanne waved her ring finger in front of her friend. "Don't play dumb with me, Jolene. You are planning to go someplace with Joe—"

"You mean Eddie." Jolene had pulled out a tube of lipstick and was applying it with a surprisingly steady hand.

"Whatever. And I do not want to be left babysitting his buddy."

"Luanne, lighten up. Nothing's gonna happen."

"Get real. It's Saturday night; these guys are out on the town. They're probably here from…where?"

"I forget."

"Jolene, these guys are looking to get laid." There were just two more women ahead of them in line.

"So what, do you have a judgment about that? Christ, Luanne, do you have any idea how hard it is to be a single mom and meet a man, let alone have sex with one?" Jolene's eyes looked mournful.

Luanne put a hand on her friend's shoulder. "No, I don't. Because I *have* a man, and whatever my problems with that situation, breaking my marriage vows is not going to solve them."

"You used to be *such* a wild woman," Jolene pouted. "What happened to you?" It was her turn now to go into the bathroom.

Luanne followed her in and pushed the latch on the door. "What are you talking about, a wild woman?"

Jolene talked through the door of the stall. "Don't you remember, when we were at Labrys? How we'd get fed up with the politics and the lesbians and the health food, and we'd take your car and drive into town and eat burgers and get shitfaced?"

Luanne hadn't remembered. It was another lifetime ago.

"And that guy, my God, that *guy*, what was his name?"

Impatiently, Luanne asked, "What are you talking about? What guy?"

"Now it's your turn not to play dumb with *me*. That guy, oh, I can see him—blue workshirt; dark hair, pretty short when almost every man was wearin' it long. I think he turned out to be a Vietnam vet or something."

Luanne's heart seemed to fall deeper into her body. Jesse. Once more she watched her face in the mirror, watched it turn back into that of a woman she could scarcely remember now.

Jolene prattled on, oblivious to the effect of her words. "I remember you goin' home with *him* the first night you met, and comin' back to Labrys with hickeys all over you. You wore turtlenecks in July because you thought the lesbians would give you shit for sleepin' with the enemy."

She emerged from the stall giggling, but stopped abruptly when she saw the look on Luanne's face. "Honey, what's the matter? Are you okay?"

"I have to go," Luanne said tightly. "I don't want to leave you in the lurch, but I have to get out of here."

"Well, that's okay. I'm a big girl; I know how to get myself in and outta trouble. Do you need me to come with you?"

"No," Luanne assured her. "I'll be fine. I hope this doesn't screw it up for you with whatshisname. Sorry to be a poop." She unlatched the door, and both walked back into the bar. Luanne headed toward the door.

"Could I ask one favor?" Jolene tugged her sleeve.

"Sure."

"If Ruthie gets back before I do, can you just look after Roger?" Jolene made an apologetic grin.

"Of course I will," Luanne promised, and walked out into the night.

The rain had stopped and the air had cooled a bit. The streets were crowded with people in the midst of their Saturday evening. She didn't know exactly where she was, and she hoped a cab driver could get her back to Rivington Street, but when she thought of the loft, she wasn't ready to go back there yet. So she walked, in a direction she guessed was uptown, along streets where she hoped she would be safe. She clutched her purse more closely to her body.

She kept hearing Jolene's voice, "You used to be *such* a wild woman. What happened to you?"

A presence seemed to walk behind her, insistent as a tiny hand tugging at her elbow. It whispered, "What about Luanne *Conley*? What about the one you've tried to leave behind?" The face in the mirror. The one who went to Labrys on her own. The one who slept with Jesse and let him cover her body with his marks. She felt the effort of breath heaving in her chest. She never walked anywhere in Detroit.

Something was happening to her, of this Luanne was certain. The woman she'd once been was catching up to her, moving back into her bones, fully occupying her skin, the face in the mirror becoming hers. She had needed to leave the bar because something was coming loose in her, something no building could contain.

The memory came from her womb, not her brain, a visceral, sensate thing; it spread through her body until it filled her living frame, stretching its dimensions to precisely fit the breadth of her inner landscape.

She'd returned from Labrys without a root, and found nothing in which to plant herself anew. The terrain of feminism had withered her, its harsh, acrid ground, yet there was no way she could set down again in the alluvial dust of her family home.

And so she had drifted across the recession-wracked territory of late-Seventies Detroit, hungry for some nutrient she could neither name nor locate. She never saw Jesse again, but one of those nights with him, she didn't even know which one, had provided the spark, a precious bud. She could feel it even now, all these years later, the swelling inside her like a promise or a threat, the gathering knot of tissue and blood, the root.

But she had pulled it, plucked it from the soil of her body. Even now she could remember the glare of the bulb in her eyes as she lay on her back, hips spread wide as their flexibility would allow. The nurses had been abrupt and matter-of-fact; they had given her a local anesthetic, told her she'd feel nothing, but Luanne knew she had felt it all, could feel it still. There, on Twenty-eighth Street, her womb contracted, her ovaries cramped, those hands once more reached into her, their instruments, unearthing that radicular flesh.

She hadn't asked them; they'd warned her not to ask, but it didn't matter—she knew anyway, knew the baby, the little curled fist of a life, had been a girl. Luanne Conley didn't know if she believed in God, but she did believe in punishment. And years later, when Ted was born, she knew that she had lost that girl forever, the phantom child she could only nurture in her dreams.

Seated on the blue bedspread in this blank, anonymous hotel room, Elena found her respiration had grown shallow, her lungs scarcely billowing with breath. As she struggled to take in air, there were pains in her chest, cold and sharp, and she was swept with a surge of fear. Not another heart attack, she chided herself, as if she could scold herself out of it.

She was holding the address book open to the page with Ricardo's name, her body curled on its side on the bed, the leather book pressed just below her diaphragm. She closed her eyes and willed her breath to slow and deepen, and after a while the tightness in her chest began to ease.

She could almost breathe her way back to those days at Georgetown, days that now seemed a lifetime ago. Ricardo had dated a little then, those few *gringas* who saw in his *indio* features and exotic background the opportunity for revolt against all that their parents held sacred. She did not date at all. Men did not figure in her plans. Men, she knew, had somehow always known, were dangerous for women. Not for her the role of submissive *esposa*, devoted, sacrificing *madre*, her own life torn from her like a fragile web.

It was not until after they'd both passed the bar exam that Ricardo fell in love with her, their easy camaraderie stiffening with an intensity she found at first amusing, then annoying, and finally frightening. She never slept with him, and though he often claimed to be moved past the point of endurance, he never pushed her to make love with him. In his heart, she believed, he was a traditional man; he wanted to marry a virgin.

What Elena remembered most about that time was that the more he declared his undying devotion, the more her heart recoiled. Despite the respect he professed for her, she saw he cared more for what he wanted than for her needs. She had told him when they first met that she would never marry; now he was intent on changing her mind. Her ally turned to adversary. When at last she severed her friendship with Ricardo Zunaya, it was like tearing away a chunk of her own skin.

It was not until 1982 that she had seen him again. To her amazement he was calling himself Richard, and he worked for the Justice Department under the Reagan Administration. CORR was fighting a test case on abortion rights that was slated to be heard by the Supreme Court. She ran into Ricardo when he appeared to file a brief urging the Court to uphold the state's right to restrict abortion.

Over dinner he confessed that he had followed her career, always fearing they would wind up opponents on a case like this. She lectured him for an hour on the importance to Chicanas of reproductive rights and chastised him for abandoning his values, even his identity.

"What's the idea of calling yourself 'Richard'?" she'd demanded. "Do they call you 'Rick' at the office?"

But really, Elena thought now, who was she to talk? The dark skirt wrinkling under her weight was nothing but a uniform; English the language of her thoughts and dreams.

Ricardo had made no effort to justify his choices. He had only looked across the dinner table with genuine sorrow and said, "Oh, Elena. You never should have turned me down." And, seeing her expression of surprise and discomfort, he added, "I promised you I would never forget."

When Elena made love with him that night, their coupling was passionate and tender as it might have been years before, but it was also suffused with sadness. Before they fell asleep he asked her one last time to marry him. "It's all I ever wanted, Elena," he whispered into her hair.

Gently she turned in his embrace to stare deep into his eyes. "*Lo siento, mi hermano,*" she told him. "It is something I cannot do."

She had not seen him since that night, fourteen years ago. He lived in New York now, a partner in a prestigious corporate firm. Each Christmas he faithfully sent her a card, which was how she came to have his address in the small book she still clutched to her rib cage.

She was not an impetuous person. She measured every gesture, weighed each word, always calculating her course of action for maximal effect. So she could not explain to herself what she did next. Maybe it was the dream, or the memory, so long pushed down, that was pressing her chest like a heavy fist. Maybe it was the tiredness she could not chase out of her bones, or the spasms of pain that wreathed her heart.

Without sitting up, without analyzing her reasons for doing it, without planning what she would say, without knowing whether it was late or early, Elena reached for the phone and dialed the number she had written next to his name. When she heard Ricardo's voice, she would simply say, "It's Elena," and then she would wait to see what happened.

There was a long ring, then another, then a third. Perhaps he is out, she considered, and almost laid the receiver back in its cradle. Instead she continued to count the rings and pace her breath accordingly, as if each exhalation could move her closer to hearing his voice.

At last the ring was interrupted and she heard the word, "Hello?" It sounded clogged with sleep.

"Ricardo Zunaya, please," Elena requested in the tone she used with secretaries and administrative assistants, the one that always got her put through to the person in charge.

"Ricardo?" The voice on the other end of the line was flat, midwestern, Anglo. Female. "Oh, you mean Richard. He's in Washington. May I help you? I'm his wife."

Elena pressed her eyelids shut at the same time she closed the leather book and let it drop to the floor with a dull thud. The blue walls of the room loomed above her, leaning closer, surrounding her in their empty embrace. "No," she whispered, tired right through to her core. "*Gracias, pero no.*"

Night drew a filmy curtain of darkness over the city, a veil of cinder that blotted the stars. Kendra unbolted the door to the crumbling warehouse, and the sky disappeared, giving way to a thin, watery light cast on walls of scarred concrete.

As the young woman led the way up five steep flights of musty stairs, Lee grumbled, "I'm too old for this." Inspired as she tried to be by the undulation of Kendra's ass ascending before her, she found the setting put a damper on her lust. Her knees ached from the climb, and the squalor of the dank old building did not fuel the aura of romance.

The loft they entered after Kendra released three locks was large and filthy, full of decrepit furniture scavenged from curbside and strange configurations of objects arrayed in a manner meant to be artistic. Perhaps there had been a time when Lee might have found the scene exotic, the proverbial walk on the wild side, but now it only wearied her. She longed for the neutral luxury of her hotel room, its gleaming tub outfitted with Jacuzzi jets, the chocolates left on the pillow like a lover's departing kiss, crisp sheets turned down, inviting.

That was where she'd intended for them to end up, after a quiet, elegant dinner in the Village, but Kendra had refused. "It'll be so uptight, so straight!" she'd whined in protest. "Come to my place—it'll be more fun."

It was a tactic Lee had used herself, a fatal blend of reprimand and promise that had proved effective in countless situations. Now here she stood in this grimy loft on the edge of what was once the Bowery.

Sound was blasting from some walled-off corner at the far end of the room, the same robotic, vicious beat Lee remembered from the club the night before. She cocked an eyebrow in question.

"That's just Arturo," the young woman explained with a breezy wave in the direction of the noise. "One of my roommates. Don't worry, he's cool."

At this news Lee slumped into a chair, raising a swarm of dust from the hideous polyester spread that draped it. The frantic bass called forth an echoing throb behind her eyes.

"Isn't that a riot?" Kendra giggled, pointing to the bedspread's lurid pattern. "Nimo got it on Orchard Street for three bucks." There was marvel in her voice for someone who could glean treasure with such economy.

Lee could only imagine how this gamin would regard her own Malibu hideaway, its careful landscaping, its lavish Southwest decor. She had paid hundreds of thousands of dollars to make her home exactly the way she wanted it, but these kids could only have disdain for such display, reveling instead in the tacky, the banal.

"Just how many roommates do you have?" she questioned, trying to keep the sourness from her voice. They might as well make love in Grand Central Station, for all the privacy afforded by this loft.

"Four," Kendra answered, slithering onto the arm of the chair, pressing herself next to Lee. In lieu of a shirt, the girl was wearing a long-line bra, recycled from a thrift shop and dyed black, the bra cups cone-shaped, pointed as missiles. Perched as she was, she afforded an enticing view of her cleavage. "It's the only way we can swing the lease. You'll probably get to meet them. Except for Trina; she's the video artist, remember? But she's out in San Francisco for a week."

Lee made a halfhearted stab at an expression of regret over the missing Trina, about whom Kendra must have spoken but

Lee remembered nothing. She was determined to maintain a semblance of charm, though a dark mood stalked her.

She needed to regain the upper hand. She'd accomplished her first seduction at the precocious age of ten; the object of her attentions, Delores di Carlo, had been twelve at the time, with a body that had burst abruptly into maturity only months earlier. Lee had had forty years of practice since that sweet initiation, and in that time she had rarely met refusal.

Fingering the soft hollow at the base of the young woman's throat, Lee inquired huskily, "Where's your room?"

Kendra met her gaze and with a breathless, "This way," led her in the direction of the screaming sound. At the far end of the loft, both corners had been walled off; Kendra headed for the room that was not Arturo's.

A bare bulb in a wall socket illuminated the bleak space and its random contents. Lee had tried to prepare herself for the aging mattress on the floor, but when she saw it, sheets knotted in a lump and somewhat less than clean, her spirits wilted. Aside from the mattress, there was a trunk, from which spewed an assortment of underwear; a portable clothing rack hung with various raiments of leather and spandex; some piles of books, mostly art criticism and translations of French philosophers; a portable CD player; and a rough-hewn crate that served as nightstand and dressing table. Next to the bed, half-hidden by the tangled blanket, lounged a long, thick dildo the color of licorice, attached to a leather belt.

"Do you think he could turn that down?" Lee yelled to be heard above the roar of music. Her tone was frayed, but she tried to sugarcoat it, adding, "I want to feel like I'm all alone with you."

Obedient, Kendra left the room and a moment later the wall of noise dissolved. When she returned she reported, "He was just going out anyway," and gestured for Lee to have a seat on the mattress. She made no effort to straighten the sheets or clear the clutter from the room.

Still, the silence was a balm, and Lee felt herself relax into it. The secret to seduction, she believed, was all in knowing *where* to begin. She reached for Kendra's hand and pulled her to a sitting position on the bed, then nuzzled close behind her. She slid one elastic strap from a slender shoulder, the shoulder without the tattoo of a black widow, and kissed the skin where the strap had left a ridge, teasing it with her teeth. She traveled up the neck to the earlobe, tasting the salty tang on her lips and tongue, leaving gooseflesh in her wake.

Lazily, her fingers worked to untwine the skinny braid that snaked down the middle of Kendra's back, discarding the rubber band, untwisting the strands until fine ringlets hung to mid-spine, their jet color harsh against gold-tinged skin.

"You gotta let your hair go natural," Lee advised as her fingers wound through the curls. "I bet you're incredible as a blonde."

Kendra whirled to face her with a derisive snort. "You sound like my fucking mother."

It occurred to Lee that since she was probably about the same age as the lady in question, she might do well to avoid the comparison. Still, as she ran her palm across the fine black bristles of short-cropped hair that covered most of Kendra's scalp, she couldn't help but muse, "I swear I just don't understand why girls don't wanna be *pretty* anymore."

"Where did it ever get us?" Kendra sneered and swung her body off the bed. She began to peel the tight, black skirt down her hips and over her thighs. She paused, glancing up. "Do you still wanna do this, or what?"

There was a hollowness in the young woman's question, a cheerful indifference that brought a stab of fear to Lee's belly, an icy finger of apprehension protruding into her spleen. She was quick to suppress it, shaking it off with a bemused toss of her head, nodding and coaxing, "C'mere. Let me do that for you."

Kendra allowed the skirt to drop around her ankles and carelessly stepped away from it, leaving behind its collapsed cylinder like a deflated tire abandoned at roadside. Lee's spirits brightened as the girl came toward her, a vision in the old-fashioned brassiere—one strap still slipped from her shoulder—and blood-red fishnet tights.

Kendra knelt on the mattress while Lee expertly released

each of the twelve hooks that fastened the undergarment. As the corset fell away Lee caught the flash of silver—the hoop that pierced clear through the young woman's left nipple.

She found herself reluctant to examine it too closely; it made her a little squeamish even to think of it. Still, Lee cupped the breast in one hand and murmured, "That must have hurt."

"Yeah," Kendra agreed with a glint in her eye, her voice laden with feeling that Lee could not quite interpret.

She pulled the slender body on top of her own and tried to bury her uneasiness in the abandon of lovemaking. As Lee stroked the length of the girl's thighs, Kendra seemed cooperative enough, yet she remained strangely unmoved, some part of her elusive, distracted, almost inattentive. Lee liked it best when a femme was active in her response, not trying to gain control but fully participant in taking all Lee had to give.

But she didn't mind a challenge; she saw it as an opportunity to ply her considerable skill. Perhaps the young woman just didn't care for foreplay; maybe it was time to get down to serious business. Lee settled Kendra onto her stomach, then eased the fishnet tights down over the delicate hips. It was then Lee noticed the cluster of welts that covered the pale skin of the girl's ass, a crisscross of raised slashes, with the hue of an angry blush. With a finger she traced the path of one large weal and asked, "What happened to you?" She could not keep the horror from her voice.

Kendra half-turned, raised up on one elbow and gazed at the older woman with curiosity. "I was at a party," she explained with patient matter-of-factness. "I guess things got a little out of hand. Usually the 'cats' don't make any marks at all."

As she spoke she fished under one of the pillows and produced the "cat"—a cat-'o-nine-tails. Its leather-covered handle was attached with nine leather strips, each about a foot long and knotted on the end. She proceeded to demonstrate its use by lashing lightly at her inner thigh.

As she observed Lee's dumbstruck expression, a sneer of amusement began to pucker Kendra's face; it was dawning on her that she had the power to shock this unflappable butch, and the fact induced in her both delight and contempt.

"It's how I like to fuck," she continued. "I thought you knew. I like it hard or I can't feel it."

A fissure was opening in Lee's chest, a tear that pressed with the weight of boulders and yet revealed a stupefying emptiness at its core. She longed to flee, lift herself up from this makeshift excuse for a bed and escape into the Manhattan streets. But Lee Bergman did not run from women, nor did she ever admit defeat in lovemaking.

Instead, she crafted a knowing smile onto her lips, and eased her body beside the young woman's. "So you like it hard, huh baby?" A cruel purr rose in her voice. "Well, I think we can do something about that."

With a forceful tug she turned Kendra over onto her back and wrenched apart her thighs. Savagely she pinched each nipple, willing to bruise, as the body beneath her began to writhe. She taunted, "Tell me how much you want it, baby," determined to make the girl beg.

Beg she did, and for a while Lee was caught up in the game of it, the sheer mastery she felt as she donned the brutal persona required to fulfill her part. She envisioned herself growing large with it, taller, her features more angular, chiseled and ruthless.

But Kendra wanted more than just the play of dominance. It was not enough to be obedient to Lee's commands, for her wrists to be shackled with handcuffs, for her vaginal walls to be pummeled by Lee's taut fist, striking inside her again and again like a piston in a powerful machine. She wanted more than rough sex; she wanted clamps to squeeze her nipples to the color of raw meat, and the blister of hot wax spilled from candles against her tender skin. She wanted pain, sharp and immediate; nothing else seemed real to her.

"Harder," she pleaded, her voice breathy and raw with need.

"Hit me," she begged, and Lee raised her arm, palm wedged to strike. It was in the hand's trajectory from sky to the side of Kendra's face that the earth once more cracked open, and Lee felt the emptiness swallow her like death.

The hand did not make impact; its arc aborted, swung dully to Lee's side where it hung useless as she said, "I hate this. I'm sorry. It's just not sexy to me."

It was chilling, the ease with which Kendra recovered herself, the veneer of indifference returning to her eyes. "Wanna get me out of these," she suggested, nodding at her cuffed wrists, her voice vacant and flat.

Lee complied, her hands trembling a little as she fumbled with the key. She had the urge to talk about it, as if words might forge a rope to keep the connection, however fragile, but Kendra was closing like a fist, her jaw set, her gestures brusque, traveling away from her as if at the speed of light. The young woman did not look at Lee at all as she rolled beneath the sour sheet, pulling it tight over her body in a gesture that did not seek company.

Lee stood awkwardly, a bit unsteady on her feet. "I'm sorry," she said again and then, after her words were met with silence, "I guess I should be shoving off."

"Yeah, too bad." Kendra shrugged one shoulder, her face a brittle mask. "I thought we'd have some fun."

Once Lee reached the street, the sky was full of mist. It clung to her clothes and swirled gray above her head. She did not want to think about what had happened, wanted it to scab over quickly and leave no scar. She told herself the dampness on her cheeks was no more than the wet caress of fog. In vain she searched the deserted streets for a taxi, then began walking briskly toward Chinatown, where she knew the streets would still be full of lights and traffic, and morning would still seem a long way off.

Chapter 16

Once JJ's taillights blurred and blended with the stream of other beacons and then disappeared, Gwen did what any self-respecting New Yorker does when she's got the blues: she walked the boulevards. However bummed out one might be, there was something absorbing about the streets of the city, providing ceaseless distraction. The Rasta dude toking on a spliff as he ambled down Broadway. The petite, elaborately coifed woman who looked remarkably like the toy gray poodle she led on a rhinestone leash.

Though her feet hurt, and her shoes were flimsy with rain, she walked. And as she walked, she worried. She worried about Emma, though she supposed Emma was past worry now. She worried about the man who'd killed her; was he out tonight, stalking other prey? Was there a young woman who, at that very moment, was getting dressed to go out, fixing her hair, trying on different skirts, a young woman who would not be alive by morning? And was there more Gwen could be doing to save her?

She walked up Ninth Avenue in Chelsea, past crowded restaurants and darkened shop windows. She worried about JJ. Although the fear taking shape in her mind was that JJ would leave her, she'd spent enough years in therapy to recognize the idea for the projection it was. She was the one pushing JJ away, feeling the pull toward Lee. Lee, of all people! After all those years in Twelve Step meetings one would think she'd have put her self-destructive tendencies to rest.

And she worried about Howard. In all the years as her sponsor he'd never been pissed at her the way he was tonight. And all she'd tried to do was help him.

She used to like to drink or get stoned because that shut off the worry in her head. She remembered herself as being a lot more fun when she was loaded, when she didn't give a fuck about what anybody thought.

But she was sober now and so she walked and worried. What would she do if JJ and Howard had finally grown fed up with her? It was Howard's voice that interrupted these thoughts, "Ged awff the pity-pot, dollface."

Self-absorbed. Self-indulgent. Self-pitying. She knew the list of her character defects was endless.

As was often true when she was most tired, she was buzzing with restless energy. It was addiction, Howard had explained to her so many times; she was high on adrenaline.

Wired as she was, she was in no hurry to go home. She didn't want to be alone there, and she definitely didn't want to be with her houseguests, whoever might have dared to return after she'd unceremoniously tossed them out. She just wanted to stay in the sheltering arms of the gritty streets. She wanted to browse the stolen merchandise laid out on the sidewalks, trade insults with the pack of teenage boys who cruised her for a block or two.

She turned to cut across town on Twenty-third. She bought a coffee to go, drained it in a few blocks, then bought another. Yes, the caffeine might be bad for her, but it kept her walking. And at this moment walking was her prayer.

If JJ decides it's time to go, she told herself, *you'll be okay. You've known since the beginning that it was only a matter of time. What can you expect from a twenty-nine-year-old? She's gonna move on. You've got your work; you've got your program. You've survived a lot worse than this.*

When Lee had broken up with her, she'd cried every day for two months, racking sobs that came from depths she hadn't even known she possessed. It was like a spell that would sweep over her, unbidden as a sudden rainstorm, usually in the afternoons but sometimes late at night. Although, in the tempest of their four years together, it could have just as easily been herself who ended it, the fact that it wasn't allowed her to access a well of victimhood—cultivated in the Kubacky family home and nurtured by the pint of scotch she was downing every day—and she'd made an art out of suffering that betrayal. She'd even made a performance piece about it, an elaborate ritual of self-indulgent grief that actually did serve to purge something.

At the end of two months she'd stopped weeping, and she hadn't cried since. Sobriety hadn't come for another five years, and gratitude to have been delivered from the emotional maelstrom of that relationship took longer still. Howard always reminded her about keeping "an attitude of gratitude." Howard.

All right, if Howard decides to stop being your sponsor, she told herself, *well, this city is full of recovering drunks who would probably take you on.*

"Quit thinkin' about yerself," she heard Howard say as she turned down Second Avenue. "Service is recovery. Get outta yer head, do something fer somebody else." Fifteen feet in front of Gwen, a homeless woman was seated on the sidewalk, her back against a brick building. She sat on a square of cardboard, soggy from the rain. Even in the heat she wore a red knit ski cap, and she clutched a tiny black kitten. Gwen fiddled in her bag for change, dropped all of it into the woman's Styrofoam cup. She heard a strangled, "God bless."

Farther up the block, the lights of a deli beckoned. She was supposed to eat every four hours or her blood sugar plummeted. Pizza with Lee had been eons ago. Gwen stepped inside, but the notion of food seemed foreign and unappealing—salad too raw and indigestible, cooked food too gluey, snack food too salty and greasy. She settled on a banana and a carton of soymilk, then went back to nab a small can of cat food with a pop-top, which she carried back to the homeless woman. Gwen ended up giving her the banana too, but the woman shook her head when Gwen offered the soymilk. This she drank as she continued down the street, the beige thickness coating her tongue.

It was almost eleven by the time she reached Alphabet City. The streets were alive with music and fights and sex and car horns and drugs and cops. Live blues spilled out the open door of a bar. Yuppies waited in line for a table outside the newest trendy restaurant. Saturday night in the 'hood. She crossed Houston, her momentum finally slackening, and practically limped her way down Rivington. She was praying that her houseguests were asleep. She had finally worn herself down to the point where she wouldn't sit up for the rest of the night obsessing, if she could just be alone and not interact with anyone else tonight. Sated with exhaustion, she climbed the steps to her loft. As her key unlatched the deadbolt, she saw the lights in the studio were low, and felt relief. She kicked off her shoes before she even looked up; only then did she come face to face with the gun that Kick was pointing in her direction.

"Hurry up and lock the door behind you," the young woman ordered. "Don't even think about running away."

Gwen couldn't have run if her life depended on it. Her limbs felt as if they were moving through heavy cream. She wasn't processing any of it. She felt fatigued beyond reason, hypoglycemic, nowhere near her right mind. It would be a hard call as to which of them was the more dangerous in that moment.

Still, some inarticulate instinct made Gwen only pretend to turn the deadbolt. Then she faced Kick. Ignoring the weapon, she said, "Kick, what the fuck are you doing here? Do you know what time it is?"

Peg interjected, "Gwen, come in, we're just waiting for everybody to get here."

Gwen turned to stare at her in amazement. "Peg, are you in on this?"

"Not exactly, but I've been telling these young people to take action, and now Kick has."

"Stupid cunt, quit yappin'. Get your hands up, and get the fuck over here."

Only as Gwen moved closer did her eyes take in the whole scene: Devon in his dress, wringing his hands. Peg, improbably beside him. She had her hands on her hips. She was missing her glasses, and without them her whole body inclined anxiously forward, as if worried that she might miss something essential.

And on the floor, trussed with rope, mouth gagged with duct tape, was a young Black man, covered in sweat. His face was bruised; blood caked one cheek. He looked up at Gwen as she approached and gurgled an imploring noise. Kick sent the steel toe of her boot into his ribs. "Shut up."

"Who is that? What is going on?" Gwen demanded.

"That's the prick who killed Emma," Kick announced. "And now he's going to find out what it's like to be at someone's mercy."

"You let them in here?" Gwen turned on Peg. "How dare you bring this into my home?"

"They rang the buzzer, said they left something. I didn't know they had him with them until they got up here."

"Kick, this is crazy. This is *illegal*. Nothing good can possibly come from this," Gwen implored her.

"Yo, all you'all been yap-yap-yappin' all weekend about is fe-mi-nist power," Kick taunted. "So here it is. I took back the fuckin' night!" She returned to the man on the floor, stuck the gun against his head. "Yeah, you were a big man, right? Who's got the power now, motherfucker?"

Gwen knelt beside the man, put her hand on his shoulder. "Are you Jersey?" she asked him, and he nodded. She slowly squeezed his shoulder in a gesture she hoped would be reassuring.

"Get the fuck away from him. I mean it, right now." The gun poked into her back. "Sit over here." Kick pushed her roughly toward a folding chair.

She had to be calm now. She couldn't appear to be afraid. She'd have to move slowly and think very carefully. Her senses grew more alert, as they did when she was in the middle of a performance, every instinct alive. She looked for the light sources, the objects she might use as weapons. She struggled to recall the self-defense classes she'd taken twenty years ago. She tried to imagine what it would feel like to be shot. She thought: *Where's my phone*, and attempted to scan the room for it without being too obvious.

She took a deep breath. "So, Kick, what's the plan here?" She willed her voice calm.

"We're gonna try him for his crimes," Kick said.

"Try him, you mean, in court?" Gwen asked, though she knew that wasn't what she meant.

"No fucking court. No cops, no judge. I thought you didn't believe in the system," she sneered. Then glumly, she asked, "Where's Dana? I thought *everyone* was supposed to be here tonight. I think we should all have the chance to cross-examine this bastard."

"That's good," Gwen told her, seeing the chance to stall for time. "We should definitely wait; I know everyone will want to do that." She couldn't envision Dana in this scene, couldn't begin to see Emma's mother cowed by this bully.

Kick was volatile, not easily managed. "I'm not gonna wait all fucking night."

Okay, maybe she just needed to play out this scene—the women confronting the accused. But Jersey might not even be a suspect. She recalled her conversation with Luce earlier this afternoon, which now seemed like years ago. Was there some way to tell Kick about the white man who'd been harassing Emma in the club?

She glanced at Peg. How could she possibly think this is a good idea? So everyone confronts Jersey in a mock trial; did Peg imagine that at the end Kick would say, "Sorry, we made a mistake," untie the ropes and let the man walk free? She tried to figure out how far Devon would go to support Kick. He didn't seem like the gun-slinging type.

She had to get to her phone. Elena had been using it in the kitchen earlier, Gwen recalled, and yes, then she'd had it in the bathroom before JJ picked her up for the meeting. That would be the best, if it were still there. Assuming Kick would let her go to the toilet by herself.

She understood it was her role to defuse the situation, to make sure that everyone got out of this unhurt. Perhaps it was alcoholic grandiosity, but she believed she was the only one who could do it. She looked at Jersey, curled on the floor. His feet were bare; they must have taken his shoes. His tank top was yellow and boasted a bright green marijuana leaf on the front. The shirt was stained with sweat and dirt and blood. He wore baggy jeans, streaked with grime. His hair was in short dreads, brown streaked with peroxided blond. He was small-boned, delicate. Nothing about him seemed capable of hurting Emma or anyone else.

To keep Kick talking, Gwen asked, "So how did you get this guy? Boy, even the cops couldn't find him," she flattered.

Kick puffed up, as Gwen hoped. "Motherfucker left town after he killed Emma. But I asked around, found out he was supposed to play a gig tonight. Devon and I waited for him outside his crib."

His crib, Gwen thought. These white kids spoke the language of *gangstas*. Her students did it, too. They picked it up, she supposed, from watching rap videos on MTV.

"That was smart," she continued. "How did you get him to Rivington Street?" Peg squinted her eyes, suspicious, but Gwen played her off, averting her gaze.

"My van," Kick said. *That's good*, Gwen thought. *At least she didn't compound her crime with auto theft. Maybe if we can explain to him that it's all been a mistake, he won't press charges.* But she was way ahead of herself.

"That is awesome," Gwen told her, and she seemed to believe it. "Look, I hate to bring this up, but I really need to pee."

Kick shook her head. "Nah, that's not gonna happen."

Gwen tried to sound more pleading. "Kick, I've been walking for the last three hours, and I had two take-out cups of coffee. Please don't ask me to piss my pants in my own house."

Kick thought for a moment, trying to decide whether to trust Gwen. "Devon goes with you," she ordered.

He didn't look one bit happy about it. He followed Gwen to the other end of the loft, and was about to step through the curtain behind her, when she stopped him. "Please," she whispered. "I've gotta change my tampon. You can just wait here, can't you?" He gratefully agreed; no matter how trans, men still had that menstrual aversion.

Thank God, her cordless was sitting beside the toilet where she'd left it, and it still had a little juice. Howard's number was already programmed into speed dial, so she peed as the phone was dialing. She waited to hear the beep of his answering machine before she flushed, and over the *whoosh* from the ancient pipes, she said quickly, "Howard, it's Gwen. Get over to my place on Rivington as fast as you can. This is 911, I mean it." She pressed "End" as the water gurgled down the toilet bowl, and turned the ringer off. Then she placed the phone in the wastebasket under some wads of tissue, where she prayed it would remain undiscovered.

She prayed too that Devon hadn't heard her and that Howard would. She washed her hands. In the mirror, the details of her face were extra sharp, every sensation heightened, as if she were high on acid.

Kick insisted on frisking Gwen after she emerged. Gwen kept her face impassive as Kick probed her waist, patted between her thighs. "Sit down over here," she directed, and Gwen did so, without argument. It must be midnight.

"All right," she announced. "I'm tired of waiting. Let's get this thing started."

Peg protested, "I thought you wanted everyone to be here."

Kick ignored her and ordered Devon, "Help me get him up."

She yanked the young man under his arms while Devon grabbed his feet; together they hoisted him roughly into a folding chair. They wound additional rope around his torso, propping him upright, binding him to the metal back of the chair. There was a distinct smell of piss as his bladder released, a stain bloomed on the front of his jeans.

"Hey, asshole," Kick whacked him on the back of the head. Involuntarily, Peg gasped.

Kick said, "Sorry, Gwen."

It wasn't the fact that she'd kidnapped someone and brought him into Gwen's home and was holding all of them hostage that she was sorry for; it was that there was urine on her chair and floor. It was such a surreal moment Gwen almost laughed. But her goal was to not provoke Kick, so she said, "I can clean it later."

Kick stood before the bound young man, grasped a handful of his dreads and yanked his head up. "Jersey Mowatt, you sit here before us accused of the brutal rape and cold-blooded murder of a young woman who had her whole life before her. Emma Firestein—remember her?"

The young man's eyes grew wider. He tried to emit sounds that were choked by his gagged mouth.

"What's that?" Kick's grin was evil. "You plead guilty?" The truculent young woman Gwen had barely observed for the last two days was gone; she'd been taken over by a glittering-eyed psychopath. For the first time Gwen felt truly afraid of her.

"Kick, you should let him speak," Peg said. There was a note of concern in her voice, quite different from her earlier exhilaration.

"Oh, I should, should I? Do you think he gave Emma a chance to speak before he strangled her with his bare hands?" Kick's forehead was beaded with sweat beneath her brush cut. "Besides,—" she began to pace, "—all he's gonna do is tell a bunch of fucking lies. Motherfucking phony cocksucking lies." With each word her voice escalated until she was yelling, her face deep red.

"Who lied to you?" Gwen asked in her softest voice. It was a technique her therapist used.

"My slimeball, golf-playing, child-molesting, rotting prick of a father," Kick answered, and her tone was suddenly matter-of-fact, as if Gwen had asked her the time.

She regained her focus then, returned to stand before Jersey. "The authorities are just men in charge, and they stand up for other men. Women have to take the power into our own hands. That's what you all have taught me."

"But Kick," Peg pleaded, suddenly waking up to how serious the situation was. "The answer is not to become just like the men who perpetrate these crimes. Yes, we want to hold them accountable, but we don't want to turn into the oppressor. That's not the kind of power we want."

"Wanna bet? I want the power to do to them what they do to us. It's the only kind of power they understand."

She raised the gun, aimed it at Jersey's head.

"Whoa, Kick..." Devon began to protest.

"Wait a minute," Gwen begged. "You can't just execute him! He might not even be the one who did it. I talked to someone today who saw Emma at the club. She said a white guy was stalking her that night."

"Oh, goddess, are you serious?" Peg put her face in her hands.

Even Devon piped up with, "Kick, we can't do somethin' unless we're sure—"

"Don't try to jerk me around!" Kick howled. "Don't. Mess. With. Me. This is the fucking guy. *I* found him, and I'm gonna..."

She was interrupted by the creak of the door opening. Expecting Howard, Gwen whirled to face in that direction.

Kick yelled, "I thought I told you to lock that door, bitch," and in the next second there was a loud boom as the gun went off. Time seemed to slow as the sound etched itself into Gwen's nervous system, as if the neurons themselves were exploding, as if for the rest of her life she would hear nothing but that sound.

But her body didn't wait for anything. She took a flying leap at Kick, knocking her to the ground. The gun skittered out of her hand. "Get that," Kick screamed to Devon as she struggled to throw Gwen off. Kick outweighed her, but Gwen was in better shape. She hung on, even as Kick punched her.

"Peg, help me," she shrieked and Peg did, decisively setting her full bulk on top of Kick. Even with two of them, Gwen didn't know how long they'd be able to hold her.

"Devon!" Kick shouted again.

But her partner in crime had moved to the door, where he was howling, "You shot her. Christ, Kick, she's bleeding."

"Who?" Gwen demanded, unable to divert one ounce of attention from restraining Kick.

"Ayisha," he reported, before the thud as he dropped to the floor in a dead faint.

It was then Howard burst through the open door with three other men. "NYPD," he announced, "everybody freeze." All had their weapons drawn. Two uniformed police and a second detective entered and surrounded the group while Howard knelt beside Ayisha and spoke into his phone, "We need paramedics at 267 Rivington Street. Fifth floor. Gunshot wound."

"Who fired?" another cop asked. Gwen recognized him from Emma's funeral. Detective Johnson.

"She did," Peg said, indicating Kick.

"You two get up. We'll take it from here."

In the presence of the officers, Kick had gone limp. She seemed almost comatose as the cops grabbed each of her arms. Gwen left Peg to explain what had just transpired as she, in slow motion, crossed the room toward Ayisha, terrified of what she would see.

The young woman was bleeding a lot from her left arm, but was conscious, sprawled on the splintery floor. A spray of red fanned the wall next to the door. Howard knelt beside her, using his jacket as a tourniquet. "It's not too bad," he was telling her. "I know it hurts like hell, and I know it's scary, but you're gonna be okay."

"What were you *doing?*" Ayisha accused Gwen. She must have seen Jersey before she went down.

"Trying to keep this from happening," Gwen told her. She didn't have the strength to say more.

She heard the scream of a siren as the ambulance wedged its way up Rivington Street. The sky outside the window was red, lit by its beacon. She heard the clatter of feet as two paramedics climbed the stairs with a gurney, a man and a woman, skin sallow, eyes tired from the night shift.

Gwen held Ayisha's hand as they took her vital signs, removed Howard's jacket and placed another tourniquet above the wound in her left arm. Then they carefully lifted her onto the gurney and strapped her in.

Howard moved over to Jersey, who had been set free. The young man fended off an offer of an ambulance for himself.

"I didn't know what they was talkin' about." His words tumbled over themselves in his haste to explain. "I was late to go meet Emma; when I got to the club she was gone, I figured she just blew me off, that night I got a call to go to Toledo, gigged with some friends in Ohio. I didn't even know she was dead."

"That's okay, son," Howard reassured him. "We have another suspect in custody." Briefly, he looked over to meet Gwen's eyes, then his focus returned to Jersey. "You're the victim here, not the suspect."

The two officers led Kick in handcuffs down the stairs. Her body was stiff and her eyes had gone hard, glassy as marbles. Devon was revived with a whiff of ammonia, and Detective Johnson read him his rights as he handcuffed him.

"Hey, I didn't do anything..." the young man sputtered a high-pitched protest as they descended the stairs.

Howard said to Jersey, "If you want, I can take your report here."

Jersey shrugged uneasily. He appeared shell-shocked. "I don' know. I never wanted nuthin' to do wid the cops. I guess I'm all right."

Howard was gentle with him. "Here's my card. You don't have to decide tonight. We'll definitely charge her with the shooting, and you can decide what you want to do."

Jersey nodded, still dazed. He wandered to the door. "I don' know where my shoes are," he lamented.

"Why don't I give you a ride home?" Howard offered, and Jersey nodded.

Peg had begun to shake. Gwen could feel her tremors as she grasped Gwen's arm. "You have to believe I never meant for *this* to happen," she entreated. "I never dreamed she would take me literally..."

She looked to Gwen for absolution, but Gwen didn't have it in her to take care of Peg right then. "We'll talk about it later," was all she could bring herself to say, as she extricated herself from Peg's grip. She needed some water.

The ambulance crew had hoisted the gurney and were about to carry it down. The woman paramedic brushed some stray hairs from Ayisha's forehead.

Jersey made his way to the door and stared into Ayisha's face. "I'm sorry you got hurt," he said.

Ayisha, drowsy with pain and blood loss, smiled up at him. "I *knew* you were innocent," she said.

Chapter 17

It was amazing to see her mother dancing, alone and in a bright red dress that clung to her thighs and dipped low at the neck to reveal creamy breasts, nothing like Marilyn would have ever worn, but now it was her favorite dress. She was dancing and singing a tune that was heartstoppingly familiar, though from where Ayisha could not recall.

Then suddenly Ayisha was alone, and she too was wearing a scarlet dress, but hers had a white lace collar and a full skirt. She was nine years old, and she stood at the bottom of a deep well. Darkness surrounded her, but miles above there gleamed a circle of blue light. She had to reach that glowing opening; there, someone awaited her.

She became aware of a rope, then, a long braid, actually, a plait of human hair and dried grasses, strips of cloth and skin, dangling in the air above her head. It swayed there, seductive, seeming to elude her just at the moment when her hand stretched up to grasp it. She strained toward it, struggling to clamber up the rough brick walls in an effort to gain height, leaping from the cold dirt floor to capture the rope's frayed promise.

Finally she discarded the red dress, her child body bare but for a flimsy white slip, and it was then she noticed how her skin was darkening, its ivory warming to the color of fawn, finally deepening to a rich umber. Her brown hands easily clasped the rope, its fibers clutched in her sweating palms. She feared she'd have to shinny her way up, didn't know if she possessed the strength. To her relief she began to be lifted, as if the rope were being hoisted from above. All she had to do was hang on.

The shuddering ascension underway, she pictured the one who would be there to greet her when she reached the top. She pictured a pair of large strong hands, brown as hers were now, tugging the rope, coiling it tight around firm biceps. The light grew nearer until she could almost see over the lip of the well.

Then without warning the rope slackened as if broken or let go, and she was hurtling down the endless tunnel, the rope swinging crazily in the narrow shaft. Just before she hit the ground, she woke up.

In the chair beside her bed sat a young man, his skin a warm brown, his hair in lighter colored dreadlocks. His face was purpled and swollen with bruises, a gash oozed below his right eye. He was staring at her with a great furrow of worry between his eyebrows, and when he noticed her opening her eyes a wide smile spread across his face.

"You awake now, tha's good."

Ayisha blinked, not sure if she was still dreaming, not certain where she was. She didn't think she knew this man who now sat grinning at her as if he'd won something. "I had a bad dream," she whimpered.

"Mus' be the drugs. They dispensin' some whack shit here in de hospital."

The hospital. That explained the sharp smell of disinfectant that scraped the insides of her nose and throat, the too-cold air. She looked down and saw the flimsy gown, stiff white sheets. As she reached to better cover herself a streak of pain shot through her left shoulder. She remembered then: She'd been shot.

"You were there," she marveled, snatches of images beginning to return to her. "But your name is..." she asked him to fill in the blank.

"Jersey." He smiled again. "Jersey Mowatt."

"You're..." She paused. "You knew Emma."

He nodded soberly. "I *met* her. Coupla' weeks ago now."

"They thought you..."

"They thought I killed her," Jersey supplied. He was quiet

for a moment. "I didn't. It's not in me to hurt someone like that."

"I know."

An awkward silence fell between them. Ayisha broke it, asking, "What time is it?"

"'Bout six, I think. I don' wear a watch."

"You been here all night?" she asked, but before he could answer, Chi came into the room, Dana just a step behind her. As always, Chi's face was the ground of a battle between the mask of composure she fiercely wore and the powerful emotions struggling behind it. "'Isha, we came as soon as we heard. Gwen called me and I tracked down Dana."

Dana came over to the bed. Stepping in front of Jersey, she sat on the bed by Ayisha's side and pressed her face into the girl's right shoulder. The hard frames of her glasses pressed against Ayisha's collarbone. In a low murmur, she crooned, "I couldn't bear it if somebody took you too."

Ayisha had never known Dana to be like this.

Jersey had stood and was backing slowly out of the room. When Chi caught his gaze, he hastily explained, "I jus' wan' to make sure she all right."

"You're Jersey?" Chi asked, her look measuring him.

Hearing the name, Dana turned to him. "I'm so sorry..." she began, but could not continue.

"Jersey, this is Dana Firestein. Emma's mother," Chi explained.

The young man's face crumpled with sorrow. "No, ma'am, *I'm* sorry," he extended his right hand, as the left reached up instinctively to hold his heart. Dana took his offered palm and held it. A world passed between them as they stared into each other's eyes.

Luanne had come back to the loft just as the ambulance was pulling away. Seeing all the police cars, she had run up all four flights in her terror that something had happened to Roger. Jolene had returned about three, high as a kite and with a bloom of hickeys on her neck, but she'd sobered up quickly upon seeing the blood on the floor and wall.

Peg called Ruthie as soon as the cops had cleared out, but they'd agreed that Ruthie not wake Roger for a few more hours. She arrived about half an hour past sunrise, with the sleepy boy in tow. Jolene scooped him into her arms and began to weep as she held him tight, as Peg clung to Ruthie.

Elena arrived at seven thirty, dressed uncharacteristically in jeans and a blue work shirt, her dark hair long and loose, not wound in its usual French twist. She was followed shortly by Kendra, eager for a final interview with Peg for her *Voice* article. She'd had no inkling of what Kick had been planning and, when told the events of the previous night, uttered, "That is lame," with a derisive sigh. By nine, even Lee had joined the group. Whatever had transpired between her and Kendra the night before, they studiously avoided each other now.

Each time someone new walked through the door, the story had to be told again, and Gwen was more than happy to leave that duty to Peg. She felt as if she had no more words inside her.

Howard had spent more than two hours interviewing her and Peg, questioning each woman separately, going over every detail of the episode. Gwen had been amazed at the painstakingly thoroughness of Howard's work. Though he'd been a paragon of professionalism throughout the long night, when she'd reached the point in the story when she'd jumped on Kick, he exploded, "Jesus Christ, Gwen, you coulda been killed."

She'd sat in a state of dumb fascination as the crime scene photographer had taken pictures of every inch of her loft, and once the photographer was done and Gwen had gotten Howard's permission, she set immediately to cleaning the blood-spattered wall and floor. Barefoot, unaware of being still garbed in her poinsettia dress, she filled pail after plastic pail with scalding water, into which she plunged her reddened hands. She scoured the urine from the chair where Jersey had been tied. She'd rearranged the chairs and swept the floor, determined to erase every trace of what had happened, as the women's conversations swirled around her. Snatches of it filtered through her haze of concentration, but she made no attempt to make sense of it.

"Has anybody called the hospital?"

"…I've decided to step down from CORR. I've given my life…"

"She's been washing that same spot for the last half hour."

"He was cute, but he didn't know a thing about how to please a woman!"

"Does Dana know?"

"From that first day I've thought that woman was disturbed."

No one tried to intervene; the others seemed to sense Gwen's need for this activity and gave her space for it. Finally, as she collapsed to the floor beside her bucket, her back against the wall, Lee came over and hunkered down beside her.

"Hey, beautiful, you doin' okay?" Her customary brashness had gentled.

Gwen couldn't even summon sarcasm. She shrugged and said, "I guess," in a voice graveled with exhaustion.

Lee reached an arm around her and, for a moment, it felt so comforting. Gwen closed her eyes and leaned into her ex-lover, wanting nothing more than to sleep now, to plunge into oblivion.

With a start, she shook herself upright, pulling a little away from Lee, scanning the studio.

"Hey, hey, it's okay," Lee soothed.

But Gwen realized now who was missing: JJ had neither called last night nor come by this morning. This recognition brought Gwen to her feet.

Lee gazed up at her. "Are you sure you're okay?" She reached to hold Gwen's fingers, as if Gwen were a balloon that might float away without tethering. "I've got an idea," she proposed. "Let's get you into a hot bath, and you can change out of this once-lovely frock."

She stood, took hold of Gwen's shoulders. "C'mon now, I'll get you set up."

And Gwen was content to be led then, told what to do. She let Lee run the water in the bath while she sat on the toilet and stared into the dim light. When the tub was full, Gwen stood. Lee began to unhook the back of her dress.

Gwen bristled. "Thanks. I'll take it from here."

"Damn," Lee quipped, "and I was so close!" Her smile was rueful, but her eyes stayed kind.

"Do you think you could find me a cup of coffee?"

"Only if you'll eat something with it," Lee admonished. "Was pizza the last meal you had?"

Gwen started, reflexively, to protest, but admitted, "You know me too well."

Lee ducked out and Gwen let the dress fall to the floor at her feet. She kicked it into the corner, as if the dress had somehow been at fault for all that had happened while she was wearing it. The rest of her clothes joined the mess in the corner and she stepped into the bath. The hot water calmed her shredded nerves.

Sinking back, she let the water soak away the grime, the heat massage her aching muscles. She pulled a loofah from the soap dish and began to drag it over her skin, as if she could scrape away the memory of the experience just as she had scoured blood from the wall.

Lee stood at the edge of the curtain. "Knock, knock."

"Lee…" Gwen began in an admonishing tone.

"I've got coffee." Lee made it a siren song of temptation.

"Okay, come in," Gwen relented, "but behave yourself." There *was* a line of propriety, she was certain, but at the moment she was having trouble discerning it.

"I know you don't eat doughnuts, which is what they're scarfing out there, but I did manage to find a bagel that wasn't too stale. I toasted it to revive it." This she offered on a plate. "With a *schmear*, of course."

Gwen reached immediately for the coffee, but Lee chided, "Uh-uh-uh, what was our deal?"

So Gwen dutifully took a bite of the bagel, which she then began to eat ravenously, washing it down with sips of coffee until nothing was left on the plate but crumbs. "I needed that," she moaned gratefully.

Lee knelt at the side of the tub and released the clip holding Gwen's hair. "How about I give you a shampoo? C'mon, scoot down and lean your head back."

Gwen did as she was told, held her breath and ducked her

head beneath the surface of the water. She stayed there a few seconds, listening to the roar in her ears. When she surfaced, Lee swirled a stream of shampoo into her palm, releasing the scent of mango. She began to spread it over Gwen's hair, squeezing it through the dripping locks, working up lather, massaging the scalp.

Gwen melted. "I take back every bad thought I ever had about you," she sighed.

"Promise?" Lee slid her hands down the sides of Gwen's neck, pressing the tight muscles on either side.

"Okay," Lee said lightly. "Do you want to rinse this under the shower?"

"I guess." Gwen was sorry to have it end. "Lee..." She turned to face her, her face open, expectant.

"Here's a clean towel," Lee counseled. "You dry yourself off when you're done, and I'll go find you something to wear. Don't worry, I'll find you something kooky."

With that she departed, leaving Gwen feeling both disappointed and relieved. *Where was JJ?* She rinsed her hair and drained the tub, stepped out and wrapped herself in a towel. The immersion had revived her, but only partially; her nerves still buzzed from lack of sleep. She plopped down heavily on the toilet seat and rested her face in her palms.

"Do you have *any* two things that match?" Lee barged into the bathroom, then stopped. "Hey, whatssa' matter?"

"Just having a catnap," Gwen mumbled, her voice thick with tiredness. She did not lift her head.

"If you want, I can call a cab and take you over to my hotel," Lee offered. "You'll never get any sleep around here."

"I need to go see Ayisha; I just have to get myself motivated." Gwen remained unmoving on the toilet.

Lee shook her head. "The most stubborn woman I have ever known," she grumbled. "Well, it's an open offer, so think about it. Anyway, I picked these out, but you'll probably think they're too conservative." She extended the clothes she held in her arms.

"I'll be out in a few," Gwen said, examining the outfit Lee had assembled, a pair of tight black Capri pants, and white cotton man-tailored shirt that might have actually been JJ's. Lee had also included a black lace push-up bra and thong, no doubt feeding a fantasy. Had it been a muumuu or a suit of armor, Gwen couldn't have cared less how she clothed herself now.

Once Gwen emerged from the bathroom, Lee was gone, but she didn't have time to wonder why. As soon as she came into the room, Elena reported, "Chi called from the hospital. They're going to send Ayisha home in a couple of hours. Dana's trying to talk her into coming home with her."

"What about Kick and Devon?" Gwen wanted to know.

"Devon's mom posted bail right away this morning." Kendra had obviously been doing some calling around while Gwen was in the tub. "Kick? I don't know. Who cares?"

There were grunts of acknowledgment from around the room.

"How can you say that?" Luanne demanded. Just yesterday she had felt traumatized by taking the unpopular position; it was getting easier. "She's one of us."

"She's crazy," Peg protested. "What she did was terrible."

"We've all sat here for the last three days talking about wanting to do something about Emma's death. *She* was moved to do something. Yes, she made a choice I disagree with entirely, but I'm not ready to exile her from the ranks of womankind over it." Luanne felt a rush of adrenaline as she spoke; it fueled her conviction. "The whole time in the Seventies, we kept splintering into smaller and smaller groups because we would only make alliances with people who agreed with us one hundred percent. That's not any way to build a movement."

"We don't build it kidnapping young Black men and threatening to blow their heads off either," Peg snarled.

"Do you think I disagree with that?" Luanne responded. "But *we* have some responsibility for her, too. What kind of world did we hand to our daughters? And our sons? What kind of lessons did we teach them?"

From the corner, where Jolene was playing cards with Roger on their pile of sleeping bags, Jolene contributed, "And what do you think that young man's mama would say about how her son was treated?"

"I find that really condescending," Kendra barked at Luanne. "Like we're supposed to see ourselves as the product of your failings! We're responsible for ourselves. Kick is just a whack job, like a loose cannon that just went off."

Luanne was undeterred. "I don't mean that women your age don't have your own free will, but you've only just begun to leave your mark on the world. Our generation has already done that, and we have to take responsibility for its outcomes. Who in this room didn't cheer when Thelma and Louise shot that guy?"

"Maybe that's the whole problem with taking the law into our own hands," Ruthie interjected. "Who among us is pure enough in our intentions to administer justice?"

"You're a fine one to talk!" Still combative, Peg returned the focus to Luanne. "What have you been doing for the last twenty years? You turned your back on the movement and just lived your little suburban life!"

"No, no, I think Luanne is right." Elena walked over from the kitchen. After yesterday, Luanne was shocked to hear those words come from Elena's lips. "Of course we didn't put the gun in Kick's hand, but what have we done to prove to her there was another option?"

Gwen slumped into a folding chair. Summoning words from who knew where, she said, "I don't really think that Kick intended to hurt Jersey. It was theater. Kick is an art student, and she imagined this grand scenario where she would have all the power and serve the cause of justice."

"I think she fully intended to kill that man," Peg insisted.

"I don't," Gwen disagreed. "I don't think she'd thought all the way through to the last act. It wasn't inevitable." She sighed, "I think it's my fault. If I'd locked the door, Ayisha wouldn't have walked in, and Kick wouldn't have shot anybody."

Elena crossed the room, squatting before Gwen's chair, so close that she could feel her breath. With gentle hands, she guided Gwen's face upward till their eyes met and held the gaze.

Elena was thinking of white calla lilies; she was thinking

of her mother, and of Kay when she murmured, "Guilt has no place in a revolution." Her voice was like rich, brown velvet, her eyes like dark water, reflecting the moon.

"This world is a very painful place where bad things happen every day." She still held Gwen's face between her palms. "Terrible things, *unimaginable* things. They happen to the people we love and to people we don't even know. And when they do, we think, 'If only we'd tried harder, if we had somehow done a better job, we could have kept these devastating things from happening'."

Elena reached to take Gwen's hands, each one in her own. "But it's not true!" The twin moons in her eyes commanded Gwen believe it. "Atrocities occur despite our efforts. We don't know why. Still, we have to keep on trying to make a better world. Guilt is a luxury we cannot afford. We must forgive ourselves and keep on trying to change the world, to make our revolution because...what else can we do?"

The zeal that fired Elena's face was also tinged with pleading; if she could convince Gwen to believe her words, she could believe them too.

Staring into Elena's eyes was like staring into darkness until shapes emerge, and Gwen suddenly understood something about herself. All these years, her feminism had been a kind of theater for her. Not that she hadn't been passionate, committed to her role. But she had continued to see this movement as an elaborate drama in which the women of the world were happily and purposefully engaged in a bloodless revolution. A revolution where no one got hurt.

Dana had known better. And Chi, of course. Perhaps Elena too. And now Ayisha. They knew, as Gwen was just beginning to understand, that there were always consequences. Of action, of inaction. How had she managed all these years to avoid that simple truth, that taking power had consequences?

Her mother, Wanda, had lived her entire life trying to escape these kinds of repercussions, avoiding risk, keeping everything clean, doing and being whatever she believed her husband and society wanted from her. This too yielded consequences that showed in the lines of bitterness that ringed her mouth, and in her ceaseless litany of complaint.

Her youngest daughter made art that offended conservative white men in the United States Senate, and Gwen would just have to deal with the outcome of that.

Kick had assumed the power to avenge Emma's death; the results for her were likely to be harsh. And Emma had wanted to live free of the constrictions of gender and sexual category. The consequences to her had been fatal.

Slowly, Gwen nodded at Elena, acknowledging the difficult truth of her words.

"What else can we do?" she echoed.

Gwen was thinking of JJ, their disconnection, pressing the hurt of it like worrying a canker sore with the tongue. Then she remembered the phone, in the bathroom trashcan, and went to dig it out. Rummaging through wads of tissue, her hands found the handset, fingers quickly pressed the "on" button.

The charge was low from too many hours out of its cradle, but she could see there were three messages. Of course, she said to herself, flooded with relief, the phone's been off.

The first call had come just after three a.m., about the time Howard had finished his interviews with her and Peg.

"*Nena*, we just got our equipment packed up, and I'm headin' home to my folks. I think it must be around three. I guess you've got this turned off because everyone's asleep there, but I wanted to say goodnight, okay? I'll call you in the morning once I wake up. Love you."

Gwen sank on top of the toilet seat, holding the receiver to her heart. The next message had come at 9:23 a.m., just as Gwen was thinking that JJ was giving up on her.

"*Cosita?* Still not there? I wonder where you are. It's weird not sleeping next to you...I don't like it! Hey, if you get this soon, call me!"

And about an hour later, as Gwen was letting Lee dress her for the day:

"*Pepita*, I'm gettin' frustrated already! *¿Donde* the hell *estas?* You know how I get when I can't talk to *mi amore*."

Whatever questions had arisen in JJ's mind last evening, it

seemed now she had worked them through. And what of her own questions?

"Listen," the message continued, "my folks roped me into going over to my aunt's this afternoon—which means all fucking day because it'll be the cousins and the babies and the whole thing. If you were there I'd make you go with me, except you probably wouldn't go. So, I'll be by tonight. I'll bring some Chinese and we can make up for lost time, okay? I love you, *nena. Recuerdeme.*"

Gwen leaned her aching temple against the cool porcelain of the sink. If she were able to cry she felt like she might do it now, but her lids remained dry, even as her throat ached. How had she ever managed to find someone who was so good to her?

As Gwen rejoined the group, women were mobilizing to leave the loft for the last time. Elena had called around and found out where Kick was being held. She and Luanne would go see her. They'd found out what provisions they could take her—a hairbrush but no comb, toothbrush and toothpaste, menstrual products, soap, shampoo, cigarettes but no matches—and made a plan to gather these.

Jolene was wondering aloud, "Roger and I have a one o'clock bus. What's the fastest way for us to get back to the station from here, not in a taxi?"

"We'll drop you," Ruthie offered. "We're headed back to Pennsylvania, to Peg's daughter's." Peg and Ruthie were busy pulling together their gear—air mattress, allergen-free pillows, special teas and foods, books—but Kendra impeded their progress as she bombarded Peg with last-minute questions: "So what *would* you say is the legacy of Seventies feminism? And what do you think my generation has to teach yours?"

Peg was improvising responses, hauling bags and bundles to the door for Ruthie to carry down. Kendra lobbed one more question. "Do you think that feminists should adopt a strategy of taking matters into their own hands to combat violence against women?"

Luanne came striding across the room. "Kendra, you can't write about what happened here last night."

Elena agreed. "Especially because we don't know Kick's legal status at the moment. We don't know if Ayisha intends to press charges."

"Kendra wasn't even here when it happened." Jolene stopped stuffing Roger's backpack to argue. "None of us was except for Peg and Gwen. What do you think, Peg?"

The older woman squinted behind her wire-rim glasses. "When Kick first showed up last night, talking about the chance to have justice, I was tempted by it. That fantasy of being powerful. It wasn't till Gwen showed up that I saw how crazy it was. It's an interesting story, but I don't trust the patriarchal media to tell it."

"Even if I write it?" Kendra was ready to take offense. "What about you, Gwen?"

"I think if the *Voice* runs it, it will be on the cover of the *Post* the next day with some lurid headline about 'Lesbian Avenges Ex-Lover's Death'," Gwen said. "They'll turn it into a freak show, and it won't matter how skillfully you've written it."

Kendra pouted; clearly this wasn't the answer she'd been hoping for. "Well, I'll think about it, but I'm not making any promises. I have to go now, I've got a deadline."

The energy that had drawn and held the women this weekend was dispersing. As everyone was preparing to depart, Gwen suddenly announced, "Wait! Before you all go, I want to show you something." It had just occurred to her, but now nothing seemed more important than this. "Don't worry," she reassured Jolene, "it won't take long. You'll still catch your bus."

She hastily pulled chairs around the battered sofa. Then she sorted through the stack of videocassettes atop her TV, extricating one from near the bottom; this she plunged into the VCR and turned on the monitor.

The screen was blank until an unseen hand began to scrawl the title in blood red lipstick, "Woman." The "W" a slash, the "O," too, angular, the "M" with its knife points, the "A" and "N" dashed off, a long trail leading past the margins of the frame. As this screen faded slowly, another appeared: "a video by Emma Firestein."

Peg made a soft inhalation of breath, as if the name were a

painful reminder.

Ever needing to assert her authority, Kendra enthused, "Oh yeah, this piece is amazing."

Gwen closed her eyes; she didn't have to look at the screen to recall these images: Emma sits at the far end of a long rectangular table. She is naked, but the camera doesn't dwell on this; it is not a nudity designed to incite. The table is raked, so that it angles slightly downward the closer it gets to the viewer. The camera pans its length, slowly zooming in on Emma's body, her face, her mouth. In extreme close-up, the lips say, "I don't want to be a woman anymore."

As the camera pulls back, Emma sends a tube of lipstick rolling down the length of the table toward the viewer.

The camera focuses on the lipstick for a beat or two, then slowly returns to a close-up of Emma's mouth. "I don't want to be a woman anymore."

This time she rolls a fistful of tampons down the table, each following their own trajectories.

The piece continues, alternating between this assertion, "I don't want to be a woman anymore," and the discarding of various objects: a dildo, a thong panty, a roll of paper towel, a serving spoon, a baby doll, one platform shoe, a breast pump, a spice jar, a circle of birth control pills, and a button—that must have at one time been Dana's—of a women's symbol with a fist in the center. In this last choice the artist seems to declare that feminism is as much a social construction as any of the trappings of femininity.

Finally, she lies crosswise at the head of the table, and begins to roll down its length. Through special effects, the table expands its measure one hundredfold, and she rolls and rolls and rolls its seemingly endless expanse, her undeniable female body—breasts and belly, back and buttocks—turning and turning in its slow descent. Her words, too, are sped up, looped, jumbled and overlapped, until what emerges is a new refrain that closes the piece, "I want to be. I want to be," the cry of a soul longing to break free from its prison of identity.

"That's what we want," Kendra said, as the screen went black. Her voice was soft; her eyes wet. Some layer of armor had slid off, revealing the young woman underneath the hard edges.

Peg moved over to her. "Believe it or not, that's what we wanted too." Then she added, "That, and to change the world." A grin of connection passed between them.

This is what Emma could have done with her art, Gwen thought. *Made a bridge where only a gulf had existed.*

But the women in the room were not appreciators of art, and they had no words to respond to Emma's performance. They returned to gathering their belongings, saying their goodbyes. They had places to go, they had schedules to keep.

Life demanded allegiance from the living; the dead could only command attention for so long.

Within minutes, Gwen sat alone in her studio, listening to the sounds rising up from the street.

Chapter 18

When JJ finally arrived at dusk with fragrant cartons from Fu Leen's, Gwen protested that she was way too tired to eat. "I don't even have the strength to lift a chopstick to my mouth," she mewled pathetically.

And even though Gwen was thirteen years older, JJ looked at her with that "what-ever-am-I-going-to-do-with-this-child?" mix of love and exasperation, and said, "Don't worry, *cosita*, I'll take care of it."

She dragged an old black serving tray to the middle of the bed, pulled out a clean plate from the cupboard and a pair of green lacquered chopsticks. From the cartons she ladled spinach in black bean sauce, steamed broccoli, sautéed tofu and garlic.

She sat on the bed cross-legged, and invited Gwen to recline with her head in JJ's lap. She plucked a cube of tofu with her chopsticks, blew on it a bit to cool it, then commanded Gwen to open wide as she popped it into her mouth. "See, *pepita*, you don't even have to lift a chopstick."

Gwen nearly wept as her tongue savored the pungent garlic and her teeth bit into the solid protein of the soy curd. JJ proceeded, alternating tofu, spinach, broccoli, a bite for Gwen, a bite for herself, and in this way fed Gwen dinner.

It was only then, fortified with food, that Gwen could begin to tell her of the events since she'd last seen her.

"*Ay, nena!* You could have been killed!" There was real fear in JJ's eyes.

Gwen shrugged. "I'm ready to go anytime," she said, because it was how she felt and because she knew it drove JJ crazy to hear it.

"Well, I'm *not* ready to have you go." JJ set the tray on the floor, the better to wrap herself around Gwen, as if she could hold her to earth with her muscles and will. They lay there for some moments; Gwen was almost drifting off when JJ picked up another thread of the story.

"Fuck, she talked to me about Jersey, but she acted like she was all on his side and everything. I didn't have any idea what she was planning to do!"

"No one did," Gwen soothed her. "It's not your fault. And he's not even pressing charges. And Howard told me they arrested this other guy in Emma's case."

"That guy you found out about at the club?"

"Yeah, I think so."

She took Gwen's face in her hands. "*Cosita*, you're a hero."

"Don't even say that." Gwen pushed away from her, sat up. "It's my fault Ayisha got shot."

"How d'ya figure? Did you bring the gun? Did you pull the trigger?"

Gwen twisted one end of the sheet in her fist. She remembered the last time she and JJ were in bed together; could it have been just yesterday morning? It seemed such a long time ago, as if she'd been a different person then. "I thought I could defuse the situation, but I couldn't. It was stupid and arrogant..."

"*Nena*, everybody got out of here alive. Don't you think that's a big damn deal?"

Gwen didn't say anything, just wrapped a pillow around her throbbing head.

"So you went to see Ayisha? How is she?"

"They were getting ready to release her, and she was gonna go to Chi's. Dana was going too. And you know who else was there? Jersey! It was...I don't know, does this sound weird? They felt like a family unit all of a sudden, the four of them."

JJ sat up up, took Gwen by the shoulders, patiently lowered

her back onto the mattress. She buried her face in the crook of Gwen's neck, wrapped an arm around her to cup her breast.

Unbidden, an image of Lee came to Gwen's mind, Lee washing her hair in the tub that morning. Lee, tender, solicitous; Lee as she used to be in those very first months Gwen knew her. Her body stiffened at JJ's touch.

"Hey, what's wrong?" she asked. Her hand moved from Gwen's breast to rest against her heart.

"Nothing," Gwen lied, "just tired." She turned on her side so JJ couldn't see her face.

Gently, JJ turned her back, looked into her face. "*Nena*, are we okay?"

Gwen said nothing, her face contorting into a grimace of guilt she could do nothing to control.

Persisting, JJ asked, "Was it seeing your ex this weekend? Have you changed your mind about what we're doing here?"

Gwen loved that JJ was fearless about the truth, but this night *she* was not fearless. How could she talk to JJ if she didn't know what she wanted? She lifted her fingers to lightly touch JJ's cheek. "Honey, I love you," Gwen told her, truthfully, "and we do need to talk, but if I have to do it before I get some sleep, my brain is going to implode, I swear."

JJ sat up, swung her legs over the side of the bed, frustration radiating from her hunched shoulders. "So what do you want me to do?" she asked. "Do you want me to go?" Wounded pride made a little knife-edge in her voice.

Gwen reached for her arm, pulled her back down. "No, honey, stay. Please stay and hold me. In the morning, we'll talk, I promise." She remained on her side, but pressed her back and buttocks toward JJ, burrowing into her. They both kept their clothes on and, once she heard JJ's breath deepen, she too finally fell into a troubled sleep.

Gwen didn't know how long she'd been asleep before she started to dream. Strange, upsetting dreams. *She was walking and walking; her bare feet grew bloodier with each step. Then she went to an AA meeting, but it was in a bar, and everyone was drinking, even as they recited the Twelve Steps. Somewhere a phone was ringing, ringing. Over and over, she answered it, but still the high-pitched ring screamed for attention* until she crashed into wakefulness and realized the phone was actually ringing, the receiver still in the bathroom.

JJ moaned but did not awaken as Gwen slipped out from beside her. She was drenched in sweat. Her eyes grazed the clock as she passed; just twelve thirty. She never went to bed this early. She reached the bathroom, plucked the cordless receiver from where it perched on the sink, and croaked, "Hello?"

"Hey, baby," a voice purred in her ear. The voice was pure Brooklyn, undiminished by absence, slurred with scotch and slippery with intent.

"Lee?" She was incredulous, but held her astonishment to a whisper, wanting above all not to awaken JJ. She gave a vicious pinch to the soft insides of her elbow, just to make sure she wasn't still dreaming.

"That's me," Lee assured her, "the one you been dreamin' about! Listen, I've been thinking…"

"Lee," Gwen interrupted, making her voice stern, "why in hell are you calling me at one o'clock in the morning?" She rallied her alertness; she would need all her wits for this encounter.

"Because all good things come in the middle of the night, baby."

Outside Gwen's open window, the night was still alive with sounds: car horns and sirens, shouted threats and laughter, music sliced from passing cars below, the unidentifiable din that was the city's background score.

"You're drunk, Lee." She strained to make this not an indictment, but a statement of fact.

"See, now, there you go," Lee protested, "I'm not drunk, Gwen, I'm…happy! Gwen, see, I was thinkin' about the old days and—"

"Lee," Gwen overrode her, "you been out in some bar and you're stinking drunk. I don't wanna talk to you like this—"

"Gwen, goddamn it!" The voice tightened like a rope, lashed out, "Just listen to me for a fuckin' minute, okay?"

Lee seemed to regain control; once more the voice turned silky and persuasive. "I'm thinking that I might've really screwed up with you, Gwen. I mean, I know you're crazy, you're an artist and all that, there was a lot to put up with, very high maintenance, but *still*, you're a very sexy girl, and we had some good times. Some good, good times. I'm thinking, maybe we should give it another try."

Somewhere in the middle of this declaration Gwen had stopped breathing; the hand clasping the receiver was slick with sweat. There had been years, literally years, when she'd dreamed of just this moment, conjured hundreds of scenarios: where it would take place, how she would be dressed, what she would say.

Early on, she'd imagined falling back into Lee's waiting arms, restored at last to the love that had been withdrawn. Later her fantasies had sought to turn the tables, spurning Lee's advances, refusing her apologies, withholding forgiveness. Now, as she sat upright on the toilet seat, she was surprised to note that what she felt was neither desire nor revenge. It was grief, painful as a knife plunged into flesh, and it made her feel heavy and old.

Into Gwen's silence, Lee planted the suggestion, "Why don't you get a cab and come uptown—I'm at the Carlysle. I'd love to see you."

Gwen recalled again that summer day, so many years before, when they'd walked along the Hudson, and Lee had vowed, "You're all I want." In those days love was dangerous, a daredevil's stunt, a leap across a chasm in a vehicle in flames. Was it age or sobriety, she wondered, wisdom or surrender that made her turn her back on that kind of perilous thrill?

"Lee," she began, "I can't..."

"No problem! I can come to you." The voice bright with self-assurance, but by its very nature the offer to come to Rivington Street revealed the depths of Lee's panic. Just yesterday Lee had berated her for living in a slum, accused her of romanticizing low life, told her to grow up.

"No, Lee, you can't." For some sick reason she felt guilty. "JJ's here with me..."

"Right," Lee's tone had turned acidic. "The Cha-Cha Queen."

"Lee, she's my lover. She's good to me." No death-defying

leaps, no flaming hoops through which to jump.

There was a pause at the other end of the line, just long enough to accommodate the lighting of a cigarette. Then an exhalation, as Lee said, "Okay, Gwen, okay." There was another pause as she summoned levity back into her tone. "Listen, it was great seein' ya', I hope everything works out for ya' with this art stuff. Remember, if you need help—I meant what I said yesterday. Look me up sometime if you ever get back to L.A."

Gwen wanted to cry out, "Wait!" She wanted the moment to freeze so she could really consider what it was she was deciding. But already Lee was gone, only the hiss of disconnection left playing in Gwen's ear. She held the receiver a moment longer, listening to that sound. Then she clicked it off. She walked into the main room, stared through the window, empty of feeling, transfixed by the smoky light, vapor swirling around the street lamp.

What do we do when we finally release our hold on the past, Gwen wondered. *Parade in the streets exulting in our newfound freedom? Catapult ourselves into uncharted heights? Or do we huddle near the gates that so long sheltered us, resentful that they've closed against us, uncertain now where we belong?*

Gwen let the tears come then; they seemed to flow from her eyes as if from an underground stream. She dropped to her knees before the window, rested her forehead on its sill. There was no shuddering in her chest, no ache in her throat, just twin fountains spurting their saline waters, washing her clean.

How do we exit the room of the past, enter into a new chamber that has yet to be built? How do we leave the security of what is known for the unimagined? Emma Firestein was looking for a new way to be a woman; none of the old clothes would fit. What might she have taught us, had she lived?

And the women of Labrys, each in her own disparate way, groped toward a new definition of liberation, the old movement too constricted, too misshapen, to contain all who longed to stand within its embrace.

And how would she grow to love JJ, tossing in fitful sleep between the sheets, really love her, now that she was finally free to do so?

The streets were quieter on this night, as if the city was turning itself back toward workaday concerns, the weekend over, its potential exhausted. She thought of Howard, and another of his cherished AA slogans that had always pissed her off: "When one door closes, another opens." She'd heard these same words spoken in meetings by people yellow with cirrhosis, people who'd been fired from their jobs, or had their kids taken away by Social Services. People with faith. Gwen's smart-mouth retort to Howard had always been, "When one door slams in your face, another hits you in the ass."

But even without Howard's prodding, she could not help but notice the doors Emma's death had opened, as if, for almost all of them, the past had finally let go its grip, nudging them—perhaps more brutally than they would wish—toward an unwritten future. And each was free to make of it what she would, to fuck it up or soar as they saw fit.

Gwen picked herself off the floor, wandered over to her worktable, rummaged in a file drawer for a new legal pad. She was a junkie for office supplies, the razor point of a new pen on a fresh tablet. A scene began to unfold in her imagination: a stage set with several doorframes, at least two stories high. By unseen hands, the doors were slammed shut, first one, then another, again and again; it would be an extended scene, the sounds becoming music, a percussive rhythm of wood against wood. When the cacophony faded, there would be a beat of silence, unforgiving spotlights on the doors' sealed faces. Then, unexpected, a trapdoor in the floor of the stage would begin to slowly creak open, a tentative aperture that slowly widened until Gwen emerged through it. Behind her, the doors would disappear as a slide was projected of the desert in bloom...

Publications from Spinsters Ink
P.O. Box 242
Midway, Florida 32343
Phone: 800-301-6860
www.spinstersink.com

ACROSS TIME by Linda Kay Silva. If you believe in soul
mates, if you know you've had a past life, then join Jessie in the
first of a series of adventures that takes her *Across Time*.
ISBN 978-1883523-91-6 $14.95

SELECTIVE MEMORY by Jennifer L. Jordan. A Kristin
Ashe Mystery. A classical pianist, who is experiencing profound
memory loss after a near-fatal accident, hires private investigator
Kristin Ashe to reconstruct her life in the months leading up to
the crash. ISBN 978-1-883523-88-6 $14.95

HARD TIMES by Blayne Cooper. Together, Kellie and Lorna
navigate through an oppressive, hidden world where lines
between right and wrong blur, sexual passion is forbidden but
explosive, and love is the biggest risk of all.
ISBN 978-1-883523-90-9 $14.95

THE KIND OF GIRL I AM by Julia Watts. Spanning decades,
The Kind of Girl I Am humorously depicts an extraordinary
woman's experiences of triumph, heartbreak, friendship and
forbidden love.
ISBN 978-1-883523-89-3 $14.95

PIPER'S SOMEDAY by Ruth Perkinson. It seemed as though
life couldn't get any worse for feisty, young Piper Leigh Cliff
and her three-legged dog, Someday.
ISBN 978-1-883523-87-9 $14.95

MERMAID by Michelene Esposito. When May unearths a box in her missing sister's closet she is taken on a journey through her mother's past that leads her not only to Kate but to the choices and compromises, emptiness and fullness, the beauty and jagged pain of love that all women must face.
ISBN 978-1-883523-85-5 $14.95

ASSISTED LIVING by Sheila Ortiz-Taylor. Violet March, an eighty-two-year-old resident of Casa de los Sueños, finally has the opportunity to put years of mystery reading to practical use. One by one her comrades, the Bingos, are dying. Is this natural attrition, or is there a sinister plot afoot?
ISBN 978-1-883523-84-2 $14.95

NIGHT DIVING by Michelene Esposito. *Night Diving* is both a young woman's coming-out story and a thirty-something coming-of-age journey that proves you can go home again.
ISBN 978-1-883523-52-7 $14.95

FURTHEST FROM THE GATE by Ann Roberts. *Furthest from the Gate* is a humorous chronicle of a woman's coming of age, her complicated relationship with her mother and the responsibilities to family that last a lifetime.
ISBN 978-1-883523-81-7 $14.95

EYES OF GRAY by Dani O'Connor. Grayson Thomas was the typical college senior with typical friends, a typical job and typical insecurities about her future. One Sunday morning, Gray's life became a little less typical, she saw a man clad in black, and started doubting her own sanity.
ISBN 978-1-883523-82-4 $14.95

ORDINARY FURIES by Linda Morgenstein. Tired of hiding, exhausted by her grief after her husband's death, Alexis Pope plunges into the refreshingly frantic world of restaurant resort cooking and dining in the funky chic town of Guerneville, California. ISBN 978-1-883523-83-1 $14.95

A POEM FOR WHAT'S HER NAME by Dani O'Connor. Professor Dani O'Connor had pretty much resigned herself to the fact that there was no such thing as a complete woman. Then out of nowhere, along comes a woman who blows Dani's theory right out of the water.
ISBN 1-883523-78-8 $14.95

WOMEN'S STUDIES by Julia Watts. With humor and heart, *Women's Studies* follows one school year in the lives of three young women and shows that in college, one's extracurricular activities are often much more educational than what goes on in the classroom. ISBN 1-883523-75-3 $14.95

DISORDERLY ATTACHMENTS by Jennifer L. Jordan. The fifth Kristin Ashe Mystery. Kris investigates whether a mansion someone wants to convert into condos is haunted.
ISBN 1-883523-74-5 $14.95

VERA'S STILL POINT by Ruth Perkinson. Vera is reminded of exactly what it is that she has been missing in life.
ISBN 1-883523-73-7 $14.95

OUTRAGEOUS by Sheila Ortiz-Taylor. Arden Benbow, a motorcycle riding, lesbian Latina poet from LA is hired to teach poetry in a small liberal arts college in northwest Florida.
ISBN 1-883523-72-9 $14.95

UNBREAKABLE by Blayne Cooper. The bonds of love and friendship can be as strong as steel. But are they unbreakable?
ISBN 1-883523-76-1 $14.95

ALL BETS OFF by Jaime Clevenger. Bette Lawrence is about to find out how hard life can be for someone of low society standing in the 1900s.
ISBN 1-883523-71-0 $14.95

UNBEARABLE LOSSES by Jennifer L. Jordan. The fourth Kristin Ashe Mystery. Two elderly sisters have hired Kris to discover who is pilfering from their award-winning holiday display. ISBN 1-883523-68-0 $14.95

EXISTING SOLUTIONS by Jennifer L. Jordan. The second Kristin Ashe Mystery. When Kris is hired to find an activist's biological father, things get complicated when she finds herself falling for her client. ISBN 1-883523-69-9 $14.95

A SAFE PLACE TO SLEEP by Jennifer L. Jordan. The first Kristin Ashe Mystery. Kris is approached by well-known lesbian Destiny Greaves with an unusual request. One that will lead Kris to hunt for her own missing childhood pieces. ISBN 1-883523-70-2 $14.95